Words of Praise
for Pat G'Orge-Walker

"Pat G'Orge-Walker is truly an inspirational writer for the New Millennium. Her brand of humor strikes chords of truth in our hearts as we reflect on the hypocritical social scene that our churches have become, as too many of us become, the Sadducees & Pharisees of the New Millennium. Write On Sis . . . I love your work! Much love and respect."

—**Crystal Cartier**
Prolific Writer 2000 recipient

"I think *Sister Betty*, created by the amazing and extraordinary Pat G'Orge-Walker, takes Christian Comedy to an all new level. You laugh, you identify with some of the characters and you actually think she's writing about people you know. In the midst of the laughter, you then find yourself spiritually enlightened and your soul blessed."

—**Joyce Griffin-Bell**
Christian Content for Net Noir
St. John Missionary Baptist Church
Meridian, Mississippi

"Pat G'Orge-Walker is proof that laughter is good for the soul . . . Her gospel comedy is literary entertainment with a purpose!"

—**Norma L. Jarrett**
Author of *Sunday Brunch*

"Point blank, Pat G'Orge-Walker is a writer to be reckoned with. I laugh and shake my head the entire time."

—**Shonell Bacon, Black Nubian Chronicles**
Author of *Luv Alwayz*

Sister Betty!
God's Calling You, Again!

PAT G'ORGE-WALKER

KENSINGTON PUBLISHING CORP.

CONTENTS

ACKNOWLEDGMENTS

This book of short stories is dedicated to my Lord and Savior Jesus Christ. I am indeed a miracle. After many years of dysfunction and abuse that should have wrapped me in a blanket of mental instability, God, in His infinite wisdom and love, instead placed into my unworthy hands a Ministry of Laughter. Psalms 126:2 *"Then were our mouths filled with laughter, and our tongues with singing. Then they said among the nations, the Lord has done great things for them . . ."*

To my editor, Karen Thomas, and my Kensington/Dafina family: Your patience will truly be rewarded. My agent, Djana Pearson-Morris: I'm so glad you listened to your heart and took a chance on a new genre and writer. God bless you all. To author and great friend Tracy Price-Thompson: I know your hands are scorched from yanking my fat from the fire so many times.

My late grandmother Lucille Acker of Williamston, South Carolina, the real "Ma Cile." Yes, she did dip snuff, wore a patch over her bad eye, never strayed from her faith, and thought television wrestling was real. It was her wisdom, a sense of humor that she kept to herself, and uniqueness that inspired the touch of comedy in many of my stories. I pray I've made her proud. Also to the people of Williamston, South Carolina, especially my third grade teacher, Mrs. Bobbie Madison-Mackey. She said in 2000, I should be a writer because I told so many convincing lies in the third grade.

My parents, the late Reverend Alonzo, and Reverend Margaret: I wish I'd done this while you were still alive. Brothers, now deceased, Herbert and Dickie . . . their encouragement had no limits.

I would like to thank the many people who have loved, prodded, put up with, and prayed for me and my Ministry of Comedy.

My husband, Robert Walker, you've stood by me through twenty-five years of friendship, and ultimately marriage as I navigated my way facing creative, personality, spiritual growth and many challenges. There's not enough space on this page for me to thank God for you and write how much I love and admire you. You are unique in your own way.

I thank my daughters, Gizel Dan-Yette Brewer, Ingrid Millsaps, and Marisa Ellis. My grandchildren, Kecia (Candi), Donald, Gary, Brian, Dasean, Garrard, Jerome, Niajia, Shyheim, Shareef, Maya, and Jada. My uncle Elbert. My aunts Ovella Harris, Mildred Brown, and Katy Simmons. To all my sisters, Shirley, Sandra, Valerie, JoAnne, Lorraine, and particularly Arlene, who prays with me constantly. My surviving brothers, Chucky, Anthony, Gregory, Rickie, and Ronnie. To my nieces and nephews, particularly ShaSean Baylor, and cousins who took to the streets to sell my books—thank you all.

My Whist Queens buddies who kept me sane and told everyone about my books, Barbara Easter, Willean Hunter, Glenda Baldwin, Connie Zephir, Ana Plummer, Anne Walker, and Susan Bride.

The Palmer-Watson family, along with Charles Carrington, who performed with me in my efforts to bring my ministry to the people. Mr. EBT—thank you for making sure that everyone at Verizon Telephone Company knew about Sister Betty. The Rochdale HIP Center and Dr. Y. Pierre-Jerome-Shulton—thank you. Carolyn Roberts—thank you for feeding my hubby so I'd have time to write—keep the oven mitts warm, I've another book to write.

For the churches who have supported my comedy ministry by constantly rehiring me. In particular Reverend Isaac Graham and the Macedonia Baptist Church in New York City, Salem Missionary Baptist Church in Jamaica, NY, Mount Ollie Church in Brooklyn, NY, Emanuel Zion in Brooklyn, NY, the United Baptist Missionary Association, and a host of others across the nation—thank you.

A very special, *thank you*, to my pastor, Reverend Stella L. Mercado and the entire Blanche Memorial Baptist Church family for their prayers and support.

Vanessa Woodward and Tina McCray (my publicists), Journeys End, Chris Whent, Esq., Carolyn Davis, Dr. Rosie Milligan. Douglas Reed, Pamela Joy Moore, Elton Tucker, Maxine Thompson (Black Butterfly Press), Tia Shabazz (BWA), Tee Royal (RawSistaz.com), Kim Grant (SistahtoSistah.com), Joyce Bell (NetNoir.com), Veda Brown (Gospel Promotions), Troy Johnson (AALBC), Kizzie Sanders, BWA-Christian Literary, Marnie Pherson and the Mormom Church (SheLovesGod.com), Cynthia Way (Gotham Writers School), AHA.com (Authors Helping Authors), Shonell Bacon (The Nubian Chronicles.com), QBR, Lloyd Hart, Zelda Miles (Mediaclique.com), the Good Book Club, Kim Lawson, Stephanie Gadlin, the BlackMarket.com, Carla Nix, Christian Fiction Writers Group, DOE, the Grits Book Club, Lena Williams, Robin Caldwell, Pooor Freddie's Rib Shack in Jamaica, NY. Akia Shangai—forty years! Who knew? All the colleges, Carnival Cruise Line, and other venues who've supported my Christian comedy performances. And to Edna Lorraine Giles: Wherever you are, you know that God does have a sense of humor.

Authors: Kimberla Lawson-Roby, Sharon Ewell-Foster, Angela Benson, Delores Thornton, Parry 'Ebony' Brown, Alice Holman, Tanya M. Evans, Susan Borden, Timmothy McCann, Karen E. Quinones-Miller, Mack and Sara Freeman-Smith, Evelyn "Mama" Coleman, Eric J. Dickey, Jacquie Thomas, Zane, Journey, Gwynne Forster, Donna Hill, Brian Egleston, Victor McGlothin, Lolita Files, Jessica Tilles, Maurice Gray, Liz Curtis-Higgs, J. California Cooper, Nancy Flowers, Vincent Alexandria, Dr. Kevon Jackson, Victoria Christopher-Murray, Dominique Grosvenor, and many others.

To the libraries, Doris Jones (Queens Library), Enoch Pratt (Dundalk Avenue) in particular, as well as radio stations WWRL (NYC) and WYCA (Chicago). Gospel Today Television. To gospel promoter Junius Griffin of Buffalo, New York, and the staff at Done Deal Entertainment, Inc.—thank you. The gospel cafés, especially the 4C's in Yonkers, New York.

Bookstores: New Life Christian Bookstore in Jamaica, NY. (I thank you for referring me to so many people when they asked for a Christian comedian). Waldenbooks, Borders, Barnes

& Noble, Cush City, APOOO- (Yasmin Coleman), Robyn Green, Mary Jones and Pamela Walker-Williams (PageTurner.net), Sable and Sand and countless others—thank you. To the thousands of readers who have loved and appreciated Sister Betty—there is no me without you.

My fellow Christian comedians: Trina Jeffries (Sistah Canteloupe) Coy LeSone (BET), Byron "da Prophet Dat Makes You Laugh" Harden, Brotha' Smitty, and Rickey Smiley . . . you crazy folks keep me on my creative toes!

Finally to Dr. Maya Angelou. Thank you for taking the time (circa 1975) to counsel me during intermission at the Broadway play, *The Wiz.* I've never forgotten your pearls of wisdom as it pertained to my writing. You told me to " . . . always write honestly." I didn't understand exactly what you meant until years later, and I've tried to never stray.

Remember, Don't let worry kill ya off. Let the Church help!

E-mail: sisterbetty@sisterbetty.com   www.sisterbetty.com

CONGREGATION MEMBERS

Pastor . . . The Reverend Knott Enuff Money
Overseer . . . Bishop Was Nevercalled
Head Deacon . . . Deacon Laid Handz
Head Mother . . . Mother Pray Onn
Choir Director . . . Brother Tis Mythang
Church Blabbermouth . . . Sister Carrie Onn
Head of Confusion . . . Sister Ima Hellraiser
Church Matriarch/Butt Whipper . . . Ma Cile

Some of the other church members

Sister Connie Fuse
Reverend and Most Righteous All About-Me
(bad kids) Lil Bit, June Bug
Sister Aggi Tate
Minister Breedin' Love
Sister Loose Gal
Sister Need Sum
Mother Blister
Ole Brother ILie A Lot
Sister Petri Fied
Council Man Hippo Crit
. . . and many others.

Sister Betty!
God's Calling You!

"Yes, she did get a phone call."

"No, she didn't."

"She did so!"

"No, she did not!"

"Lil Bit, June Bug!" Ma Cile yelled from the flower-covered front porch. "If y'all two young'uns don't shut ya mouths out there, I'm gonna whup ya like you stole sumpthin'. Y'all hears me? Me and Sister Betty tryin' to talk about de Lawd, and even He can't hear us over all the ruckuses y'all two makin'. Now shut up before I knock ya out and pray ya back!"

June Bug was ten years old. He was caramel-candy-colored but not as sweet. He was also kind of short and skinny, with a lot of attitude compared to his ten-year-old cousin, Lil Bit. Lil Bit, on the other hand, looked more like she was fifteen than ten. She wasn't chubby, but what the old folks called "thick." Her complexion was lighter than June Bug. Lil Bit was often called "high yella" or "mixed." Separately, the two cousins were little angels, but together, they could turn old Satan into a punk and make him hang a "Closed for Today" sign on hell's door and hide.

June Bug and Lil Bit always attempted not to get on the wrong side of their grandma, Ma Cile. Working Ma Cile's last good sixty-five-year-old nerve was never a good move, especially in front of company, and definitely not in front of her life-long friend, Sister Betty.

The startled children scrambled toward the safety of the wild honeysuckle bushes on the side of the house and started arguing again.

"Yes, she did, too!" June Bug whispered. He pointed his skinny index finger in Lil Bit's direction for emphasis while using his free hand to toss dirt at her.

Lil Bit ducked the flying dirt. She quickly raised her head and peeped through a gap in the wild honeysuckle bush. She didn't see Ma Cile, so they must have been out of her earshot. "No, she ain't. I just know she ain't!" She was so mad, she felt like chewing on a rock, but instead she tossed a fistful of dirt back at June Bug.

Being skinny had its advantages as June Bug fell flat, like a brown praying mantis, and ducked the flying dirt. He rolled over onto the grassy lawn and yelled, "I said, yeah, she did!" He thought he might have yelled just a little too loud, so he, too, jumped up. He carefully parted the slender branches of a full-blossomed rosebush and looked toward the house sur-rounded by colorful beds of jasmine, impatiens, and orange jack-in-the-boxes.

Not one to let a good argument go to waste, Lil Bit crouched down and then slid next to June Bug. "No, she didn't!" Lil Bit snapped. "June Bug, you are one of the biggest liars the devil ever gave birth to. You know Ma Cile told you the next time she catches you lying, she was gonna drop-kick your lips and make them look like you wearing a turtleneck sweater!"

For the next two minutes, they argued back and forth. Suddenly, the fragrance of sweet flowers was gone. A dangerous shift in the warm weather took its place. A storm was about to hit, and its alarming outline hovered over them. There was no time to build an ark or run.

"Lil Bit! June Bug! You two must think I'm deaf and blind. Y'all ain't up north with your mamas no more; you down south, where ya gonna be raised right! Now, go git me a switch—make it two switches, so I can twist 'em. Better be ripe ones, 'cause if I gotta go find 'em myself, that's two lickin's ya be git-tin'," Ma Cile said.

Lil Bit and June Bug never saw or heard her coming, but there she stood. Ma Cile was honey-colored and tall with wide hips, and she was standing over them with one hand on each hip, looking every bit like that Jolly Green Giant on the televi-sion commercial. She leaned over to get a better look-see at her two shivering grandchildren and soon-to-be victims. It was hard to do, since she only had one good eye. A blue store-bought false one replaced the brown eye kicked out, in childhood, by an uppity mule. Ma Cile wasted no time. She jerked her head around and then casually spit a glob of Railroad brand snuff from her mouth.

To the children, her head seemed to make a 360-degree turn. That action made them feel as if Ma Cile would cancel their birth certificates without a second thought.

"How many times have I told you young'uns that Sister Betty done heard from the Lawd? I said, when she comes around to visit, that y'all two keep yo' mouths buttoned! How many times, heh? Heh?" Ma Cile snarled.

"We sorry, Ma Cile; we knows—"

"Shut up! Did I tell ya to talk? Well, did I? Did I?" Ma Cile loomed over the children, breathing so hard you could almost see the snuff powder coming out of her mouth and nostrils. "Oh, now, ya li'l heathens ain't gonna answer Ma Cile, heh? Well, is ya?" she fumed.

"Yes, ma'am, we gonna ans—" June Bug and Lil Bit said at the same time.

"I done tole y'all two to shut up fo' the last time." Ma Cile plunged her hand into her white starched apron pocket as if she were searching for a weapon while she continued her tirade. "Y'all gonna burn in hell for interrupting Sister Betty and me." She pulled out a soggy tissue and wiped her lined and glistening forehead. "Git in that house, right now, whilst I go and find me them switches. Gonna whup yo' tails fo' sassin' me, too."

The children rose and started to back away. To Ma Cile with

her bad eye, they looked like they were plaited together, like two cornrows on Lil Bit's head that were done so tight, they looked like crocheted stitches.

The children picked up speed as they wobbled up the creaky steps and into Ma Cile's spotless house. They started running down the foyer, but Lil Bit was so much bigger than June Bug that as he hung on, he looked like one big brown tube sock on her leg.

They stopped running when they reached the foyer. "This here is all your fault, June Bug," Lil Bit barked. "I told you not to tell that lie on Sister Betty. Now we gonna lose some more black off our behinds." She was so angry, she could almost taste her irritation.

"I don't care what you say; I know what I heard, and I ain't lying. If you hadn't stuck that big head of yours out the bushes, Ma Cile wouldn't have heard us. It's your fault, Miss Big Butt!" June Bug hissed. He clamped his fingers against his ears because that was all he could do.

The children looked out of the foyer window just in time to see Ma Cile lumbering toward the maple and oak trees near the vegetable garden. "Oh, Lord, help us, she's gonna get one of those giant Joshua tree branches to whip us with!" they whimpered. Just when they thought they couldn't get any more frightened, June Bug and Lil Bit each felt a hand on one of their shoulders. "Oh, be Jesus!" they shrieked. "Now the Lord is mad and He's touched us!" They tried to bolt, but the omnipotent power of the hands gently pulled them back.

"Not the Lawd, but someone real close to 'em." Sister Betty whispered. The hands felt powerful, but the voice seemed tiny, almost dwarfish, by comparison. The children turned around, and there she was, the object of their argument and the reason for the whipping they were about to receive. She was pecan-brown-colored, elderly, and real short, like one of those little people in *The Wizard of Oz*, and she wore white from head to toe.

Sister Betty always wore a big cross hung around her tiny, wrinkled neck, carried a much-too-big Bible, and constantly smiled for no apparent reason. The children had heard that no matter what the situation was, she would just clasp her petite hands together, look up toward heaven, and give you a smile. Sometimes while laying her hands on your head and praying, her false teeth would fall forward. Before they hit the floor, she would snatch the teeth by their metal hook. She'd put them in her pocket and keep right on smiling, showing her pink, rubbery gums. Every so often, she mumbled some words that she claimed only she and God understood, but which would benefit whomever she prayed for.

The children willed their feet to move, but nothing happened. Sister Betty held both their chins in her small hands and proceeded to smile as she whispered again, "Sister Betty has to leave now, 'cause I must be about the Lawd's business. There be so many people that the Lawd must have Sister Betty see about." She stepped back and looked up at the children. "Y'all two young'uns look like ya been crying. Ya wanna tell ole Sister Betty what's wrong? 'Cause all things are possible for them that love the Lawd, ya know. Come on, tell Sister Betty yo' troubles."

It seemed to Lil Bit that Sister Betty put a tattling spell on her, because before she knew it, she told everything June Bug said. " . . . And, Sister Betty, I didn't believe a word that lying June Bug was saying about you. I know Jesus ain't gonna call nobody up on no telephone and tell them nothing. I don't know why June Bug would say sumpthin' so stupid, and especially about you, Sister Betty." She leaned down to Sister Betty and whispered, "I think he's gone and got himself possessed." Rising back up again, Lil Bit ranted, "Now Ma Cile has gone to get some braided switches or tree limbs, and she gonna whip us because June Bug is possessed. I don't know why I got to get a whipping, too; June Bug the one with the lying demon!"

Lil Bit was talking so fast while pleading her case that she didn't realize that she had twisted the hem of her dress into a knot. Poor child wore panties that read *Tuesday*, exposed to everyone who knew today was Friday.

Sister Betty stood there with her eternal smile etched on

her wrinkled face and chuckled, which caused her false teeth to slip. She shoved the teeth back into place and laughed, "Hush, chile, ya done gone and got ya'self all hypered." She backed a few steps away from the children, turned, and pointed one tiny brown finger toward the living room. "Y'all go on in there and sit down on that sofa."

The children looked at one another in disbelief as their voices went up several notches. They shrieked in unison, "Oh, no, ma'am, we can't do that, Sister Betty. Ma Cile said that sofa just came out of layaway and she put plastic covers on it just for her company. We ain't company. She catches us sitting on her *good sofa* and we'll be dead for real!" Each child kept inhaling air on every syllable. They sounded like they had just swallowed nitrous oxide without the laughter effect.

Sister Betty stopped laughing and spoke in a hushed voice that suddenly sounded like a command, from God Himself, breaking through the sky. "I said for y'all young'uns to sit down on that there sofa, and that's what me and the Lawd mean!"

June Bug and Lil Bit didn't doubt her. The soles of their floppy shoes scattered the multicolored throw rugs that lay from the foyer to the living room. They stopped just in time to push aside the strings of colored beads that served as a partition. Entering the living room, they picked up speed and dove for the sofa, thought about it, and screeched to a complete stop. Lil Bit wiped a bead of perspiration from her cheek and firmly grabbed the still-terrified June Bug by his shoulder for support. Together they slowly turned around and sat down on the *good sofa*, giving it all the respect it deserved. Sister Betty followed with her eternal smile still etched on her face.

From the outside and through the large picture window in the living room, they heard Ma Cile holler like she'd stumped her big toe, the one with the Band-Aid-covered corn. "June Bug, Lil Bit, I got my switches for yo' butt training, and I'm fixing to stomp some sense into y'all heathens. Where ya be? Y'all best have off dem *good clothes* I bought ya. I ain't whuppin' no clothes, 'cause dem clothes didn't do nothin' wrong. Now, where in the house y'all be at? Don't make me come lookin' fo' ya!"

Ma Cile's voice was getting closer and stronger. The children knew they had crossed the line that time. They would rather have woken a bear from his hibernation than to have embarrassed Ma Cile. Of all the people to embarrass her in front of, they thought, why did it have to be the most holy and God's best friend, Sister Betty!

June Bug and Lil Bit stood up and started to run for the stairs up to the attic to hide. In their panic, they tripped each other several times. They looked like two brown toy Slinkys as each one kept pulling the other down. When they did recover, they got up so fast that they almost knocked over Ma Cile's snuff-spitting can. Again they panicked. All they needed was to be caught sitting on her *good sofa* and knocking the snuff spit and ashes out of the spittin' can onto the *good rug*. They stopped in front of the multicolored beads and stood completely still because they didn't know where or how they should move. They looked sad. June Bug's usual big-mouthed attitude had vanished long ago back into the jasmine bushes, and Lil Bit wished she weren't so big, so that she could hide under the *good sofa*.

Sister Betty's softened voice coaxed them back to reality. "Y'all young'uns, please, jist sit down. Don't worry about ya ole Ma Cile. I'll tell her the Lawd had sumpthin' fo' me to say to ya and everythang will be all right." She waited to see if her words had any effect on the children, who stood as stiff as statues. They didn't. She tried again, this time adding a little more sweetness in her voice. "Y'all do believe me, don't ya?" she implored, smiling that smile again. If June Bug and Lil Bit did not believe her, they did not show it; instead they moved backward toward the *good sofa* and again, with deference, sat down.

Sister Betty had them right where she wanted. The children continued to act as if they were hypnotized. If she told them to go and hitch a wagon to a flea's butt so it could tote the wood to town, they would do it.

Sister Betty and the children heard Ma Cile wheezing as she

entered the house, seconds before they saw her. "Whew, them steps is gettin' harder ta climb every day, especially when I got ta go and git the whuppin' switches myself. I might have ta sit a spell befo' I whup them heathens' behinds." She stopped and smoothed a wrinkle on her apron and then used that same hand to fan her face flushed with perspiration. The trip to get the switches had taken its toll. She needed an excuse to rest, but she had promised her grandchildren a whipping and she did not want to appear to soften. She said aloud, "Maybe if I don't whup 'em right away they be extra good, 'cause they don't know when I'm gonna do it." She threw in the last part to keep them on their toes.

Ma Cile stood still long enough to catch her breath and then continued down the hallway. As she waddled her wide hips past the living room, she remarked, "Be right back, Sister Betty; excuse me a minute whilst I go and find them young'uns—" Quicker than two rabbits meeting for the first or fifteenth time, Ma Cile backtracked and looked in disbelief at the two children sitting on her *good sofa.*

"Oh, my Gawd! Y'all done sho'nuff lost ya little minds. Lawd, look at 'em; they done desecrated my *good sofa.*" Ma Cile found that all her strength returned as she launched toward the children and, at the same time, knocked over her snuff-spitting can. Now she was madder than the ugly girl that always watched the pocketbooks at the dance club; there was ashes and snuff spit on her good carpet. Her brown good eye and the blue store-bought one kept rolling around in their sockets as she tried to regain her balance. Ma Cile started toward them again; she couldn't wait to get her hands on them. With outstretched hands, palms wide and arthritic knees stiff, she went after the kids like an evil, out-of-control robot.

Saving grace was on the children's side. "Ma Cile, let dem young'uns be!" said Sister Betty, once again sounding like the voice of God in a tunnel. "I'm fixin' to tell them what thus saith the Lawd."

Ma Cile was moving so fast, the crusty calluses on the soles of her feet burned to cinders as she stopped just inches away from the children. Moving slowly, out of breath and wheezing like an asthmatic turtle, she turned around and, in her haltering, sweetest voice, said, "Well, if'n they ain't no bother, Sister Betty, they can sits here on my *good sofa* and listen to what ya has to say. Lawd knows they sho'nuff needs to be reminded of they place if they expects to survives in dis here cruel world."

That's what she might have said to Sister Betty, but what the children actually heard was, "When Sister Betty leaves, y'all's souls may belong to Gawd, but ya black behinds belongs to me!" At that very moment, the children just gave up their plans of ever reaching eleven.

It took a few moments, but Ma Cile finally recovered and tipped over to her rocking chair. She gave the chair a light push, and as it came forward, she timed it so she could shove her wide hips onto the calico chair mat. Because of her anger, her timing was off. She swayed to and fro as though the rocking chair were pushing her away. After several tries, which looked more like she was getting ready to skip double Dutch than sit down, she fell into the seat with a loud thud as the southernmost part of her flesh hit more wood than chair mat. Of course, it sounded more like an involuntary release of gas than a splat. Her anger and embarrassment grew, but instead she held her peace and smiled at Sister Betty again. After adjusting one of her elasticized taupe-colored Knee-Hi stockings, which had fallen around her ankles, Ma Cile gestured for Sister Betty to proceed with the story.

Sister Betty was sitting on Ma Cile's blue-eye side—the false one—so Ma Cile didn't know that Sister Betty saw her when she turned back and gave the children deadly, silent threats. Once again, Ma Cile gave them her renowned *"Oh, yeah, y'all definitely gonna be some dead young'uns come sundown"* stare. That time, the children almost passed out completely.

Once again, Sister Betty's commanding voice pulled Ma Cile and the children back. "Now, Lil Bit, from what you done tole me, everything June Bug said about me was almost true, but what ya don't—"

Ma Cile had barely rested her head against the headrest of the rocking chair, still trying to get her second breath and plan phase two punishment of her grandchildren. When she heard Sister Betty say June Bug's name, she sprung forward like she was shot from a circus cannon and butted in. "That June Bug was talkin' 'bout ya, Sister Betty? Oh, Sister Betty, I'm so sorry fo' that. That's another reason why June Bug gonna git his sorry behind whupped fo' sure. I ain't givin' no mercy to 'em. He done known better den to talk 'bout folks, especially you, Sister Betty!" Ma Cile didn't try to hide it this time. She pointed a fat, stubby finger and laid her one *good eye* on June Bug, and without saying a word, she gave him her *"I'm not only gonna whup yo' behind, but I'm gonna set it on fire, and when it's done burnin' up, I'm gonna burn da ashes, too!"* glare. June Bug started whimpering, and his behind suddenly filled up with gas, as if that would save it!

As though she could read Ma Cile's mind, Sister Betty smiled and put a finger to her lips to caution her to be quiet. Sister Betty's false teeth slipped, which caused them to make a *tsk-tsk* sound; she pushed the teeth back in, turned back to the children, and continued speaking. "As I was trying to say befo' I kept getting interrupted . . ." She stopped long enough to see if Ma Cile caught her hint. Ma Cile did. "Most folks around these here parts only know a little sumpthin' about me, because I pretty much keep my business to myself. Although I was born and raised right here in Pelzer, South Carolina, I've been a member of the Ain't Nobody Else Right but Us—All Others Goin' to Hell Church since I was younger than y'all two. Why, I even remember when the late Reverend Wasn't Evencalled delivered the first sermon there. It was, 'Don't Let Worry Kill You Off. Let the Church Help.' Anyway, now I'm gonna tell y'all out of my own mouth what happened on that Wednesday afternoon in nineteen eighty-four. That way, y'all know the truth, and ya won't have to be out there hiding in dem bushes, arguing about whether or not I got a telephone call from de Lawd."

Sister Betty leaned forward and winked at the children as

she spoke. The children, however, were too busy trying to make their minds go blank and wishing that a spaceship would come and abduct them to safety. They couldn't figure out how she knew they were hiding in the bushes. Could this old woman read minds, too? They didn't mean to, but out of nervousness, they found themselves glancing over at Ma Cile.

Luckily, Ma Cile didn't see the children looking in her direction. She was too busy readjusting her false blue eye, trying to line it up with her *good* brown one, so she could dispense another double whammy. A whammy that was sure to have the children lying on a psychiatrist's couch well into their fifties. Ma Cile may never have finished high school or even middle school, but she majored and received honors in Emotional Abuse 101, and in her mind, she did it out of love.

Sister Betty continued to ignore them as she folded her hands in prayer. She smiled as she continued. "Ah, yes, I remembers it like it jist happened yesterday...."

As Sister Betty rocked and fingered the big cross around her neck, she told them about the day she got her telephone call from God.

Pick Up de Phone. It's Gawd Callin'!

Old Sister Betty always lived by herself and had what some might consider the typical "faithful servant" type of home. In the sitting room there was a big armchair, encased in clear plastic covering, with lace doilies on each arm, and a big family-sized Bible on the brown glass-covered wooden coffee table. One white painted wall proudly displayed a giant red, velvet-backed, lighted picture of Christ with a metal chain that hung from its side. On the mantel over a faux fireplace was a bottle of Blessed olive oil, the extra-virgin kind.

Every day, in good health or bad, Sister Betty had prayer at exactly twelve noon. She knelt beside her plush green-brocaded sofa protected by its zippered triple-layered plastic covering, without benefit of a cushion to support her sometimes swollen arthritic knees. After humming a verse of her favorite hymn, she offered up enough thanks to make any self-respecting Pharisee proud. She also fasted often and made sure everyone knew about it. She was aware that the Bible taught to fast in private, but she told because she didn't think most people, other than herself, read the Word. She wanted people to know it was the right thing to do.

From all outward appearances, everyone knew she was definitely one of God's chosen people.

One day, as usual, Sister Betty was home alone. She had just barely gotten up from kneeling after her noon prayer, when her tiny fingers raced to reach for her television remote on the table.

Sister Betty was a creature of habit. Her daily ritual was to start prayer at noon but be sure to be finished by one P.M. She would get up, throw her hands up in one swooping gesture, then reach over and grab the remote control. She did not want to miss one moment of her favorite soap opera, *She's Having Every Man's Child.* Knowing whom the characters Erica and Tad slept around with at that moment was very important to her. She barely got the word "Amen" out of her mouth before she turned on the television.

Sister Betty took no prisoners when her favorite soap opera was on. She was a soap opera addict and watched her favorite little thirteen-inch color screen with the intensity of an eagle. The television set was old, and a metal coat hanger replaced a broken antenna. She had saved fifty books of S&H Green Stamps to get it. The knob had been lost long ago, and the vertical worked when it wanted. She held onto the television out of loyalty, even though she needed a pair of pliers to change the channels.

When Sister Betty watched her soap opera, she would either scold the characters or praise them. Whether or not she really thought they could hear her was the subject of many back-of-the-church discussions.

As the hour dwindled, Sister Betty relaxed during the commercials by drinking a cold glass of her favorite flavored Kool-

Aid: red. She was busy yelling at the television, giving it a piece of her mind, when she thought she heard the telephone ring. It rang one time and she hesitated. She didn't want to miss one word of what Erica Kane was saying about her ninth husband not appreciating her. It rang a second time. She became annoyed. Anyone who knew her knew better than to call around that time of day. The telephone rang a third time, and that time, she turned down the volume on the television. She sounded like a pit bull singing *Aida* in patois as she spoke into the phone.

"Praise de Lawd—Sister Betty speakin'!" Suddenly, her expression changed from resentment to one of sheer surprise and humility. She stood as still as a rock and listened to the voice on the other end and pulled the telephone closer to the big armchair. In her most devout tone she replied, "Yes, Lawd, is this really the Lawd? Ya callin' me?" She stopped blabbing long enough to check her own pulse, to make sure she hadn't crossed over. Seeing she wasn't hallucinating, she continued babbling. "I'm the least one of ya chosen people? Y'all say ya comin' by to see me! When, Lawd? When ya comin'?"

Sister Betty leaned forward in her chair with a look of serenity upon her face. She placed a hand on one of her skinny knees and pictured herself sitting on the left side of the Lord. She was so full of herself, she was about to add another book to the Bible and call it "Sister Betty 1:1." She cackled on, daydreamed, and never heard the other end hang up.

When Sister Betty finally came to herself, she could not believe what she had heard. Was that really the Lord calling her? Well, of course it was. The more she thought about it, the more sense it made. After all, wasn't she one of the most faithful members of the Ain't Nobody Else Right but Us—All Others Goin' to Hell Church? There was no one else who could moan, sing, or "amen" the pastor on as well as she could. She even knew all twelve made-up verses of "Jesus on the Main Line." On Easter Sunday, wasn't she the one that made crosses out of the palm leaves and gave them to the children? She was a super saint; why wouldn't the Lord be calling on her?

Everyone in Pelzer, South Carolina, may not have known much about her personal business, but they knew how long Sister Betty had been a God-fearing woman. They knew she had been saved, sanctified, and Holy Ghost-filled longer than the current pastor, the Reverend Knott Enuff Money, because she never let them forget. Those who paid particular attention to her finances knew she paid her tithes when she could and never went to church without looking real neat and color-coordinated. She had proper church manners; she even held up her index finger when she rose in the middle of service to go to the bathroom. Why it was necessary to hold up that particular finger, few if any knew, but most were obedient and did it anyway. It was only natural that the Lord would want to visit her; she was a fine example of how a chosen child of God ought to be.

Sister Betty needed more time to praise herself, but there was a lot to do. After all, she was Sister Betty and her house should be spotless for the Lord when He came. Too bad He hung up before she found out exactly what time that would be.

Sister Betty started to do a little church dance, but something on television caught her attention. She turned up the volume and laughed aloud. "Well, who said I cain't clean up my house while I watch a little television? The Bible sho' didn't." Sister Betty went about her dusting. Well, actually, she was doing some light dusting, because this was Sister Betty's house and it never got too dirty. All the while she dusted and cleaned, her attention was on the television, so she missed a few spots, especially a big spot where her coffee cup had lain. She also forgot to wipe the dust from the cover of the big family-sized Bible.

Sister Betty was interrupted by a knock at the door. She chose to ignore it. Cleaning her house and watching television was what she wanted to do. The knocking persisted, so she threw down her dust rag and took off the fishnet cap, which covered the *good wig* she wore.

My goodness, what if it was the Lawd? she thought. Much to her disappointment, when she got to the door, there was only a young boy standing there. He looked to be about eight, skinny, and wore "sometime" clothes—the Southern custom where some-times you wore the clothes and sometimes others wore them, thereby making them *sometime* clothes. She looked at the little boy and asked impatiently, "Chile, what do ya want!?"

"Sister Betty, ma'am, it's me, Buster Junior from down the road. I'm so hungry; could you please spare a sandwich or sumpthin'? Mama said come and see you 'cause she ain't got no food to feed me today, and you is the most Christian-like folk around."

Sister Betty didn't budge. Instead, she fingered a couple of her chin hairs. While still staring at the child, she thought to herself, *Hmmm, now, if I invited him in, that would mean I'd have to stop cleaning and go into the kitchen to fix sumpthin'. That also means I'd be missin' more of my soap opera, and that ain't an option; besides, the Lawd is comin'.*

Sister Betty stopped staring at the little boy and smiled as she said, "Honey chile, I don't have time to fix sumpthin' for ya, but y'all wait right here." Turning around, she ran back inside and grabbed a handful of candy Now and Laters from her mason jar, then rushed back to the door and snatched skinny little Buster Junior up by his collar. She slapped the rock-hard candy into his hand. "Here, take these. Eat one now and save one for later," and before the little boy could say, "Thank you, ma'am," Sister Betty was back in her living room, watching television and dusting, waiting for the Lord to come by.

When a commercial came on, Sister Betty dashed into her kitchen and seized the straw broom. She rushed back into the sitting room and gave the floor a lick and a promise. After she had put the broom away, she spotted a few untouched places. No one was around to see her, so she kicked the dust balls under the couch; she could get it later. Who would know?

As she opened the bottle of ammonia to clean her mirror, the doorbell rang again. She really got annoyed this time. Every time something good was about to happen on television and she was getting into her cleaning, there was an intrusion. She slammed down the bottle of ammonia, spilling some of it on her-self. Using the hem of her old paisley apron, she wiped her hands and stormed toward the door. She slowed down a few feet from the door and laid her hand over her heart. "Oh my, what is wrong with me? This time it must be the Lawd!" she panted. Sister Betty pushed a loose strand of hair back under her *good wig* and continued toward the door.

When Sister Betty opened her door, a strong, and unpleasant odor, like a combination of raw chitterlings and cheap buttered popcorn, whiffed into her house. The odor was overpowering and pungent, so she grabbed for the doorknob with one hand to keep from passing out. She closed her eyes and blinked at the giant garbage bag, with head and limbs protruding, on her front porch. She started to scream but stopped when she realized the plastic bag clothed a homeless man.

Giving no thought to the homeless man's feelings, Sister Betty immediately pinched her nostrils tight until flashes of electrifying light ripped through her head. Between the stink and the streaks of light, her *good wig* started sliding to the side of her head, taking her dignity with it.

"Excuse me, ma'am. Er, good day," he grunted. The homeless man was taller than Sister Betty by about a foot, but he began to shrink to her size as she gave him the evil eye.

He shuffled his feet from side to side. She didn't flinch.

The homeless man's legs buckled as he ran his dirty fingers through his blond hair. Hair, long ago camouflaged by dirt, was matted and stuck to his scalp, with several hairy mounds that dared to peek out.

For a brief moment, Sister Betty continued to stare at the man in disbelief, and then she, too, replied with a grunt, "Huh?" He looked like someone too lazy to work and too nervous to steal, she thought.

Sister Betty didn't finish, because she spied a small metal spade on the shelf by the door. It was her favorite gardening tool. Favorite tool or not, she thought to herself, if the man made a wrong move, she'd plant him deeper than Jimmy Hoffa.

The man's face was so masked with the cruel scars of a hard life, she could not tell his true age. Instead, she looked at him with the intensity of the killer shark from the movie *Jaws* as she tried to determine whether he was Caucasian or Creole.

"Uh, I'm sorry—my name is—" was all the homeless man had a chance to utter. He wanted to flee because suddenly she looked hungrier than he, but he could not move. The sweat, created inside the plastic bag that covered his skinny and infested upper body instead of a clean shirt, began pouring. As uncomfortable he was, running he was not.

Again Sister Betty ignored his feelings. She quickly decided his race didn't matter. He would have smelled the same.

"Hmmmm . . ." was Sister Betty's response as her eyes darted between the man and the spade. But she refused to let go of her nostrils, and the palm of her hand covered part of her mouth, causing her speech to sound slurred. "You'd better move from my door" was what she meant to say. It sounded like "Yo butter mo' dough."

The homeless man felt defeated. He hung his head with more shame than he thought he had, as he reexamined his tattered pants protruding from the garbage bag. He looked at the rags as though it were for the first time. It took a few moments, but the man regained his courage and spoke again. "I need prayer. Can you just pray with me?"

Sister Betty ignored his pleas. Instead, she focused on his lips. They were gray and crusted. With everything the man was going through and the fear she felt, all she wondered was if ChapStick came in a spread.

Sister Betty rebounded. She could not have this man, tattered, stinking, dressed in a Ziploc garbage bag and looking like the last of the mentally challenged, at her door when the Lord arrived.

Sister Betty finally took her fingers away from her nose while her palm still covered her mouth. Her other hand still gripped the doorknob like it was found money. She held on to it just in case the man's obvious mental problem paid a visit. Of course, having the spade within reach made her feel a little braver.

She carefully moved her palm away from her mouth for a second and spoke. "What do you want? I'm not home alone."

Sister Betty felt she could stretch the truth a little; after all, she did have God on her side, so she wasn't actually alone. And, she was expecting Him any moment.

Without waiting for the homeless man to answer, Sister Betty raised her hand and pinched her nose again while slowly backing through her door.

The homeless man did not try to follow Sister Betty into her doorway. He was only homeless, not stupid. "I'm sorry, miss. My name is Ellis—Ellis Alonzo Turner. I know I must look a mess—"

Sister Betty cut the homeless man off with the display of another shocked look on her face. She thought, *A mess? A mess is something children or pets make, this man is a walking, talking wreck.*

The homeless man took a chance and proceeded with caution as he again spoke. "I really do need prayer. I need it now. I don't know how or why I knocked on your door. Can you please help me?"

Sister Betty took about sixty seconds to compose herself. She was torn and didn't know what to do. An answer suddenly came to her when she realized she was probably missing more of her soap opera. She was certain. She knew what she had to do.

The homeless man looked at her, and she thought she saw a tear start to form in one eye. For a brief moment, she felt compassion. The moment passed quickly.

"I don't have time. This is not a church. I'm waiting on special company. Maybe another time we'll have prayer." She was lying, but she'd repent later.

Sister Betty started to close her door, but she stopped. She was, after all, a child of God, so she whispered and made the sign of the cross. "Be blessed, Mr. Ellis Alonzo Turner." That should take care of that little white lie she'd told, and then she slammed her door.

When Sister Betty returned to her living room, she realized

that she had forgotten to lock her door. She could not be too sure that the homeless man would not return. Just in case, on her way to the front door, she grabbed the fishnet cap and placed it over her *good wig*. As she reached her front door and tried the knob, her doorbell rang again. She threw her hands up in the air, whirling them like twin helicopter blades as she said aloud to herself, "Now this is ridiculous. I told that homeless man that I wished him blessings and now he's back. I sho' hope the Lawd don't come and find this man on my doorstep."

When she opened it, there stood a young woman. To say Sister Betty was disappointed would have been an understatement. She eyed the woman up and down and then snatched the eyeglasses that hung around her neck and put them on. She peered over the glasses at the woman and then stepped closer to her. The young woman was some loose gal named Kecia, who Sister Betty had seen around the neighborhood but had never spoken to. The woman looked to be about thirty and wore a screaming-red halter dress with tiny spaghetti straps. She looked like she should have been wearing a size twelve, but the store only had size nines—so she wore the size nines. Her large breasts were escaping from the top of the dress and had no intention of returning until a size twelve was found. She also wore a bright-red, waist-length wig. Her dark-complected face was covered by wingtip eyeglasses without the lenses but lined with rhinestones anyhow.

Sister Betty crossed her arms, tapped her foot, and asked the woman what did she want. The young woman cringed but said she was there to talk about helping another neighbor who had lost her home and possessions in a fire.

Sister Betty was only half listening. Why come to her? It wasn't like she and Kecia really knew each other. She only saw the woman when she went to church, which was probably about two or three times a week. Sister Betty made it a practice not to speak to anyone on her way to church.

Sister Betty liked to keep her mind on the Lord, praising him in her heart, so that when she got there, she could almost walk in the door shouting. She didn't want to be one of those so-called Christians who had to wait for the music or the preaching to start before they could get into the service. When Sister Betty got to the church, she was ready. "Sister Ready Betty" was what she was called. So what if she always shouted "Amen" during the service and especially while the pastor was preaching. What could he say that she hadn't heard before? After all, she had been attending the Ain't Nobody Else Right but Us—All Others Goin' to Hell Church for a long time. She knew all the sermons by heart.

She unfolded her arms, stopped tapping her foot, and told Kecia she didn't have the time to discuss the situation; perhaps later she would. Then she slammed the door, almost ripping away one of Kecia's too-hot-to-trot-red press-on fingernails.

Kecia was stunned and looked like a chocolate Barbie Doll with her hand caught in the collection plate. Instinctively she had moved her hand out of the doorway. She quickly glanced down at her too-hot-to-trot-red press-on toenails. They were still intact. She was grateful the old woman didn't rip them off when she slammed the door in her face.

Sister Betty had barely gotten back into the room and put the fishnet cap back on her head when she realized that the soap opera was over. "What else could go wrong?" she thought aloud as she roughly hit the television's *Off* button. Sister Betty did not stay angry for long. The idea of the Lord's impending visit lifted her spirits again, and she continued cleaning and moaning while singing the old spiritual, "Only the Meek and Humble Shall See Gawd." When she sang, she sounded like a tomcat being neutered without anesthesia.

The afternoon wore on, and Sister Betty started getting tired, so for the last time she removed the fishnet cap from her head and used it to wipe the perspiration from her face. The old armchair felt like a welcome lover when she sat down in it. She laid her head back and smoothed the lace doilies on each arm of the chair. Next, she leaned over and rested one of her little wrinkled hands on the big family-sized Bible, looked up at her giant velvet-backed picture of the Lord, and smiled. She was exhausted to the bone, but she had done a good job of cleaning her house. The Lord would be very proud of her. Now all she had to do was wait on Him.

Sister Betty was also sleepy. It had been several hours since she got the phone call from the Lord. What was keeping him? There was no doubt in her heart that the phone call was from Him, but where was He? She had started to get annoyed again. Her patience needed a lot of work, but "God knew her heart," was what she always said.

Once again, the phone rang. Sister Betty debated whether or not to answer it. She needed to be able to hear the Lord when He came to the door. Whoever was calling better have a good reason for disturbing her.

Sister Betty got up and answered the phone. Before she could say anything, her face went blank. Her hands moved behind her in all directions as they tried to find the cushion in the big armchair before she collapsed.

Hardly able to speak above a whisper, she cried, "Lawd, I don't understand! Ya say you came by to see me, but I wouldn't let ya in. Lawd, how could that be? I've been home all day. Every time there was a knock at my door I opened it!" Sister Betty felt the room spin around, and as she put her hand to her head for balance, her *good wig* fell to one side, exposing tiny braids that resembled a long-ago-forgotten cornfield.

"Lawd, ya telling me that you was that little boy that was hungry. I should have known that, Lawd. You did say in yo' Word that unless we become as a chile, we can in no wise enter into yo' kingdom." She continued to hold her phone in disbelief.

"My goodness, Lawd, the homeless man that smelled so bad—that was you?"

Sister Betty could feel the heavy weight of remorse as tears started to roll down her cheek. "Of course, I should have known that. Didn't you send the demons out of a homeless man and send them into the swine?"

Sister Betty suddenly tried to perk up and spoke with confidence. "Well, Lawd, I feel comfortable in knowing that the woman that was obviously a prostitute—"

Suddenly, Sister Betty's face, ashen with terror, seemed to

shrink as she continued her conversation with the Lord. "Y'all was the young lady that needed my help with my neighbor! Lawd, I didn't know you could've been Kecia! Lawd, I should've remembered it was a harlot that wiped yo' feet with her hair and gave her best from an alabaster box. I just wanted to clean my house up for ya, to show you what a good Christian I was. Oh, Lawd, please give po' Sister Betty another chance. Please, dear Lawd, just one mo' chance!"

Sister Betty fell limp to the floor with outstretched arms and continued her pleading. . . .

Everything had come to a complete stop as Sister Betty told her story. She had Ma Cile and the kids' complete attention. Not even a breeze moved. When Sister Betty spoke, the elements knew to stop and listen.

"Aw, come on, y'all young'uns stop staring at me with ya mouths all wide open. Sister Betty is jist fine now." She turned to Ma Cile, who had somehow managed to maneuver over to the *good sofa* and sat down next to her grandchildren. "Now, Sister Cile, you know I ain't one to be in yo' business about these here young'uns, but if ya don't lighten up, ya gonna mess 'em up."

Still in a state of shock, Ma Cile and the kids stood up at the same time. Collectively they looked like the three monkeys, See No Evil, Hear No Evil, and Speak No Evil. Ma Cile recovered first. "Sister Betty, this is the first time I done hear with my own ears about yo' telephone call from de Lawd. I don't know what ta say to ya." She didn't realize that she had twisted the switches into the shape of a cross. Ma Cile wasn't even aware that she was waving the cross-shaped switches she still held at Sister Betty. It looked like she was trying to ward off some spirits or something. Maybe it was just her nerves.

"Please, don't ya say nothin' for a minute, Sister Cile; jist listen for a change. The Lawd fo'give Sister Betty 'cause I needed to really know what being His child meant. He humbled me right to my knees. When Gawd got finished with me, I had ta put down my coordinated clothes, my thinking that didn't nobody know him better'n me, and anythang else that smelled like pride. I don't limit praying time no mo', either. If I start praying at twelve noon and I don't finish till twelve midnight, well, that's okay. I don't turn help away from folks, 'cause they could be angels from Gawd."

Ma Cile and the children wanted to move, but they still couldn't. June Bug was really in a pickle. His bladder was kicking and yelling at his feet to move, but the feet was more afraid of Sister Betty and Ma Cile than it was of the bladder. The bladder had no choice but to back off or it could boss around the intestines. It decided it would bully the intestines if for no other reason than to see what would happen with the gas June Bug was holding in.

"Now, Sister Cile, I ain't gonna sit here and preach, but y'all best get rid of that notion of yo' *good sofa*, *good rug*, and yo' *company sittin' room*. Treat yo' grand-young'uns like they jist might be Gawd's li'l angels. Raise 'em right when they's young, and when they's older, they won't forget it."

Sister Betty straightened the little white, brimless hat on her head and murmured as she went toward the door with her tiny feet barely touching the floor. "I want y'all to turn to each other and say, 'I love ya and there ain't nuthin' ya can do about it.' "

Ma Cile and the children didn't waste any time obeying. They kept repeating the words, "I love you" to one another as if it were their mantra.

Sister Betty smiled to herself as she watched them. "I best be getting on now. You young'uns behave yaselves so Gawd can use ya."

To Ma Cile and the kids, it seemed like she just levitated and disappeared. They still couldn't move. They looked like gape-mouthed statues as they nodded together in agreement at Sister Betty's message of patience and tolerance. They might have still been standing in the same spot today if something strange hadn't happened. From out of nowhere, they all heard a telephone ring. They did not have a telephone.

And the second is like, namely this, "Thou shalt love thy neighbor as thyself. There is none other commandment greater than these.

—Mark 12:31

Flee all youthful lusts; but follow righteousness, faith, charity, peace with all them that call on the Lord out of a pure heart.
—2 Timothy 2:22

Train up a child in the way he should go: and when he is old, he will not depart from it.

—Proverbs 22:6

Sister Connie Fuse Makes a Grave Mistake

It was a warm and breezy summer evening in Pelzer, South Carolina. The fragrance of purple lilacs and the shimmering lights coming from the butts of bloodthirsty lightening bugs filled the air in Ma Cile's front yard. She stood in one spot on her porch as if glued and said, "Ah, I just wanna say thank you to ya, Lawd. Ya done brought me through yet another day."

Ma Cile muttered to herself as she absentmindedly twisted the faded gold wedding band on her brown, wrinkled finger and remembered its history. It was a seldom thought-of memory, one almost as faded as the ring. A memory of a marriage that took her innocence at the age of fifteen and left her raising two young daughters by herself. Her life changed forever when her husband, Charlie, was forced to spend their meager earnings on necessities such as food and mortgage instead of a doctor that might have saved his life from pneumonia. She was nineteen when Charlie, a day laborer at odd jobs, died at the young age of twenty-two. "Yes, Suh, I just wanna thank ya." She folded the memories of her late husband back into the recesses of a place in her mind that held all her painful memories. She unclasped her hands and looked up in wonder at the marvel of God's sun and the orange haze that accompanied its surrender to the oncoming night.

Ma Cile worked as a cafeteria cook at the Caroline Elementary School for the past forty-five years. She looked forward to the end of each school day for a quick nap and a few well-deserved pinches of snuff. She finally moved from the spot and slowly rocked in her favorite brown mahogany high-backed rocker, giving in to her tired body. Every time she would doze off, frantic scenes of marauding children throwing lumpy mashed potatoes and soggy peas throughout the school cafeteria entered her mind. She awoke, felt around inside the deep pockets of her perfectly starched white cotton apron, and found the little tin canister that held her pleasure.

On the real side, Ma Cile had a snuff habit.

The setting sun that early evening seemed exceptionally bright, and with each dip, it became brighter. She tilted her head back, laid her hands across her huge bosom, and looked around her flower-filled white porch. She smiled to herself, which was something she seldom did. Pious children of God did not smile too much, she was always told.

Placed around the faded and chipped white front porch were elephant ear plants with yellow and red roses, mixed in with red and green pepper plants. Her love of snuff and hot, home-grown jalapeño peppers was infamous, although, if she started dipping snuff and eating those raw peppers in front of company, they made their visit short. If she decided to chew a mouthful of Argo starch, then they made their visit very short! She believed that letting out gas was a natural act, and if Ma Cile was anything, she was natural.

Inside on the electric stove, a large aluminum pot of lima beans, seasoned with smoked ham hocks and vegetable bits, bubbled and sent tantalizing soul-food smells to anyone with a nose. Adding a pinch of baking soda to the beans was supposed to alleviate intestinal gas, but that only worked if someone did not dip snuff and eat raw hot peppers. If they, like Ma Cile, decided to eat a little Argo starch with it, then they could have just saved the baking soda for the biscuits or something else useful.

Everything about the warm summer evening seemed so peaceful as she continued rocking and enjoying the satisfying euphoria of her snuff. It was so quiet, neurotic cats could be heard whispering and jumping on cotton.

Unusually well behaved this evening were Lil Bit and June Bug. The kids were playing a competitive game of "country Scrabble," using letters cut out from magazines. Normally, they would argue and make up words that only the one who made them up had ever heard. Then each would call Webster "stupid" because he did not include their made-up words in his dictionary. They knew since Sister Betty's visit to Ma Cile a few weeks ago, when the Lord showed her how not to be materialistic, that Ma Cile was trying to change her ways. That is what she said, but the children were still not convinced. They thought she was biding her time and giving them plenty of rope to hang themselves; they were cautious.

As time passed that evening, the kids would aggravate Ma Cile and then retreat, each time becoming a little bolder. Normally, they did not see her take the snuff dip, but tonight they had. Therefore, they cut aggravation some slack.

Ma Cile finally felt relaxed and had just got her *good* brown eye lined up just right with her store-bought false blue one, when it happened. She was relaxed but shot forward from the rocker like a Scud missile when someone yelling out her name startled her. Ma Cile's neck stretched like a piece of brown taffy as she tried to readjust from euphoria to reality.

It was Sister Connie Fuse. Despite a full mane of fiery-red waist-length hair that whipped her body like she had done something wrong, the lithe, twenty-five-year-old woman came running like an Olympic sprinter across Ma Cile's lush, green lawn. She wore a pair of Pay Little hard, clear plastic thong shoes that threatened to sever a toe with each step. With one hand held over her heart, she ran huffing and puffing.

Everyone in the town of Pelzer knew not to walk on Ma Cile's grass; it was not worth running the risk of one of her "eye whammies."

Although she loved Sister Connie Fuse like a daughter, tonight she was not in the mood for her particular kind of company. But when Ma Cile heard the panic in Sister Connie Fuse's voice, she knew her much-deserved peace and quiet was finished.

However, Ma Cile was not giving up her peace and quiet easily. Jamming her hand into her apron pocket, she pulled out her little tin canister and yanked the lid off. She then lowered her head slightly, opened her mouth, pulled her lower lip forward, and instead of delicately taking a pinch of snuff, she poured the pungent powder into her mouth. Wham! A heavy-duty dose of "snuff giddiness" hit Ma Cile like one of those crash-dummy race cars hitting a brick wall. It seeped into the veins under her tongue and caused her eyes to line up all on their own. She felt like she could have taken on *I, John the Conqueror*, but this was Sister Connie Fuse, so she took another pinch while waiting for her to finish running through her lush, green grass.

Sister Connie Fuse finally made it to the front porch steps. She was crying from a combination of the loss of circulation in her toes from her hard plastic shoes, and her current dilemma. When she finally reached the porch steps, her creamy skin had a bright-pink hue. With the wet, matted, stringy red hair flapping in her face, she blurted out to Ma Cile that she was in trouble and needed her help.

Ma Cile, by now quite mellowed by the snuff, asked Sister Connie what was wrong.

In between her wailing, which had reached a high pitch and caused her emerald green eyes to look like penicillin mold, she managed to get her story out.

From what Ma Cile could understand, apparently the church mother, Mother Pray Onn, had asked Sister Connie Fuse to run an errand. Mother Pray Onn, about ten years Ma Cile's senior though she would never admit to it, quite often got the congregation members to do her bidding by saying, "The Lord told me to ask you." Since she always testified to having a close walk with God and acted like she was a direct descendant of a Pharisee with clout, no one disobeyed her without a trip to the altar for forgiveness.

After Mother Pray Onn asked the favor, Sister Connie Fuse, whom Ma Cile also thought was a bit naive and about ten cents short of a dime, became just that: *con-fused*.

"Hush, now! Jist explain to me exactly what happened," Ma Cile said.

"Ma Cile . . ." Sister Connie Fuse could hardly get the words out. "Ma Cile, Mother Pray Onn asked me to take her grave layaway payment down to Mr. Bury 'Em Deep at the They All Dyin' to Git Here Cemetery. . . ."

"So, what's wrong with that?" Ma Cile wanted her to get to the point before the night was over, and prodded her along. "Can you please jist git to the problem?"

"Well, I couldn't decide what to wear and so I got downtown late."

"So you wuz late; that ain't no big deal to git so upset about!" Ma Cile was really becoming agitated.

"But I made a mistake."

"We all make mistakes, chile."

"I know. I made a big mistake. It's one of those humdingers."

"Being late ain't no bigger mistake than not gittin' there at all," Ma Cile countered.

"I might as well have not gotten there. I accidentally put Mother Pray Onn's grave layaway payment through the mail slot of the We'll Haul Your Ashes Crematorium."

"Ouch!" That was all Ma Cile could say.

"I came from shopping downtown about two hours later. Ma Cile, I was so happy to have been able to help Mother Pray Onn. A song was all in my heart—"

"Yeah, chile, I git all dat. You had a song and ever'thang and you wuz jist sanging yo' li'l ole heart out, but what happened?" Ma Cile was losing her patience and her snuff high, and that was a lethal combination for sure.

"Well, like I was saying . . . What was I saying, Ma Cile?"

"Ya wuz sanging a song to yo'self!" Ma Cile screamed. She suddenly smiled when she saw she'd frightened Sister Connie Fuse even more than she was already. Ma Cile didn't want to frighten her. She just wanted her to finish her story. "You wuz jist as happy as a bear in an empty beehive with a giant spoon."

"That's right. Anyway, when I got home there was a message on my answering machine from Mother Pray Onn. The crematorium had called her and told what I'd done. They didn't know it was a mistake. They didn't have Mother Pray Onn's ash and they wanted someone to bring her ash downtown."

"Oh, Lawd. Mother Pray Onn's ashes—I'd spend my snuff money to see that!" Ma Cile laughed so hard, her bladder filled up, but she refused to budge. "What happened next, chile?"

"I could tell by how slowly Mother Pray Onn was speaking that she was gonna get me."

" 'Cause she was speaking slowly don't mean she's gonna git ya. What makes ya think she gonna do you some harm?"

"She said, in a real slow voice, that she was gonna get me at Wednesday night's testifying service and there was no place on earth for me to hide. She said I'd better hop up into the butt of the next buzzard flying out of Pelzer and over the Atlantic Ocean and hope it never crapped. That buzzard's butt would be the only safe place for me."

"We ain't got no buzzards in Pelzer, South Carolina," Ma Cile laughed.

"I know; that's why I ran to the next ark of safety." Sister Connie Fuse cried again.

"Where would that be?" Ma Cile asked as she looked all around her.

"Your house is my ark of safety."

Sister Connie Fuse kept hopping from one foot to the other as she continued to blurt out her story. Ma Cile was trying to keep a straight face while again lining up her eyes, which by now had sobered up from the snuff's effect.

"Oh, Ma Cile, what am I gonna do? Mother Pray Onn is going to have a vision or something about me. I just know she will! Allah's gonna give her a vision . . . !" ranted Sister Connie Fuse.

Mother Pray Onn prays to *God*," mocked Ma Cile. "Aren't

you in enough trouble with Mother Pray Onn without switch-ing her over to Allah?" She continued to laugh.

"Ma Cile, please don't tease me. I didn't mean Allah; I meant God. Sometimes I just get so confused," pleaded Sister Connie Fuse.

"Now, you wouldn't be fooling your old Ma Cile, would you, honey? You? Confused? Who would have thought it?" said Ma Cile as she continued to mock Sister Connie Fuse. She looked distressed, so Ma Cile took pity and stopped teasing her.

Ma Cile turned around and yelled into her house, "Lil Bit, June Bug, you two heathens git out here and bring a chair for Sister Connie. Make it very quick and don't bring my *good* rockin'—"

Ma Cile stopped herself as she suddenly remembered her friend Sister Betty's last visit. It was during that visit that Sister Betty had told her about the telephone call from God. That call had changed Sister Betty's life. She learned that people should not worship their material possessions.

Ma Cile felt a chill down her back and quickly added, "Never mind; just bring a chair."

Lil Bit and June Bug dragged Ma Cile's *good* sitting-room rocking chair out onto the porch and set it down by Sister Connie Fuse. With the sudden appearance of company, bold-ness revisited the children, and they decided to test Ma Cile just one more time, for old times' sake. They did not realize that the snuff had worn off and her neurotic *good stuff* feelings had returned.

Ma Cile shifted her bulk in her chair and smiled at Sister Connie Fuse. She waved her hand and motioned her to come and sit down. Ma Cile then turned around toward Lil Bit and June Bug.

Ma Cile took a deep breath and innocently swatted a mos-quito that was buzzing, minding its own business, with her bare hands. Throwing the stunned mosquito to the floor, she slowly leaned forward and stepped on the bug. All the time, she never took her eyes off her grandchildren. In fact, she didn't even try to line her eyes up.

The children knew that she was about to pull that proverbial rope and that they were hanging themselves. June Bug slunk back and tried to hide behind Lil Bit. He did that just in case Ma Cile dispensed one of her whammy-eye curses their way and they ended up like the dead mosquito: flattened.

After Ma Cile finished putting the fear of her and God into the children, she adjusted the tattered stocking cap that covered her short, tight, curly gray hair. She smiled, reached into her apron pocket, and again pulled out her snuff canister. As she was about to open the lid, she remembered that Sister Connie Fuse was still there. She didn't need everybody in her personal business, so as quick as she pulled it out, she put it back.

Ma Cile let her head lean back against the chair's headrest and spoke softly. "Now listen, chile, you gotta stop being so afraid of Mother Pray Onn. She ain't got no heaven or hell to put you in. She's trying to make it through them pearly gates just like you and me. You just need to calm yo' li'l antsy self on down a bit."

Sister Connie Fuse tried to muffle another tear. "Ma Cile, I'm trying to be a good Christian. That's why I spend so much time in church." She looked up sadly toward the evening sky and continued, "I've been searching for God for so long and in so many places that until I joined the Ain't Nobody Else Right but Us—All Others Goin' to Hell Church, I had just about given up hope of ever finding Him."

"That's what I'm trying to tell you, chile. You keep running from church to church, and prophet to prophet. Every time you hear about a tent meeting, temple meeting, mosque meeting, or a camp meeting, you end up running there. I even seen you at the last PTA meeting and you ain't got no kids," Ma Cile said, as she struggled to sound serious.

The need for snuff had a strong hold on Ma Cile. The more she rocked and talked to Sister Connie Fuse, the more she excused herself to go inside and take a much needed snuff break. The more she dipped, the better she felt, and the better she felt, the funnier Sister Connie's dilemma.

It was good Ma Cile felt quite jovial. She needed a jovial spirit and a taste for burned lima beans. As often as she excused herself to go inside the house, she never checked her pots. The beans and ham hocks had cooked long past simmering and were on their way to meltdown.

When the odor of burnt beans reached Ma Cile's nose, she sobered up quick. When she smelled the burned beans, so did Sister Connie Fuse. The two of them jumped up at the same time, leaving their rocking chairs still rocking. Not wanting to be the cause of Ma Cile's dinner being burned, Sister Connie Fuse excused herself and apologized for being a bother. With her red hair fanning out like a peacock, she raced back down the porch steps as fast as she had run up them. The last thing she needed was to be on the *teed-off* list of both Ma Cile and Mother Pray Onn. She decided to run back home using Ma Cile's walkway instead of the lush, green grass—just to be on the safe side.

Lil Bit and June Bug stopped laughing when they realized that they should have told Ma Cile the beans were burning when they first smelled them. Now they would have to eat mayonnaise-and-jelly sandwiches for dinner.

Ma Cile came back onto the front porch with both hands on her hips. She looked up and spoke to the heavens. "Lawd, maybe if these two li'l smart alecks had more mayonnaise sandwiches and Kool-Aid, they might jist straighten up." Looking at the frightened children, she looked toward heaven again and sighed. "Probably not, Lawd—these two got about as much chance of straightening up as that crazy fella Jeffrey Dahmer had of being a vegetarian."

Sister Connie Fuse's wet clothes clung to her body the way they did when she once modeled skimpy swimsuits for *Dirty Ole Men's* magazine, which was before she found God. She wanted to go home and change, but she needed to talk to someone who knew why she feared Mother Pray Onn. Although she knew Ma Cile was not afraid of Mother Pray Onn, and she was usually someone that you could talk to, obviously that night was not the right night.

Sister Connie Fuse stood for a moment on the sidewalk, willing the warm summer night to dry her clothes. Without further hesitation and with damp clothing, she made up her mind. She started walking toward Brother Tis Mythang's house. He was the young choir director of the church. His boyish good looks, over-the-top flair, and flashy clothes made him another convenient victim for Mother Pray Onn. Being who Sister Connie Fuse was, of course, she headed in the wrong direction. She soon found herself standing in front of Sister Carrie Onn's house.

Sister Carrie Onn was Mother Pray Onn's immature and stuck-up, way-past-forty daughter. Actually, she was an uptight old maid.

As Sister Connie Fuse realized her mistake and started to walk away, she thought she heard a familiar voice. The closer she listened, the more she was certain she knew that voice. She did know it. It was the wheezing, clacking voice of Mother Pray Onn! Sister Connie Fuse felt the ground move and her world spin like a top. She tried to calm down but was too afraid to move. She stood completely still in the shadow of the bushes and started counting the rosary beads she secretly wore around her neck. After having been a member of so many churches and faiths, it made old habits hard to break.

Sister Connie placed one foot in front of the other, hesitated, and then looked around, and that's what she continued to do until she finally got to the end of the block. Then she dashed around the corner. She was running so fast, she tripped over a rock and fell into the outstretched arms of Deacon Laid Handz, the Chairman of the Ain't Nobody Else Right but Us—All Others Goin' to Hell deacons' board.

Deacon Laid Handz had just attended the church fund-raiser pre-banquet meeting and was busy humming to himself the melody to the "Electric Slide." That particular tune was number one with a bullet on the church's "approved listening" chart—that one song and "Bad Luck." He was stepping and sliding, stepping and sliding, did a half turn, took a step up and then back, dipped and clicked his heels together, and did another half turn. He added one of the dance steps from the "Macarena" for effect.

Deacon Laid Handz looked at his reflection in the glass and, as usual, liked what he saw. He thought, *Forty years young and I still got it going on. I'm a fella that's tall, a mellow-yellow complexion, full, thick, black, wavy head of hair and mustache to match.* There was a lot more fat in the word *fat* than he had on his body.

As a precaution, Deacon Laid Handz adjusted his big yellow apple cap, checked out the crease in his purple, double-breasted retro zoot suit, straightened his bright-yellow tie, and made sure he still had his expired "Playa card" in his pocket. At first, he did not see Sister Connie Fuse—yet, as soon as she bumped into him, he was at full attention. Helping the ladies was like second nature to him, and his arms just naturally fell forward and caught her.

Deacon Laid Handz did not skip a beat. "Whoa, there, Sister Connie Fuse, be careful. Where you running to so late this enchanted evening?" He ogled the beautiful bounty bestowed upon him. The good deacon liked to lay hands, and he never limited himself to doing it just in the prayer lines.

"Oh! Thank you, Deacon," Sister Connie Fuse said as she stepped back in embarrassment. Looking around to make sure that no one was around to hear her, she said softly, "Mother Pray Onn—it's Mother Pray Onn. You know she don't like it when you do something wrong. I didn't mean to do anything wrong!" She leaned in closer, crying as she whispered, "I am scared to death of Mother Pray Onn. She's always having them visions and speaking with God."

Deacon Laid Handz barely heard a word Sister Connie Fuse said. He was too busy sizing up his options. He needed to find a way to turn Sister Connie Fuse's bad luck into his good luck.

The good deacon leaned back, placed one arm across his chest, stroked his chin with his other hand, and continued staring and scheming, never taking his eyes off his *femme du jour*, Sister Connie Fuse.

Sister Connie Fuse continued without a clue. She calmed down and again whispered, "Deacon Laid Handz, you seem to get along okay with Mother Pray Onn. Can't you say something to her? I don't want to have to miss Wednesday night testimony service, but I don't want to face Mother Pray Onn, either. Please."

"Yeah, I get along with Mother Pray Onn. Why not? Heck, everybody knows I ain't scared of her. I mean, she's old and only—what?—about four feet tall. I'm the chairman of the deacon board. Why I got to be afraid of her? She needs to stop wearing her hair in that tight bun. She looks like she's wearing a lightbulb on the back of her head, that hair is so tight," Deacon Laid Handz whispered as he looked all around. Telling Sister Connie Fuse this was one thing; letting someone hear him say this was another.

For the past ten years, Deacon Laid Handz had stayed off Mother Pray Onn's teed-off visions list, or at least near the bottom of it, and he saw no reason to change his status.

Deacon Laid Handz's plan was formulated. "Listen, my dear, why don't you let me drive you to your home? While we are riding, we can think of a way to put you back in Mother Pray Onn's good graces."

Deacon Laid Handz took Sister Connie Fuse by the arm. He continued to look around, to see who might be watching as he led her across the street. Pointing toward the end of the block, he bragged, "You know, everybody around here in Pelzer knows me and my ride. You have seen my new purple Mercedes, haven't you? That car makes anybody's driveway or parking lot look good. Makes it look like nothing but classy folks come around."

Before Sister Connie Fuse could say yes or no, Deacon Laid Handz spoke again. "My car is parked over there in the Homeboyz

'All Nite-All Day' parking lot where the old Ben Gaye Arms Nursing Home used to be. To be on the safe side, though, we got to hurry before they close."

About the same time they arrived at the front gate of the parking lot, they heard someone call out their names.

"Good evening. Praise the Lord. How you two doing?" Brother Tis Mythang called out as he happily skipped across the street in their direction. He was in a particularly good mood, having just finished a foot-stomping, funky, and successful recording session with his radical band, God's Posse.

Deacon Laid Handz stopped and glared at the young, flashy choir director. "He's always where he ain't wanted. Wearing that tired old garage sale Armanee-moochin' outfit," he muttered beneath his breath. However, what he said aloud was, "We are doing just fine, Brother Mythang. Now, if you don't mind, I need to give Sister Connie Fuse the benefit of my counseling, and we're in a hurry," he added.

"Um-hmm, I know that's right. It seems like every woman who receives your benefits usually ends up needing benefits like food stamps, Medicaid, government cheese, and free health clinic visits!" Brother Tis Mythang snarled. He did not like Deacon Laid Handz any more than the deacon liked him. However, he did like Sister Connie Fuse. She was like a kindred spirit, and he saw how upset she looked.

Brother Tis Mythang took a few steps and brushed Deacon Laid Handz aside. Pulling Sister Connie Fuse close to himself, he asked, "What's wrong, Sister Connie?" He turned and yelled right into the deacon's face, "Is the good deacon here trying to force some of his expired and unhealthy benefits on you? Is he trying to take you for a ride in that old, tired, and used *Mercedes*?"

Suddenly, Sister Connie Fuse knew Brother Tis Mythang must have felt a little suicidal. Even she knew you could say something nasty about the deacon's mama and even his clothes. If you wanted him to shoot you with poisoned words, or his cousins, Smith and Wesson, then say something defaming about his car. She tried to step back a safe distance from Brother Tis Mythang. If she really wanted to die, she wouldn't be worried about meeting up with Mother Pray Onn.

Deacon Laid Handz's eyes got as big as saucers as he took a few steps toward Brother Tis Mythang, waving his finger in the air at the same time. "When *one* owns a Mercedes, it is never referred to as being 'used!' You fool! It is called, 'previously owned.' At least I don't drive a scratched-up, gas-guzzling Ford, like you!" Madder than a neutered bull, he continued, "You do know what Ford stands for, don't you? It means 'Fix Or Repair Daily!' Now, sit on that and . . ."

Sister Connie Fuse rushed forward and stepped in between them and took each man's hand. She ignored the tension and instead told Brother Tis Mythang how happy she was to see him. When she related to Brother Tis Mythang what she had told Deacon Laid Handz, he broke out in hives at the very mention of Mother Pray Onn's name.

"Well, I got to agree with Deacon Laid Handz this one time. Mother Pray Onn ain't nobody you got to be afraid of," Brother Tis Mythang whispered.

To Brother Tis Mythang, acting hard was difficult in any situation. When it came to denouncing Mother Pray Onn, it was almost impossible, and he was no different from most of the other congregation members, who secretly feared the church mother.

However, without missing a beat, Brother Tis Mythang continued his frivolous boasting. "That old fish has been a pain in my neck since the first day I stepped foot through the doors of Ain't Nobody Else Right but Us—All Others Goin' to Hell Church." He sucked his teeth and hissed, "She's always complaining about me not finding her 'key' when she sings. There's eighty-eight keys on that piano. I keep telling her to select her key from one of the black or white ones and stick with it. Not only can't she find one of them eighty-eight keys, but she gets mad because I cannot manufacture an eighty-ninth key to fit that squeaky voice of hers. She couldn't carry a note if I gave it to her in a paper bag and stapled it to her hand."

Brother Tis Mythang's ranting turned into background noise, as Deacon Laid Handz was too busy trying to devise a scheme to get Sister Connie Fuse back on track and in his car.

"I'm gonna forgive you for that nasty and vicious remark you made about me. I can do that because I truly know how to be humble. Now, Sister Connie Fuse has a real problem, and the hour is late. I would like for she and I to continue our conversation about her private problem *in private*." Deacon Laid Handz spoke slowly and patronizingly.

Brother Tis Mythang let go of Sister Connie Fuse's hand and stepped up toe to toe with Deacon Laid Handz. He placed one hand on his hip and, using his pointing finger, jerked his neck back and forth Egyptian-style, and then shouted as loud as he could, "How private can it be when she just said that she told you, Ma Cile, and me? Now, since it was me she was first looking for, I'll see that she gets home and that she gets the *right* advice!" Then he added, in his own patronizing manner, "After all, I'm just looking out for your reputation, Deacon— the little bit you got left." He snapped his finger in the deacon's face for extra measure, twirled around, and quickly led Sister Connie Fuse away.

Deacon Laid Handz stood there boiling mad as he watched them leave. He decided to teach them a much-needed lesson. When it came down to teaching folks a lesson, he knew just who to get: the devout and feared Mother Pray Onn. She always brought home the gold. He straightened his tie, smoothed down the creases in his polyester purple pant legs, and ran to his car because class was about to begin.

The Deacon was driving on pure, anger-driven adrenaline. He left deep tire tread marks in the dirt as he put the car into reverse and headed toward Sister Carrie Onn's house, hoping Mother Pray Onn would still be there. "I don't know who them two think they messing with. I'm the head of the deacon board. I ain't the one to mess with!" Deacon Laid Handz said aloud to himself, pounding the steering wheel. "I've had enough of that Brother Mythang. Gonna see that *his thang* is gonna hang like a chicken wing when I put Mother Pray Onn on his behind." He was driving down the block like a madman and did not see Sister Betty passing out Bible tracts in front of La Femme Chippendale's, but she definitely saw him. She did not have a choice, since he came *thisclose* to running her over on his way to 666 1/2 PMS Boulevard—the home of Sister Carrie Onn.

It was Tuesday evening, and as usual, Mother Pray Onn and her daughter, Sister Carrie Onn, sat at the kitchen table talking about the moral decay and cheapness of some of their maternal family members. Their family, the infamous "Hellraisers" clan, was run out of Williamston, South Carolina, in 1959 after starting a rumor that the Grand Wizard Rednec Noguts and the good Reverend Plenti Panties had a thing going on. The town's local news rag, the *Rumor Mill Gazette*, printed the story on their front page. It was the first and last time the combined efforts of the NAACP and the KKK were used for the town's good. *Banding together to rid the town of those Hellraisers was a stroke of genius*, the paper reported. Their collaboration was a little too successful. The NAACP and the KKK, fearing that they might like each other as human beings, decided never to agree or cooperate on anything again. Those Hellraisers spread out, and now there is one in every town and church. When that conversation exhausted itself, Sister Carrie Onn decided to carry on about something else.

"Mother, you know I'm with you on this one. Sister Connie Fuse can't mess with my mother and think she gonna get away with it," Sister Carrie Onn carried on while drinking a cup of saltpeter-laced iced tea at her kitchen table.

"Don't worry. I left a warning message on her answering machine. Tomorrow night at prayer and testimony service we gonna settle a few things. One simple little errand, that's all I asked that woman to do—one simple little thing and she messed it up. I'm living the best I know how so I don't go to hell, and that crazy woman gonna give my grave layaway money to them folks over at We'll Haul Your Ashes Crematorium to burn me up!" Mother Pray Onn shouted, with veins popping up in her wrinkled neck. "As a matter of fact, make sure when we go over that list of folks that I don't want at my funeral, that Sister Connie Fuse's name is at the top. Put it up there in big bold letters!"

Sister Carrie Onn took a quick look at the "funeral service attendees" list on which she and her mother had been working. Since becoming a widow ten years ago, Mother Pray Onn revised her lists weekly. They had worked out a color-coding system. There was a list written in blue that contained the names of everyone who had gotten on her nerves that past week. Written in yellow were the members who, in the past five years, had only gotten on her mother's nerves once or twice. Since in her mind it would be a packed church, the people on this list would have to sit near the bathrooms. Written with a green magic marker were those who had failed to recognize or respect her regal position within the church and, therefore, would not be allowed to sit or speak. Everyone knew that Mother Pray Onn could not stand other hypocrites. Sister Connie Fuse's name was written with a red permanent marker, a color used only for the elite of Mother Pray Onn's teed-off list of those who couldn't get in even if the church was empty. The list of people *not* welcome was getting longer than the ones that were. She started to bring this to her mother's attention but thought that perhaps another time would be better.

Mother Pray Onn pounded the table. "I know the Lord gonna give me a vision on how to handle her, but in case He don't, I am gonna give her one of mine, and it's gonna be real clear."

"I'm with you on that one, Mother. You want me to call Bishop Was Nevercalled? What about Reverend Knott Enuff Money and Minister Breedin' Love? They need to know about this! After all, Mother, you know by now Sister Connie Fuse is probably crying on Ma Cile's shoulders, and we gonna need some help . . ." Sister Carrie Onn carried on.

"Chile, just shut up! I don't need no pastor, bishop, and nobody else to take care of Sister Connie Fuse," Mother Pray Onn boasted. "However," she whispered to herself, "now, that crazy Ma Cile may be another matter."

Sister Carrie Onn continued pacing around her kitchen. "Well what about Sister Betty? You know she's gonna be at the prayer meeting, and lately she has been acting stranger than usual. I guess thinking I was getting telephone calls from God would make me act a little weird, too, but Sister Betty act like breathing hard is a sin. Personally, I don't believe she got a telephone call from God at all."

Sister Carrie Onn had what seemed to her a reason to rant and rave. She was over forty, or as she liked to tell folks, she no longer celebrated birthdays—just anniversaries of her thirty-ninth one. She did not have a man and could not get a man. She always said, "Jesus was the *only* man." Meanwhile, she was always looking for a man in particular: Deacon Laid Handz. Because there was no man in her life, she carried on and on and on. She had the looks. Not having a man in her life made her work extra hard at keeping herself man-ready. She spent a lot of money to look "chic cheap." She was definitely in the high-maintenance category. However, her good looks could not cover up that *bad attitude* Hellraisers DNA she inherited from her mother—Mother Pray Onn.

"I don't know if she had a chance to speak with her protector, the great Ma Cile," said Mother Pray Onn sarcastically. "Maybe I'll stop by there on my way home anyway."

Sister Carrie Onn started wringing her hands. "I don't know, Mother. Maybe I should go with you. You know, in case Ma Cile gets riled up and start throwing them lopsided eyeballs around! Just give me a moment to grab a sweater. We'll go out the back door and get my car out of the garage. Ain't no sense in you walking this time of night by yourself." She laid a hand on her mother's shoulder and then helped her from the table. "You wait at the back door and let me check the front to make sure my doors are locked."

Mother Pray Onn gathered her Bible in one hand and her large can of scientifically concocted mace in the other and headed toward the back door.

Sister Carrie Onn grabbed a sweater from the hall closet and went to check her front door. She heard the loud squeal of tires. Curiosity got the best of her. Parting the curtains at the living room window, she saw her man *du jour*, Deacon Laid Handz, rushing from his car toward her house. She got as giddy as a bedbug and suddenly did not know what to do. There was her mother about to go out in the late hour to, of all places, Ma Cile's house by herself, and here was a good-looking, sexy man rushing up to her front door. Moreover, not just any man but *the* man, *her* man, Deacon Laid Handz himself. What a dilemma! Now what should she do? She rushed back through the living room to her mother, who was still waiting at the back door.

Sister Carrie Onn was sweating as she blurted, "Mother, I tell you, I'm just so mad about what Sister Connie Fuse almost did to you that I can't even think of where I laid my car keys." Her mind was racing away and left her mouth to carry on. "I know you in a hurry. Don't you worry about nothing; you got your Bible and your mace. You gonna be all right." Sister Carrie Onn pushed her mother out the back door—just in time, for there stood Deacon Laid Handz looking good, fat-free, and about to ring her front doorbell.

Before Mother Pray Onn could protest, she felt and heard the back door slam behind her. Her daughter had thrown her out the door with lightning speed. It took several seconds for Mother Pray Onn to gather her wits about her—one moment she was waiting on her daughter to find the car keys, the next she was standing in the backyard. Mother Pray Onn slammed her fist against her Bible and then apologized to God.

Daughter or no daughter, if Sister Carrie Onn did not watch herself, she could find herself on her mother's ever-increasing teed-off list.

Sweating from brow and armpits, Deacon Laid Handz stood hopping in place and rapidly pressing on the door buzzer. He was too angry to be bothered by the loud, irritating gongs of the doorbell, which played a "Here Comes The Bride" melody in four-four meter on a funky Stevie Wonder harmonica.

Sister Carrie Onn also heard the sound of bells. The rapid chiming did not irritate her. By the time the sound reached her ears, it was the sweet tolling of wedding bells anxiously played by her imagined intended.

If Mother Pray Onn had not been deep in thought—or rather, plotting on how to neutralize and manipulate Ma Cile—then perhaps she might have seen Deacon Laid Handz standing on the front steps. But she didn't see the deacon looking like a poor man's purple version of Cab Calloway visiting Minnie the Moocher, as she walked toward the gate.

Mother Pray Onn took her time as she walked out the side gate and onto the moonlit sidewalk. She hugged her Bible, the Know-It-All unabridged edition, tightly to her chest and popped the safety cap off her mace spray. She had purchased it on the down-low, from the back room of El Diablo's Soul Food Kitchen shanty. That was a run-down diner over on *Tomaine* and Poison Streets, where they sold stir-fried collard greens and spicy chitterling fajitas hot enough to singe your brain cells. She took off its cover and cocked it into its lethal and ready position. That was just in case somebody in Pelzer, South Carolina was new and did not know that they may kill a wounded grizzly bear with their bare hands, and even swallow bleach and live. However, Mother Pray Onn could swallow a bottle of industrial-strength bleach, then go ten rounds with a wounded black bear, and run a triathlon. She was no joke.

Mother Pray Onn continued the short walk to the corner taxi stand. She took tiny steps to avoid the many small mounds of dog droppings on and around the sidewalk. Too bad she was not that cautious in dealing with her own life or that of others.

Back at 666½ PMS Boulevard, Sister Carrie Onn could not believe her good fortune. She almost ripped her sweater apart taking it off. She snatched her unused man-getting, bargain lilac-colored Victoria's Secret robe from her closet. She had ordered one from the February 1996 issue of *Desperate Old Broads'*

Man Catching Outfits and Other Myths catalogue. She had decided she was suffering from youth deficiency and, therefore, purchased a lifetime subscription. It was apparent that Victoria did not keep the secret to herself, because not everybody can or should, wear what Victoria wears.

Sister Carrie Onn thought that since Deacon Laid Handz was all adorned in purple, her lilac-colored robe would help him to see how compatible they were.

Sister Carrie Onn's guerilla man-hunting hormones and lonely single-woman reasoning were unique. Sister Carrie Onn had issues.

Sister Carrie Onn went to her dresser and lifted up several layers of frilly and laced scarves. She pulled out a red velvet box. Smiling, she quickly lifted the lid. From the velvet box, she pulled out a brown perfume bottle shaped like a man's muscular biceps, wrapped in scented tissue.

Another impatient gong from the doorbell caused Sister Carrie Onn to hasten. She wrestled the top off and sprayed. She anointed her entire body with half the quart bottle of Mary Kay's Forever Alone Parfum. Emulating an old B movie, she twirled and flung open the front door.

"Hello," Sister Carrie Onn said in a low, sweet, and syrupy voice. No one was there. She stuck her head completely out the door and rapidly looked from side to side as she searched for Deacon Laid Handz. She looked like she was watching a very enthusiastic tennis match or was a hungry owl looking for her dinner from a tree. It was too little and too late, because Deacon Laid Handz had spotted Mother Pray Onn as she came out of the side gate, and had taken off after her. Poor Sister Carrie Onn; she was alone—again.

Sister Carrie Onn stepped back inside and slammed her door. *No sense in wearing a parachute if you ain't gonna fly,* she thought. She then slowly took off the lilac-colored Victoria's Secret robe and stepped into an old cotton flowery one with a ripped pocket and missing buttons. She sank down on her couch and grabbed the remote control to watch a rerun of the eighties comedy show *Amen.* She cried because it was the episode where the character Thelma finally got the preacher to propose to her. "Why that can't happen to me and Deacon Laid Handz?" she sobbed.

It did not happen for her because, unlike her life, *Amen* was a television show with a script; she, on the other hand, was a forty-plus-year-old woman without a man or a script.

Outside, the moonlit street was practically empty with the exception of a few people that were obviously minding their own business. It was a fact that had escaped Deacon Laid Handz as he called out Mother Pray Onn's name as he ran up and grabbed her arm. It was a costly mistake because the next thing he knew, there he was, crumpled up in a ball, lying on the sidewalk, crying in soprano, smelling like week-old rotten, unclean gizzards and pig feet, and he was temporarily blinded.

The small, shadowy figure of Mother Pray Onn walking slowly by the light of the moon had seemed nonthreatening. She had been deep in thought, but not so deep that she was not aware of her surroundings. She hesitated when she heard the sound of threatening footsteps. Since she was already in a foul mood and somebody needed to suffer for it, somebody would. That somebody would be whoever was running up behind her.

Mother Pray Onn chuckled to herself as she balled her left hand into a tight fist. She licked her lips and gritted her teeth with anticipation as she thought, *You got to bring some to get some.* She carefully turned her custom-made Bible around with its sharp, serrated edges to the outside and made ready her Equalizer Mace canister James Bond style. She then pushed the spray lever up a notch past "lethal weapon part five" to "better recognize" and then got ready. As soon as she saw the shadow on the sidewalk and felt the tug on her arm, she went into action. She lowered her head and spun around like a Texas tornado. Throwing her hands up like Bruce Lee, she lit on the shadow's owner like a Tasmanian she-devil in menopausal distress. She was kicking it in the behind while screaming and yelling, "Somebody help me! I'm being attacked!" What she would have yelled if she were losing the fight was anyone's guess.

When Mother Pray Onn got finished with the shadow's owner, Deacon Laid Handz, he looked like a smashed purple, fat-free eggplant with dabs of ketchup. His yellow apple cap had landed atop a mound of dog poop.

Mother Pray Onn was just about to reload and go into her full-assault mode when she recognized the crumpled-up purple eggplant singing falsetto as the good deacon. She wanted to move closer to say she was sorry, but the putrid smell was overwhelming. As she rushed away from him, she pulled out a handful of tissues, threw one at him, and held several to her nose. With a quick glance, she looked back over her shoulders and yelled out, "Oh, my Lord! Deacon Laid Handz, I am so sorry. Why didn't you say something before you came up on me and grabbed me like that? Old defenseless and fragile women like me can't be too careful these days."

The odor was getting worse, so Mother Pray Onn cut her insincere speech short. "I'll speak to you about it tomorrow night at prayer and testimony service. Got to go 'cause I got something to do!"

Even though Mother Pray Onn obviously won, the fight had taken its toll on her. Instead of continuing to Ma Cile's house, she decided to go home and rest up for her next fight: Sister Connie Fuse.

Several of the onlookers that had forgotten that they were supposed to be minding their own business commented, "That old woman has fighting skills that could put the Cripps and the Bloods gangs to shame."

Deacon Laid Handz lay totally messed up. He did not know where he was or how he got there, and he was seeing double. Soon, the crumpled-up eggplant-looking deacon's mind and vision began to clear. Below his pants belt, he felt like a bag of chipped marbles as he tried to climb to his feet. His throat was dry from screaming and crying, and of course, he smelled something awful. He looked around the neighborhood and hoped no one had seen what happened. But he had been wrong all night, and this time was no exception. Most of the people on the street turned around and pretended to cover their faces. Some of the neighbors yanked down their curtains. For a while, they were laughing hysterically at the drama that had unfolded. Sister Carrie Onn was no exception. She laughed the loudest as she grabbed the neck of her torn robe.

Unlike the other neighbors, Sister Carrie Onn took her time closing her curtains. She made sure that she savored every moment of Deacon Laid Handz's humiliation as he lay there in payback hell. She even went so far as to turn on the two big and bright 500-watt spotlights by her front window. She wanted to make sure he saw her looking. The entire neighborhood saw her looking.

Deacon Laid Handz finally got to his feet and promptly fell again as he stumbled to his car. He had forgotten that when he bought his big, sleek purple Mercedes, he had special alarms installed in it. As he ambled toward the car, the entire neighborhood heard the ten different alarms sound off with an automated voice that repeatedly threatened, "Get away from the car!" He could not stop the alarm because the deacon did not have his car keys. They had fallen out of his pocket and lay innocently beside the big yellow apple cap that was lying on top of the dog poop.

If anyone kept score that night, it was bad luck, a plus ten; deacon, a zero.

Sister Carrie Onn had seen and heard enough. She ran to the kitchen and did what came natural to her. She grabbed the telephone, hit the speed and conference dials, and carried on and on. Of course, she edited the story as she went. She was in that rabid Hellraiser payback mode. Her mother would have been proud.

Brother Tis Mythang rode along under the moonlit sky without saying a word as Sister Connie Fuse sobbed. There was not much traffic, so Brother Tis Mythang and Sister Connie Fuse arrived at his building in no time at all.

The slow elevator ride up to his fifth-floor apartment was as uneventful, with the exception of sobbing, as the car ride. The fresh smell of Pine-Sol and ammonia that hung in the elevator's air helped to revive Sister Connie Fuse, who by now was near dehydration from all her crying.

After fumbling around inside his pants pockets and finally finding the right key, Brother Tis Mythang opened the door and told her to go in and relax. Brother Tis Mythang had often described his apartment as art deco. Fuchsia-colored silk curtains were supposed to embrace luxurious maroon drapes, which adorned each of the four large living-room windows. Two black Grecian urns also supposedly stood guard on each side of the elaborately tiled wall mirrors. An ivory-colored plush carpet completed the decor. That was the way Brother Tis Mythang had often described his apartment when he thought he was in the company of those whom he believed God had blessed more than himself.

Now what Sister Connie Fuse saw was entirely different. What she actually saw were several pair of faded red, mismatched linen curtains at each window. Instead of the windows being large, they were the type you had to find the handle for, fit it on, and then struggle to get it open. The Grecian urns turned out to be two old dingy plastic birdbaths left over from a 1994 John's Bargain Store going-out-of-business sale. She had been there herself last week, and the sale had apparently been going on for several years; perhaps if she told him, he could hurry and find a matching pair. Sister Connie Fuse was confused. Was there anybody in her life who was what they said they were?

Brother Tis Mythang returned to the living room, proudly carrying two tall glasses of cold lemonade, making polite conversation as he handed her a paper towel with the glass. He waited until she took a sip, concerned that she calm down enough to have a serious conversation about Mother Pray Onn.

He never seemed to notice that his home was not the way he had often described it, nor was he embarrassed that Sister Connie now knew differently. Nearly all his life, Brother Tis Mythang had been trying to live up to everyone's expectations but his own.

"Now, tell me. How are we two gonna disarm that old biddy?" Brother Mythang smirked as he sat down next to her. He used another napkin to gently dab her swollen eyes, much the way he'd wished his mother had done when he would come home crying after being tormented by neighborhood bullies, both boys and girls.

Brother Tis Mythang's mentioning of Mother Pray Onn immediately brought Sister Connie Fuse's mind back to the problem at hand. "I don't know what to do!" she cried again. "How could I have been so stupid and done something so wrong? I should know a cemetery from a crematorium."

Taking her hand in his, Brother Tis Mythang asked, "Are you sure she said she was gonna speak to you *tomorrow* night at prayer and testimony service?" He wanted to make sure that Mother Pray Onn wasn't out that night looking for her and found out she was over at his house.

"That's what she said, and I know she means it, too. I guess I'll just have to miss service tomorrow night, and I really don't want to do that. I told Sister Loose Gal that we would go together and I don't want to disappoint her, but I don't want to face Mother Pray Onn, either."

"You won't have to skip service. We'll call Sister Loose Gal and tell her what's going on. Who knows? Maybe she can help us defang Mother Pray Onn."

Although Brother Tis Mythang made a great speech aloud, what he really thought was, *If Mother Pray Onn can really be reasoned with, then just maybe pigs aren't pork, grits ain't groceries, and Mona Lisa was a man.* They were not dealing with world hunger, which would have been easier.

"Her answering machine picked up, so I left a message," Brother Mythang announced as he hung up the telephone. "Do you want to stay here tonight? I am not going to worry about

Mother Pray Onn calling my house, and I am confident that you should not, either." He did not tell her that the caller-ID connected to his telephone gave him the quasi-macho confidence.

Brother Mythang and Sister Connie Fuse sipped ice-cold lemonade and talked long into the night, and each plan they devised sounded more ridiculous than the last.

The moon was still hanging high as Sister Betty arrived home around ten o'clock. She was hungry, tired, and humming her favorite hymn, "Amazing Grace," as she walked up the steps to her house. She laid down her Bible on the mantel next to her bottle of blessed oil. Sister Betty sat down in her oversized leather armchair, looked at the red-velvet-backed picture of Jesus on her wall, and smiled. She rested a moment and meditated on how the Lord had used her that day. "Lawd, you sure been good to me, and I'm so grateful."

It had been a successful day for Sister Betty as she handed out the Bible leaflets inviting the raunchy people patronizing the La Femme Chippendale's club over on Sodom Avenue to give their lives to Christ. Only a few dared to ignore the little old church lady dressed from head to toe in white. Armed with her large Bible and the giant cross hanging around her neck, she always went through the neighborhood smiling and preaching.

Suddenly, thoughts of Deacon Laid Handz came to Sister Betty's mind. Where had he been going in such a hurry? Why hadn't he stopped after nearly running her over? Something was not right, but what? She felt an inner chill, got down on her knees, and started to pray. She began praying very softly and reverently, but then the face of Deacon Laid Handz kept reappearing before her along with Mother Pray Onn's face, and that could only mean one thing—trouble of the Armageddon variety.

Sister Betty stretched her short, thin arms and tiny hands palm side up toward heaven and again began to pray in earnest. On her knees, with her body swaying from side to side, she cried uncontrollably as she pleaded for her God to intervene and remove the mysterious burden that she now carried. She cried out loud as Moses did when he pleaded for the freedom of his people. She wept as strong as Ruth and as courageously as Esther.

As Sister Betty moaned and went deeper into fervent prayer, she achieved her spiritual grace, and peace came unto her. She closed her eyes, and through a vision, she saw the confusion that Mother Pray Onn and her daughter were about to create at the prayer and testimony service. She also saw why she was concerned about Deacon Laid Handz.

Soon, Sister Betty was exhausted and drifted off to sleep on the floor beside her couch, on her tweed carpet. She would need her renewed spiritual strength for tomorrow—that and a miracle.

Meanwhile, back at 666½ PMS Boulevard, Sister Carrie Onn was running back and forth between her living room and the kitchen with her cordless phone in her hand, like an Energizer bunny on drugs. She had called only a few of the church members when she decided to try a different tactic. Why neuter Deacon Laid Handz's already questionable reputation over the telephone when she could easily remove his ego-driven manhood in person? True to her nature and just like her mother, she, too, would wait until tomorrow night at the prayer and testimony service. Her mother could testify and signify on Sister Connie as much as she wanted, but Deacon Laid Handz belonged to her. She planned to break him down to a Y chromosome nub in front of the whole congregation.

Well past midnight, Sister Carrie Onn carried on in her mind exactly what she was going to do. As she wrote out her attack strategy on a wide-ruled yellow pad, she started humming the hit song by R & B diva Toni Braxton "Love Should Have Brought You Home Last Night." She hummed that particular tune for motivation in her quest for revenge.

It was not actually a humming sound—it was more like a whine.

With what Sister Carrie Onn had in mind, some people might have almost felt sorry for Deacon Laid Handz—almost.

Wednesday Night Prayer & Testimony Service At the Ain't Nobody Else Right but Us— All Others Goin' to Hell Church, Better known as The Bake 'Em and Rake 'Em Over Congregational Hootenanny

The huge two-story red-brick-veneer building, its steeple adorned with a large crucifix, had been on the same corner of Hell and Redemption Avenues in Pelzer, South Carolina for the past sixty years. The church sat approximately thirty feet from the immaculately kept sidewalk and had a giant glass-covered billboard in front. Written in small letters were the order of the weekly services and a Bible verse. The words AIN'T NOBODY ELSE RIGHT BUT US—ALL OTHERS GOIN' TO HELL CHURCH," along with the words FOUNDED BY THE LATE REVEREND WASN'T EVENCALLED AND PASTORED BY REVEREND KNOTT ENUFF MONEY were in larger gold letters on a black background.

A rich, deep-piled, fiery-red carpet and solid oak pews with Bibles and hymnals neatly placed in each slot decorated the sanctuary. Evenly spaced throughout the church were twenty extremely expensive crystal chandeliers paid for by the family of the late missionary Staid Holm. A large painting of Jesus praying in the Garden of Gethsemane hung behind the pulpit, bathed in an iridescent aura of crisscrossing floodlights. The picture gave the church a more peaceful and holy appearance and also hid the fact that there was an ATM bank machine placed in the gray, wood-paneled vestibule alongside the metal blessing dispenser.

Several nosy people, previously alerted by Sister Carrie Onn, arrived early and were reacquainting themselves with the church protocol, handed to them by sour-faced ushers. Most of them, especially those who had not been to church in months, elbowed one another as they dashed toward seats with a view and waited for round one to begin.

Much of the smart money was on Mother Pray Onn and her grouchy, Geritol-filled, geriatric prayer posse, who were there in full force with Sister Carrie Onn leading the pack. The few who secretly hoped that Sister Connie Fuse would come out on top sat safely in the middle pews located near the back exits, with car keys and automatic buzzers in hand, just in case they needed to get away quick.

Inside the lavishly purple-tiled pastor's study sat the Reverend Knott Enuff Money and the Bishop Was Nevercalled. They were in a deep discussion, hashing over their latest fund-raising scheme. Both were divorced and always spent their free time together in collusion, causing more confusion than conversion. They made the Watergate burglars look like choirboys.

Strong, cold air coming from the air conditioner caused a mound of Lotto gambling tickets on the desk to fall to the floor. Some people would haven taken it as a sign to pay attention to what was happening inside the sanctuary, but these two were not like most people. Instead, they picked up the tickets, checked them to see if any were overlooked winners, and placed them back on the desk, using a paperweight shaped like a dollar sign to hold the tickets down.

Opening the door and looking out to make sure no one was lurking around, the Reverend Knott Enuff Money then closed the door and whispered, "Now, Bishop, we got to make sure that whoever is in charge of the collection plate tonight recites that verse from the nineteenth chapter of Numbers."

"What's the nineteenth chapter of Numbers?" asked Bishop Was Nevercalled, stroking one of his several chins and scratching his shiny white, bald head. "It has a familiar ring to it."

He never picked up a Bible and read it for himself; if he had, he would not have had to ask.

The Reverend Knott Enuff Money closed the study door. He laughed and said, "That's the money-draw chapter them bigtime preachers up North always use when they start off the collection. Just telling these folks that they suppose to give at least ten percent of their money in tithes ain't bringing in the kind of cash money we need. I'm telling you, my cousin, Reverend Clockin' Dollars, up North in New Jersey, swears by it. He also says that you must say it with a certain rhythm so that it sounds hypnotic. Then you let the people see you putting your own fifty-dollar bill in the plate, and them church folks can't give it up fast enough."

"Percent, you say? Where did that come from? Is that in the Bible?"

The Reverend Knott Enuff Money didn't bother to respond. He simply shook his head in amazement.

The bishop kept on speaking, oblivious to the snub. "You know what else? I've been giving this new idea a lot of thought. I think if we can shame a few folks, they'll dig a little deeper and bring out some of those King Kong dollars they've been holding out for them television preachers and their Save Them Kids charities."

The bishop stood up and moved around to the side of the desk. He checked the vents in the wall for hidden listening devices and said in a low voice, "You see, what we do is, we tell the person in charge of the collection to announce some special names. The ones that have given up the big bucks will have their names announced using the cordless microphone, and we'll even have the congregation give them some standing applause. Those who only give a little money don't get the microphone or the applause treatment. Whoever gives money that make noise, we'll give them a nasty look."

"Hmm, I hear what you saying, but I don't know if that's gonna work. Most of the people here ain't got much shame to begin with, but it's worth a try. I do know we need to do something quick; that's for sure! We also got to make certain we bring Mother Pray Onn in on this. She does not like for policy changes to be made without her being included in it," said the Reverend Knott Enuff Money. "By the way, has the old gal arrived yet?"

Before the bishop could answer, they heard a loud commotion in the sanctuary. They hesitated for only a moment before jumping up and almost knocking each other to the ground. Whenever they heard any sudden noises, immediately they would always run and grab their briefcases. These held their

passports, necessary funds, and other secret documents. Both
men recovered, got up, and dashed for the door. Much to their
delight and surprise, instead of the IRS, they came face-to-face
with more people than normally attended the Wednesday night
service. They cautiously closed the door and tiptoed to the
back of the pastor's study. Right away they started to giggle.
They gave each other high fives. They yelled, "Woof, whoop"
like late-night *Arsenio Hall Show* audience members, and
added a little shouting dance. Running toward each other, they
did a couple of belly smacks and began estimating the people,
which to them meant five dollars a head. Whatever was the
real reason for the discord among the unexpected crowd that
night never entered their greedy minds.

A master game plan would be needed to turn around the
two old shysters.

The reverend continued speaking while greedily rubbing his
chubby hands together. "These people could not have come at a
more opportune time. Don't you think this is the perfect night
to test our new collection plan?"

"But, I thought you said that we needed to have Mother
Pray Onn in on the plan first. I don't think she's here," replied
the bishop as his bony hands began to perspire. He could not
speak for the reverend, but he took Mother Pray Onn's ap-
proval policy very seriously.

"You slow, you blow!" the reverend scoffed. "Come on, now,
can't you see the congregation is a bit anxious tonight? Let's do
this! And don't you forget to say your hallelujahs on time!
Lately your rhythm has been a little off."

They celebrated with another round of high fives as if they
were entering the play-offs. They bolted the study door shut
and started toward the sanctuary. They crept across the plush,
deep-piled carpet, stopping only to make sure the blessing dispenser was refilled with green-scented money candles, enemy-
crushing handkerchiefs, and multicolored ribbons. They slipped
a five-dollar bill to one of the ushers whom they instructed to
do a special limited-time-only promotion on several of the blessing items during the service.

The reverend and the bishop, strutting like used-up peacocks, proudly ascended the steps to the posh pulpit while visions of dollars still danced in their heads. Together they looked a little bit like Don "Scary" King and the basketball star, Reggie "Skeleton" Miller. The Reverend Knott Enuff Money was resplendent in a tailored blue Versace tuxedo "Homeboyz'-style robe, which made his short, round frame seem shorter. The robe had little telltale signs of Jheri-curl juice from the reverend's greasy hair. Bishop Was Nevercalled, who was about ten inches taller than the reverend and completely bald, with blond mustache and eyebrows to match, opted for a green Tommy Hilfiger bomber jacket, complete with high-top black sneakers. Neither of them looked out of place, because the dress code for the Wednesday night services was always casual.

There was not a calm person in the church. Everyone fidgeted in their seats, tapped their toes, talked trash about each other, and waited for the contenders to arrive and the vocal mudslinging to begin. Wednesday night's prayer and testimony services were always more entertaining than spiritual, and tonight's festivities had all the makings of a World Series or a championship bout. They could promote it as "Beauty and the Beast" or the "Night of Black Babylon" or better yet, "Testilying Made Easy."

Eager for a good, vocal mudslinging event, the congregation began to calm down as word spread of Sister Connie Fuse and her entourage's arrival. Surrounded by Ma Cile, and Brother Tis Mythang, and with June Bug and Lil Bit taking up the rear, the frightened challenger entered the sanctuary. Sister Connie Fuse's walk was somewhat unsteady as she unsuccessfully tried to hold up her head, which for this occasion was wrapped in a black scarf. Earlier, she had sent June Bug in to survey the crowd, so she knew that Mother Pray Onn had not yet arrived. However, that did not make her feel any less nervous, and only news of Mother Pray Onn's actual disappearance would.

Brother Tis Mythang left Sister Connie's side and sat down at the organ. He began playing a few inspirational melodies usually meant to soothe some of the savage beasts that had attended. Then, he started playing the movie theme to *Rocky*. It made a bad situation worse.

Meanwhile, in the pulpit, the Reverend Knott Enuff Money and Bishop Was Nevercalled rehearsed the verses they would use to keep the longtime absentees and their wallets coming back. They whispered back and forth so much that they began to look like two brown speckled barn owls locked in a kiss while repeating, "Hallelujah."

The two pious phonies thought they were going to collect a few new dollars; little did they know that some of the less spiritually minded, better known as "space savers," had a betting pool going on.

The reverend and the bishop were also happy that the good Minister Breedin Love, who was out of town on a speaking engagement, would not be returning to Pelzer until tomorrow. He was their thorn, always trying to do everything exactly by the Word of God and spoiling their plans.

They sat back in their high-backed seats and proceeded to squint their beady little eyes while examining the financial pickings, all the while intoxicated with greed.

Brother Tis Mythang continued playing the organ with gusto, alternating between Mendelssohn's "Messiah" and Dorothy Norwood's "Shake the Devil Off." He gave Sister Connie Fuse nods of assurance.

Ma Cile looked over her shoulder at potential troublemakers sitting over in Mother Pray Onn's cheering section. She crooked her neck and shook a finger at each one as if she were aiming at sitting ducks at a carnival.

One by one, the members turned and hung their heads. None of them wanted Ma Cile's eye whammies.

That was just the tip of the iceberg; Ma Cile was actually looking for the biggest troublemaker of them all, Sister Carrie Onn.

Sister Carrie Onn had already seen Ma Cile enter the church, so she slipped away to the ladies' bathroom to hide. There she would wait until she heard the crowd announce Mother Pray Onn's arrival to show herself and, of course, carry on.

It had been about twenty minutes since the service had begun, and Brother Tis Mythang's repertoire was about to be exhausted. He nodded toward the pulpit, an indication that testimony and prayer service should begin. It was not a moment too soon because the Reverend Knott Enuff Money liked to keep to a schedule that was exactly one and a half hours. He called the congregation to order. Then he asked a volunteer to lead the devotional service.

Deacon Laid Handz, blissfully unaware of Sister Carrie Onn's prior evening's broadcast of his humiliation at the hands of Mother Pray Onn, strutted to the podium dressed in another one of his off-the-rack beige ensembles. He ignored the giggles coming from the congregation, because he thought they were meant for someone else—certainly not him. No one in the congregation, other than Sister Carrie Onn and Mother Pray Onn, should have known what happened to him last night. He knew that Sister Carrie Onn had a thing for him and would never jeopardize the possibility of their getting together by telling anyone.

Most of the members just looked at poor Deacon Laid Handz and felt he needed to hurry back from his mental visit to that state of denial if he thought they didn't know about his previous night's beat-down. They laughed and lightly elbowed one another as he strutted across the floor and led devotion service.

As the evening progressed, the hearts of a few of the members were stirred. Some stood up to sing a song and testify about the goodness of the Lord. Others, however, eagerly glanced at their watches and wondered when Mother Pray Onn would show. Some of them had sacrificed their favorite Wednesday night *Frazier* and *Jamie Fox* shows, as well as an unauthorized Pay-Per-View cable movie, to see this event, and they did not want to be disappointed.

Sister Betty managed to arrive without any fanfare or recog-

nition. If any did see her, they paid little attention. She was just
glad to be there and to be left alone. She knew that everyone's
focus was on Mother Pray Onn and Sister Connie Fuse.

Calmness covered Sister Betty as she walked down the outside aisle to her seat. She clutched her large family-size Bible
and quietly sat down next to Ma Cile. Happy to see each other,
they embraced and gave each other a little peck on the cheek.
Sister Betty leaned over Ma Cile and touched Sister Connie's
arm to get her attention. She gave her a smile that said everything would be okay.

Sister Connie tried to return Sister Betty's smile with confidence. She clutched the colorful blessed handkerchief she had
purchased earlier from the church's blessing dispenser. Then
she bowed her head and silently prayed for guidance. At the
same time, she also hoped that Mother Pray Onn would never
show up.

As the time passed, many members started to relax, while
others showed their disappointment by crossing their arms or
swatting flies with their fans and looking just plain bored. They
muttered, to no one in particular, that if they had wanted to
hear testimonies of God's goodness, they could go to other services. This one was supposed to be different.

Brother Tis Mythang stretched his fingers in preparation to
play and sing the old hymn "A Storm Is Rising." It was a remix
he'd created using the melody from Isaac Hayes's hit "Shaft."

Before Brother Tis Mythang could tap the first note, someone yelled out that the champion, Mother Pray Onn, had arrived. They might as well have hollered, "Fire!" The effect
would have been the same.

Congregational necks arched and jerked around all over the
church trying to catch a glimpse of Mother Pray Onn. Of
course, Sister Connie Fuse's nerves went into overdrive, and
she almost passed out just thinking of confronting Mother Pray
Onn.

When the sounds of excitement reached the women's bathroom, Sister Carrie Onn gathered her courage and rushed in.

She arrived just in time to see another old lady, who resembled her mother, appear in the doorway.

The congregation looked in disgust as the old lady, who wondered what she'd done that was so wrong, slowly made her way to her seat. Sister Carrie Onn wanted to make a hasty retreat back to the safety of the women's bathroom, but it was too late. She could feel Ma Cile's eye on her as well as Sister Betty's prayers. She sucked her teeth in rebellion and threw her head back. She then eyed the crowd, acknowledged the few that sent conspiring smiles her way, and sat down proudly and fearfully in the pew in front of Ma Cile and Sister Betty.

Before Deacon Laid Handz could continue the devotional service, the Reverend Knott Enuff Money signaled Brother Tis Mythang to play something that would urge the people to give freely. Brother Tis Mythang, feeling a bit playful, started playing a funky rendition of the O'Jays' "For the Love of Money."

Some of the members familiar with the routine stood up and, in a stiff manner, made their way to the offering table. Welcomed in the collection plate was currency of any kind, including food stamps, as long as the five-dollar-and-over stamps were still in their original books. However, the Reverend Knott Enuff Money did not like the music Brother Tis Mythang chose to play. "For The Love of Money" was his power-hour theme song reserved for the pastor's collection—his own. He slid to the edge of his seat and glared over at Brother Tis Mythang, gritted his teeth, and gave him a warning look.

Brother Tis Mythang returned the look with pretended innocence, smiled back, and even added a wink. He wanted to have a little fun while Mother Pray Onn was not there.

After the offering had been collected, it was presented to Bishop Was Nevercalled to say a prayer of blessing. He glanced at the basket and mentally counted the bounty, because the size of it would determine what kind of prayer he said, and for how long. After determining that the collection was adequate, he asked God's blessing on those who gave and those who were too cheap to give better. Taking a pink polka-dotted polyester handkerchief from his pocket, he wiped his brow and frantically waved it toward Deacon Laid Handz to continue with the service.

Deacon Laid Handz nodded back toward the pulpit on cue. Grasping the cordless microphone in one hand, he extended the other hand toward the congregation.

"Brothers and Sisters, Saints and friends, let us not sit down on our praises. I know God has done something for each of you. You need to testify and let us know what has happened in your life since our last testimony meeting. We need to be like popcorn—popping up for the Lord! Let us see some Jiffy popcorn testimonies or Orville Redenbacher popcorn praises. Don't be like that government-issued, won't-pop popcorn!" prodded Deacon Laid Handz.

What he really wanted was for this part of the service to end. Like the others, he, too, wanted Mother Pray Onn to show up and put Sister Connie Fuse in her place. As for Brother Tis Mythang, the good deacon had other plans for him.

The deacon just did not know when to quit.

"Well, since no one will stand up, I might as well 'pop up' and say a little something!" Deacon Laid Handz shouted with a gleam in his eye that coincidentally found its way over to Brother Tis Mythang. He continued, "Some folks need more things to do in their lives and not spend so much time intruding on others."

Turning back toward the congregation, the deacon continued, pronouncing each word precisely and with authority.

"One of the gifts that the good Lord has given me is the gift of 'assisting'—and when I'm 'assisting,' it's not good to interfere with the work I'm trying to do!" he said, this time raising his voice.

Before he could say another word, Brother Tis Mythang, who had returned the good deacon's stare with equal ruthlessness, started softly playing the Funkadelics tune "Why Must I Chase the Cat? Maybe It's the Dog in Me."

Sister Carrie Onn was unrelenting in her quest to get revenge on the deacon, old-maid style. Joining instant forces with Brother Mythang, she started mimicking "Get away from the car" in her best electronic voice. It was her confirmation to the deacon that the previous night's experience was a complete embarrassment, and she was going to make sure everyone knew about it.

Sister Carrie Onn's poor mimicry gave the bored congregation permission to laugh. It also reconfirmed to the good deacon that hell hath no fury like an eager and matronly daughter of Mother Pray Onn, scorned.

Before things could get too far out of hand, Brother Tis My-thang, knowing he had gotten even with the Deacon, played another song. This time it was the Isley Brothers' hit "It's My Thang." He did it with a gospel tempo.

Lil Bit and June Bug sat still, their minds uncluttered with stubborn opinions and falsehoods. It was the reason Lil Bit, who had watched everything that had been going on, could not quite understand the overwhelming tension in the air. She turned to June Bug and asked softly, "June Bug, why do you suppose Sister Connie Fuse is so scared of Mother Pray Onn? Didn't Minister Breedin Love say in Sunday school that God is the only one we got to be afraid of?"

Making sure that Ma Cile was not looking, June Bug inched closer to Lil Bit and whispered back, "Yeah, God is who we suppose to fear—Him and Ma Cile! You heard what Sister Connie Fuse said about taking Mother Pray Onn's grave lay-a-way payment to the We'll Haul Your Ashes Crematorium. You know Mother Pray Onn don't play that. She don't allow no mistakes."

Lil Bit had begun to squirm in her seat as she said, "That's what I'm talking about. How come in Sunday school, they say that God forgives, but Mother Pray Onn is the church mother and she don't have to? God does it. How come she don't?" She shook her head sadly.

Ma Cile, uncharacteristically, was concentrating on the service, waiting for her turn to testify, and, for whatever reason, did not hear Lil Bit and June Bug whispering. If she had heard them, she would have given them a backhanded slap for talking during service—while she praised God at the same time.

Sister Betty heard the children. She just kept smiling and praying while saying to herself . . . *and a child shall lead them.* She was not the only one to hear the whispering; so did Sister Connie Fuse, who, by now, was petrified.

Lil Bit continued with concern, "I still don't get it, June Bug. Sister Connie is so pretty and nice, and she got more going on than practically anybody else here. Why she so nervous and scared all the time?"

June Bug stopped and began to move away from her. "Ooh, hold on, you feel something?" His IBW (Impending Butt Whipping) alert system was very sensitive tonight.

Sure enough, there was Ma Cile sending her eye arrows at him and Lil Bit—never saying a word, just staring. Just as Ma Cile was about to line up an industrial-strength gospel-eye whammy and her pinching fingers, Sister Betty cautioned her.

"Let the Lord do His work His way, Ma Cile," Sister Betty whispered in her syrupy manner.

As usual, only Sister Betty could restrain Ma Cile when Ma Cile had made up her mind to do something.

Sister Connie Fuse's mind, for the first time in a long time, became clearer. She meditated awhile longer on what she had overheard the children say. She felt ashamed. Suddenly, different Bible verses began to return to her memory. She remembered in particular Psalms 27:1: *The Lord is my light and my salvation; whom shall I fear? The Lord is the strength of my life; of whom shall I be afraid?* No matter what else was going on around her, for the first time, she was totally focused as some of the words and music of "I want Jesus to Walk with Me" played in her head.

. . . *I want Jesus to walk with me while I'm on this tedious journey, I want Jesus to walk with me.*

The tears poured from Sister Connie Fuse's eyes. Her body shook with spasms as her confidence and faith increased. Finally, she, like so many others, was beginning to see the error of her ways.

It had taken a great deal of effort, but resistant members, who, after being skillfully prodded and humbled by Deacon Laid

Handz and passionately moved by Sister Connie Fuse, arose and gave spirited testimonies. Some praised God while others continued to air their and others' dirty linen, as well as to point accusatory fingers. Those testimonies mattered little to Sister Connie Fuse that night. Only what the children were saying did. She clasped her hands in prayer as she continued to listen.

Feeling somewhat braver and encouraged by the fact that Ma Cile did not backhand him, June Bug boldly moved back closer to Lil Bit.

"Where do you suppose Mother Pray Onn is?" asked June Bug, echoing what was on everybody's mind.

"Don't know and don't care. She ain't gonna mess with us as long as Ma Cile's around," replied Lil Bit with confidence. "Look at all these crazy folks. I ain't seen no picture of Mother Pray Onn hung on a cross—have you? Even the pastor won't say anything to her when she goes off. Remember when she started praying and hollering when that woman from Prayers to Go Church started prophesying about Mother Pray Onn not really getting no visions from God? Mother Pray Onn started screaming about how God didn't visit no little store-front churches, so that woman didn't know what she was talking about. And, I don't even wanna think about that argument she had with Mother Sweet Lee before she died."

Lil Bit, as usual, began to hyperventilate from talking too fast. June Bug seized the opportunity to interrupt her.

"Lil Bit, why you getting so upset? You know why Mother Pray Onn act the way she does. Don't you remember Ma Cile told Sister Betty that Mother Pray Onn life's going through a change?"

"I don't know what her change is! I don't care whether she changes her mind, changes her clothes, or just needs change for a bus—she ain't got no business upsetting folks all the time!" Lil Bit argued.

"Shush, you two!" whispered Sister Connie Fuse as she began to rise from her seat. As she rose, she looked like a flag ascending its flagpole. She looked majestic and yet still afraid.

When she finally stood tall, the activity of the entire congregation came to a halt. Ma Cile attempted to take Sister Connie Fuse by the hand, to sit her back in her seat. Sister Connie nicely rebuked Ma Cile by gently pushing her hand away and resumed her standing position with confidence. Had she realized that Ma Cile, like many others, had seen Mother Pray Onn arrive, slowly strutting peacock-style to her place on the mothers' bench, she might have heeded Ma Cile's warning, or perhaps she was beyond that.

Another storm was brewing on the horizon. Mother Pray Onn took Sister Connie Fuse's act of standing up before she had a chance to go through her customary Mother's arrival bench routine as another apparent slap at her authority. She usually walked slowly to her seat, pretending to be bothered by arthritis. After making sure that she had everyone's attention, she made a frail attempt at kneeling in prayer before she sat down, while indicating to all that whatever was going on could continue.

Everyone knew Mother Pray Onn's routine.

Sister Betty ignored Mother Pray Onn. She was very proud of the new take-charge attitude of Sister Connie Fuse, who now took her time taking off the scarf revealing her beautiful fiery-red hair.

Sister Connie Fuse stared ahead with conviction, her eyes focused and looking like newly mown grass. She avoided the dumbfounded looks from the congregation.

The Reverend Knott Enuff Money and Bishop Was Never-called decided that that would be the perfect time for them to finish their business in the rectory. They slithered from the pulpit. As they made their exit, a swarm of flies trailed behind them. Flies always followed the scent of something rotten.

Ma Cile also marveled at Sister Connie Fuse's newfound courage. She and Sister Betty went about their smiling, praying, and giving thanks. Each one knew that something in the form of a miracle was about to unfold.

All of a sudden, the church bell rang. Although everyone knew that it always rang at nine o'clock in the evening, tonight when it rang, it had the tone and enthusiasm of the start of round one.

Sister Connie Fuse's Testimony

The church became quiet except for the whirring sounds of a few handheld minirecorders and VHS camcorders. A few of the members with entrepreneurial ambitions had decided to develop and sell the recordings of that night's event in the front of a few supermarkets and on street corners.

Sister Connie ignored the lights from those cameras and started speaking.

"First, I want to give honor unto my Lord and Savior, Jesus Christ. To the pulpit, though it be empty now, and to all that are gathered here tonight under the sound of my weak voice."

Sister Connie Fuse placed both hands on the pew in front of her and started walking toward its end. She then leaned over quite close to the place where Sister Carrie Onn was sitting, and continued.

"I've got a lot to thank God for this evening. I've got my health, I'm not homeless, and my mental status is not as bad as some!" She said this with defiance while looking at Sister Carrie Onn.

Ma Cile gave an eye rebuke to some of the members that laughed at the last remark. They responded by shutting up, letting Sister Connie Fuse take small breaths as she continued her testimony of praise and thanksgiving.

Sister Connie Fuse had listened intently to what the children had said, and played it over repeatedly in her mind as she spoke. She decided that she did not like living in fear of another human being, and it would end that night. She made her way past the children.

June Bug, in an act of desperation, tugged on the hem of her dress to warn her, but she kept on moving, making her way to the aisle. Lil Bit sat up straight in her seat as a sign that she was proud of Sister Connie.

Sister Connie Fuse further surprised everyone, including herself, as she then turned and walked toward Mother Pray Onn. Everyone at this point thought she had completely lost it and was about to attack the church mother.

Even the brave and most-feared Mother Pray Onn became alarmed and squirmed down toward the end of the pew, which by now was empty. Her Geritol posse had moved out of the way. She then sat there like a statue or a deer caught in headlights as she locked eyes with Sister Connie Fuse. She decided she had better be quiet instead of interrupting the crazed woman with the flaming red hair and wide green eyes. Backing down was a strange reaction for Mother Pray Onn.

Sister Connie Fuse now had Mother Pray Onn trapped between herself and Brother Tis Mythang. Her persuasive voice and their need to see what would happen next held the congregation captive.

Sister Connie wiped away her tears with a tissue given to her by one of the blank-faced ushers, who also used a clean one to dab her own eyes. As if some protecting force guided her, she took the cordless microphone away from Deacon Laid Handz, who dared not resist her. With her bosom heaving with emotion, she continued to testify.

"I've had many experiences in my life. Some of them were terrifying and a lot of them were okay. All during those times, the good and the bad, I have been searching. Searching for God, the Creator, the Almighty, Jehovah, Allah, Buddha, any higher power. It was a full-time quest for me. My parents died when I was very young, and although I barely remember them, I have always felt something or someone would still protect me. I don't want to go through all my troubles, but ever since I came to this church, a year ago, because of some of the members, it has felt like home." The tears began to swell again in her eyes.

For the next ten minutes, Sister Connie Fuse continued her blazing testimony. She had finally understood. She knew that it was God she was to fear and not man. Her mind would take some time and much prayer to erase all the mixed-up beliefs she held in it, but the process had already begun. She decided never to live in fear of being alone again.

Upon ending her testimony, Sister Connie Fuse calmly asked the congregation to repeat with her the twenty-third Psalm of

David, and many did: *"Yea, though I walk through the valley of the shadow of death, I will fear no evil: for thou art with me . . ."*

She had gone from testifying to preaching.

Sister Connie Fuse won most of the congregation over. Choruses of "Hallelujah!" and "Praise God!" echoed throughout the sanctuary. With obvious skepticism and deceit, both Mother Pray Onn and Sister Carrie Onn halfheartedly joined in with them.

It was now Sister Betty's turn to show her pent-up emotions. She closed her eyes and clutched her Bible as her overdue rivers of tears begged release. She turned toward the nearest window. For a brief moment, she thought she had seen something she had only heard about. She saw a shooting star blazing a white-hot path through the night sky. A warm sensation enveloped her small body, and she felt a stirring that began in her stomach and traveled rapidly to her mouth. She began to utter short, staccato-toned words that were foreign to her, yet traveled with complete clarity toward the heavens.

Sister Betty believed that all the angels in heaven sang and rejoiced when one soul embraced righteousness. She let the tears flow freely because she then understood. She believed that the shooting star she had witnessed was an angelic message that Sister Connie had finally understood it all and that God had answered her prayers and was pleased.

Of course, the Reverend Knott Enuff Money and Bishop Was Nevercalled were still in the pastor's study counting money and did not witness Sister Connie's metamorphosis. In the pulpit was where they should have been, and then they would have known that Minister Breedin' Love had arrived.

Minister Breedin' Love returned from his trip, rushed to the church to make the testimony service, and did not realize what he'd walked into. Although he wondered briefly why the pulpit was empty, he did not have time to dwell on it. He witnessed Sister Connie Fuse's moving testimony. He was grateful for whatever happened to change her. Even through her tears he could see a powerful glow about her, a glow he had never seen before. She was in the church aisle, shouting and praising God as Brother Tis Mythang again played Dorothy Norwood's gospel rendition of "Shake the Devil Off."

Ma Cile, June Bug, and especially Lil Bit were emotionally drained. Sister Connie Fuse was like a part of their family, and they rejoiced in her change and sang praises as well.

The hour was growing late, and Minister Breedin' Love offered a few words of apology for his late arrival.

The apology was lost on most of the women, married and single, because they thought he was a gorgeous hunk of eye candy. They would rather look at him than listen to what he had to say.

As the benediction was about to begin and hands were raised toward heaven for the departing prayer, both Bishop Was Nevercalled and the Reverend Knott Enuff Money returned. They had been gone for so long that most of the congregation forgot they had ever been there. They were both surprised and upset to see that the young and extremely handsome Minister Breedin' Love had returned.

Mother Pray Onn gave them a killer look of condemnation for abandoning her when tonight was supposed to be her victory.

Not letting Minister Breedin' Love have the last word—even if it was the departing prayer—outweighed a double dose of Mother Pray Onn's anger, so the Reverend Knott Enuff Money interrupted him. Whatever rebuke she had in mind, and he was certain she had one, would have to wait until after the service.

Minister Breedin' Love had barely adjusted the microphone to speak, when he heard heavy, stomping footsteps climbing into the pulpit. He turned aside slightly as soon as he saw the Reverend Knott Enuff Money rushing to claim the microphone.

The reverend was not fast enough. He tripped and fell face-down in his Jheri-curl hair, which to everyone looked like a wig. He jumped up, baldheaded, with the wig still on the floor, quickly spat the Jheri-curl juice out of his mouth, and started shouting around the pulpit like he had tripped on purpose or was simply humbling himself before God.

The Reverend Knott Enuff Money, embarrassed, stopped shouting and acted as though he had been there during the entire service and, with a ritualistic upraising of his hands, blessed and dismissed the congregation.

Deacon Laid Handz made a conscious choice to stay at the altar podium, out of the fray, until most of the church cleared out. He did not want to take sides, so he stayed in the middle.

He had better make a choice, because there is no middle ground with God. Heaven or hell, those are the choices.

Several of the stoic-faced church ushers frantically waved their fans in a futile effort to cool off the perspiring and sobbing Sister Connie Fuse, but Sister Betty and Ma Cile waved them aside, and each took Sister Connie's arms to help her stand to leave.

With Lil Bit, June Bug, and Brother Tis Mythang taking up the rear, Ma Cile laid an eye toward several members who stood in their path, and automatically cleared a path.

To those walking along the street that night, they appeared to be a strange entourage. A beautiful young female supported by two elderly women—one tiny, dressed in white, the other big-boned with one blue and one brown eye—descending the church steps. The tall, slender, and colorfully dressed choir director held the hands of two young children and skipped happily behind them.

Most of the congregation had poured out into the warm summer's night and conversed about the events that had unfolded. However, several stayed behind to see round two. It was not over. There were Mother Pray Onn and Sister Carrie Onn surrounding the Reverend Knott Enuff Money and Bishop Was Nevercalled. Between the two old jackleg preachers and the exit door stood Sister Carrie Onn, legs and arms spread wide. She was moving from side to side like a football linebacker, pushing and blocking their escape. She had learned how to do those maneuvers as a child to avoid some of the hormone-driven Hellraiser uncles in her family.

Mother Pray Onn dug deep down in her church bag, which

had the words *More Than a Conqueror* inscribed. She pulled
out her newly refilled giant-size Equalizer Mace canister and
steadied her aim. She adjusted the lever from "better recognize" to "jackleg preacher removal" and let go.

Deacon Laid Handz, who had shifted closer to get a better
view of the impending bedlam, had a flashback of the night before and took off running.

Those outside the church heard shouting and crying. Some
people thought the service was still going on. They did not
know a service was being held indeed—Mother Pray Onn's ex-
termination service for those who had betrayed her.

As they walked toward the bus stop, Ma Cile and Sister
Betty were deep in their conversation of praise when they
heard someone call their names. They turned around and found
Minister Breedin' Love running toward them. He greeted
them and then asked if he could offer a ride home. There was
also enough room in his station wagon for Sister Connie Fuse
and the rest.

After making sure everyone was in the car, Ma Cile related
to Minister Breedin' Love the entire evening's event, including
what had happened to cause it.

Minister Breedin' Love was not surprised at anything he
had heard, and as was his habit, he apologized for the inatten-
tiveness of the Reverend Knott Enuff Money and the bishop.
He stopped short of apologizing for Deacon Laid Handz, because he himself was not perfect and he did not like the deacon.
He rebuked himself without saying why. He asked Sister Betty
and Ma Cile to pray along with him as he asked God to put
more love in his heart.

Surrounded by conversation and good friends, Sister Connie
Fuse felt overcome by the new emotion of self-confidence and
faith. She wanted to wallow in it. Absorbing each new thought
in its clarity obsessed her.

Lil Bit moved closer to Sister Connie. She wanted to be a
part of whatever it was that Sister Connie was feeling. Her
feelings for Sister Connie had grown tonight, and in her ten-

year-old mind, she envisioned herself becoming like her.

Sister Connie Fuse understood and placed Lil Bit's hand in hers and gently squeezed it. She allowed the little girl to lay her head in the fold of her arms. If her mind were to become as clear as crystal, she still would never be able to tell the ten-year-old little girl how much the conversation she had over-heard had meant to her. With no words spoken between them, they leaned back in their seats to enjoy the beautiful night sky embedded with thousands of shining stars. The stars were beautiful and twinkled as if they were notes vigorously played on a vibraphone.

June Bug took advantage of Brother Tis Mythang's good mood and asked him if he would teach him how to play one of the latest gospel songs. They agreed on a time and place and then laughed as they imagined what Mother Pray Onn was probably doing to the good reverend and the bishop. They then decided that Kirk Franklin's hip-hop, gospel-like song "Stomp" would be perfect.

Soon all conversation ceased, and the car became quiet as each one reflected on the lesson they learned at prayer and tes-timony service. They knew no one should fear man, because those fears lead to unnecessary despair. It was a lesson they hoped never to forget.

However, the praise and fear of God will always lead to peace and blessings.

So that contrariwise ye ought rather forgive and comfort, lest perhaps such a one should be swallowed up with overmuch sorrow. Lest Satan should get an advantage of us: for we are not ignorant of his devices.

—2 Corinthians 2: 7, 11

For God hath not given us the spirit of fear; but of power, and of love, and of a sound mind.

—2 Timothy 1:7

It's Only a Hat

The Fourth Sunday in August, Time for the Annual "Friends and Family Day" At the Ain't Nobody Else Right but Us— All Others Goin' to Hell Church.

Sister Betty woke up early with a big smile on her face. One of her favorite church events, the annual Friends and Family Day celebration, was about to happen. Since Old Mother Centennial first announced it, months ago, she'd been preparing. There was only one day left before the celebration would start, and she needed something special to wear. She had gone to her neat little bedroom closet, and from among her array of white and green dresses—the only colors she ever wore—she had picked out a conservative green cotton dress that was appropriate for a sixty-year-old, and caught the bus to go shopping downtown.

The downtown Pelzer bus was very crowded and the air-conditioning was not working, and Sister Betty did not care. She was armed with a lot of patience, but not too much money.

After arriving downtown, Sister Betty went inside one of her favorite boutiques, the Cost A-Plenty. That's where most of Pelzer's poorest folks shopped. You could put everything from a hatpin to one glove on layaway for years. Finally, she found the perfect hat to go with her "I'm Saved, and You'd Better Know It" outfit. After haggling with the sales clerk, they agreed upon a price that would at least leave her with bus fare and a semblance of dignity. The surly clerk placed it in a much-too-large hatbox that was very cumbersome, yet nothing could dampen her spirits.

The long bus ride back to her house didn't seem too long at

all, since she had her hat for the "special occasion." She arrived home still smiling and put the hatbox in her neat hallway closet. After eating a light supper of fried peanut-battered catfish, grits, and cheese, with a bottle of Diet Pepsi to quench her thirst, she went to bed. In her dreams, she saw herself praising the Lord in her beautiful new hat.

The next morning, the buzzing sound of the alarm clock softly poured into Sister Betty's ears. She sat up, wiped the spittle from the corners of her mouth, turned off the clock switch, and took about five minutes giving God praise for allowing her to live another day after several trips to the bathroom during the previous night's revisit of that peanut-butter-battered catfish.

Sister Betty, never a big breakfast eater, maintained her weight of 105 pounds on her five-foot-two-inch frame with no problem, despite her healthy dinner appetite. She decided to skip her usual breakfast of Spam and poached eggs. She doubted there could be anything left from the previous night's dinner, so she opted instead for a bowl of double-strength bran flakes. There would be all types of ghetto cuisine served at the annual Friends and Family Day celebration, and she wanted to save her appetite.

After putting away the dishes in her neat kitchen cupboard, Sister Betty performed several menial chores around the house, waiting until it was time to get dressed. She could not wait to put on her new hat. Sister Betty took her time primping. After looking in the mirror, she gave her outfit of white on white dress and short-sleeved jacket a glowing self-endorsement. Suddenly she began to perspire. She had a feeling that all was not well, but she dismissed the feeling. Nothing would spoil her day.

It was close to twelve o'clock noon. Almost time to leave. Sister Betty took a moment to peep through the vertical blinds in her living room. She took a deep breath of the summer fresh air and got into a waiting taxicab. She relaxed and enjoyed the ride.

That Sunday was beautiful by both heaven's and earth's standards. There were no clouds or the appearance of a threatening thunderstorm. However, the climate inside the church was going to be another matter.

Inside the church, clouds and thunderstorms infused with little drops of pure insanity were starting to form. That thunderous dark cloud's name was Sister Ima Hellraiser. Nobody in the church hated peace and quiet like her. Whether it was during a baby shower, or a funeral, she could be counted on to set off a riot. Friends and Family Day would be no different.

Sister Betty's taxi finally pulled up in front of the church. She looked one last time at the reflection of her beautiful hat in the car door glass. She was more than satisfied. Her tiny feet barely touched the steps as she hurried inside. Suddenly, from a far corner of the sanctuary, came a nice-nasty, purring voice that sounded like a buzz saw. The voice deliberately assaulted Sister Betty's peace and quiet.

"Sister Betty, that's a nice little hat you're wearing," Sister Ima Hellraiser whispered as she smirked and slinked her way across the plush red church carpet. She stood there model-thin and gorgeous, dressed to the nines in a two-piece, inappropriate, sure-to-start-tongues-wagging, belly-showing mustard yellow dress, and basked in the bright sunshine, which poured through the church's stained-glass windows. "I guess we must be one of the first to arrive." She liked to set up her victims with niceties and small talk before she attacked.

Suddenly, Sister Hellraiser thought perhaps her eyes were playing tricks. However, she knew even Ray Charles could see that Sister Betty was wearing the same hat as she. How could that be? That went against all female logic. Two women could not wear the same hat, at the same time, on the same occasion, and in the same place.

The sales clerk who sold her the hat at the Cost A-Plenty Boutique told her it was a "one of a kind." Evidently, she'd lied, and Sister Hellraiser couldn't stand folks lying unless it was her doing the lying. That sales clerk would pay dearly come Monday morning when the store reopened. She was going to beat the woman down to a discount.

Sister Ima Hellraiser eyed Sister Betty with the intensity of a cross-eyed, calypso-dancing she-devil, and with about the same sincerity. She had as much use for Sister Betty as one tomcat had for another. For many years, Sister Hellraiser had thought the elderly church lady had a little bit too much religion for her taste, and even worse, whenever she was around Sister Betty, her conscience tried to bother her. Sister Hellraiser and her conscience had an understanding—she didn't bother it and it wouldn't bother her.

On such a lovely day and at such a wonderful spiritual event, most would have tried to act like they had a little religion or upbringing. However, Sister Ima Hellraiser was not like most people. She had been dragged up instead of raised up.

It took a moment, but Sister Betty regained her composure. The subtle yet nasty attack from Sister Hellraiser had come from out of nowhere. "Well, thank you very much. I see we are both, definitely, wearing the same nice little hat." She stared suspiciously at Sister Hellraiser to see if there was a hint the woman was teasing. There was none.

Sister Betty was no fool. More than fifty years had passed since becoming a member of the Ain't Nobody Else Right but Us–All Others Goin' to Hell Church, and forty of those years were spent ducking and dodging Ima Hellraiser's mother, Sister A Real Hellraiser. The one thing she knew for certain was the apple didn't fall far from the tree. So no matter how much she wanted to relax and enjoy this beautiful event, she knew she'd better watch as well as pray. "I'm gonna go inside and get a little prayer time in before things start. Would you care to join me?"

No one would blame Sister Betty for being leery. Sister Hellraiser was the type of person that could make the Holiest of Holy trap her in a corner, call the police, and report that someone had been shot. Next, that same Holiest of Holy would put down the phone and shoot her. Of course, that same Holiest of Holy person would have to rush to the altar, lie stretched out, decked out in sackcloth and ashes, and then ask for forgiveness for malice aforethought. Sister Hellraiser had that effect on people, both the saved and the unsaved.

Sister Hellraiser ignored Sister Betty's attempt to leave and invitation to join in prayer. She jeered as she circled Sister Betty, "I didn't know you could afford a *hat* like that, living on a fixed income." She still couldn't believe her eyes. Her one-of-a kind hat, supposedly handmade by Sister I Lie Alot from the Cost A-Plenty Boutique, was staring right back at her, atop the head of Sister Betty. It was like letting the late comedienne Moms Mabley wear a thong bathing suit. It just wasn't right.

The hat that had Sister Ima Hellraiser in such a snit, and poor Sister Betty wondering why she ever got out of bed, defied description

The hat was made of bright-orange shellacked straw and shaped like a triangle. There were so many red, blue, and mauve flowers on the right side of it, Sister Hellraiser had to pretend her head was leaning, because that was the attitude needed to go with the hat. The only thing that kept her from completely falling over was the big matching orange-and-mustard-yellow pocketbook, which she carried in her left hand for balance. As strange as it would've looked on anyone else, it looked good on her.

Sister Betty was wearing the same hat, so she leaned the same way. However, in her left hand she had her big family-size Bible that she always carried. That Bible kept her from falling over. Together, they looked like Frick and Frack runaways from the Fun Mirror in an amusement park.

The gasoline-laced situation was about to turn up another notch because the church's choir director, the always effervescent Brother Tis Mythang, was about to stick his nose where it didn't belong.

"My, my, don't you two ladies look special," Brother Tis Mythang teased from the other side of the church vestibule. He stood by the blessing dispenser. He was deep into admiring his two-piece green-and-beige suit, complete with matching tie, when his attention was diverted. He saw what he knew was sure to be an unscheduled yet exciting event.

Brother Tis Mythang could not believe his eyes as he put his pocket mirror away. Two church sisters wearing the same hat.

This event was just too delicious. Without thinking, he started toward them with his hand moving like it was shooing flies away. He almost knocked down Sister Carrie Onn, the church's premier blabbermouth, as he tried to get a closer look at what was about to go down.

Walking was taking too long, so Brother Tis Mythang ran up to them, completely out of breath, and blurted out, "Are you two singing a duet or something? I didn't know anyone was wearing uniforms today. All I can say is that y'all working them hats . . ."

He would have continued, but he felt the knives thrown by Sister Hellraiser's fierce brown eyes. He was bubbly, not stupid. When he looked around and no longer saw Sister Carrie Onn, he knew she had gone to tell everybody about the hats. He mentally gave her five minutes before the vestibule would be filled with folks vying for front-row spots to watch the cat fight that was sure to take place. He was already writing his op-ed piece in his head to submit to the church's newsletter, the *Daily BLAB* (Braggarts, Liars and Busybodies) *Report*.

Five minutes was a long time for Brother Tis Mythang to wait. One of his main pleasures was stirring things up, but that event was too good to waste, and besides, he loved an enthusiastic crowd. "Let's get ready to rumble." He could hardly keep still as he giggled to himself.

Sister Betty didn't have to be a rocket scientist to know what was about to go down. She decided she would try to do whatever she could to stop it. She would make the sacrifice, even if it meant taking off her brand-new exquisite hat so that Sister Hellraiser could have bragging rights. It was a good and well-meaning intention until she remembered her hat was pinned to her good church wig. She had intentions of being buried in that wig. No one had ever seen her without it. No one would.

In no time, Sister Carrie Onn returned with about thirty spiritually challenged congregation members. They were elbowing and jockeying for places to see the impending bout between Sister Betty and Sister Hellraiser. Many were returnees from the bout between Mother Pray Onn and Sister Connie

Fuse, which never took place. This time they were not to be denied a Hellraiser-and-Carrie Onn-sponsored event in the making.

Sister Betty suddenly felt she would have been better off if she had stayed home and watched "World Championship Wrestling." Now she was in danger of involuntarily participating in a title bout. If she took off her hat, then her good church wig would come off with it. She'd already made up her mind that she certainly didn't need to do that in front of Sister Carrie Onn.

She was about *this close* to figuring out what to do. Then it happened! Something faster than a locomotive and able to leap over the truth in a single sentence occurred: Brother Tis Mythang's big mouth flew open—again. He gave the term, *quick of tongue* a new meaning.

Brother Tis Mythang took one look at the advancing Sister Carrie Onn and her ruthless estrogen-laced entourage. He knew he had the Dream Team backup.

Brother Tis Mythang twirled, snapped his fingers as if he were Zorro without the sword, and jerked his neck, Egyptian-snake-style. He looked like an asp. "If fashion were a candle, you two would be unscented, flickered, and burnt out in no time." He laughed as he glanced back over his shoulder and winked. Seeing the crowd behind him gave him extra courage. He was hunting without a clue, and his reality check was lost in the mail. "Ooh, Sister Hellraiser. Girl, I didn't know that was a two-piece suit you were wearing. Those stretch marks on your stomach made it look like you were wearing a one-piece corduroy suit. I wondered why you was wearing corduroy in this hot weather with such a lovely twin hat. . . ." His mouth was on autopilot, but his safety radar was turned off.

Brother Tis Mythang was about to star in his own drama. His supposed ally, Sister Carrie Onn, was a renowned blabbermouth but no ordinary fool. She was a fool with special skills. She was Sister Hellraiser's first cousin and knew firsthand when to play with her and when not. "Fool, you are on your own." She laughed, and slapped high fives with someone standing close by.

Sister Carrie Onn and her cousin, Sister Hellraiser, were about the same age and had many similar character issues. Sister Carrie Onn had spent several of her most traumatic childhood summers with her cousin and her aunt, Sister A Real Hellraiser. Those summers were the training ground for the vicious and lonely woman she became. It was during that time, after a few unsuccessful and infantile escapades, that she learned how not to get in Sister Hellraiser's way.

The only reason Sister Carrie Onn brought the crowd to the vestibule was to see how Sister Betty was going to get herself out of her current dilemma. Like most of the people in the church, she thought Sister Betty's mind was about ten cents short of equaling a dime. As much as she did not care for Sister Betty, she still did not intend to help Brother Tis Mythang. Since he stuck his big nose into the mess by himself, she was going to let him pull it out—by himself.

Just like Brother Tis Mythang, her reality check had been returned, marked *undeliverable*. She knew better than to bring a crowd into the vestibule. She just didn't care. Her participation would be required, and she felt up to the task.

Sister Betty's dilemma worsened. She wrung her hands and prayed that her best friend, Ma Cile, would be around somewhere inside the church. She was right. Ma Cile was chomping on a pigfoot fajita in the church dining room when she heard the commotion, and came lumbering into the vestibule. Sister Betty explained her situation to Ma Cile.

"Sister Betty, you ain't got nuthin' to worry 'bout. Jist let me finish my pigfoot fahidah. We'll pray some mo' and handle this here situation."

With Brother Tis Mythang, Sister Hellraiser, and Sister Carrie Onn on the attack, Sister Betty knew she could wait for prayer. She did not know if she could wait for Ma Cile to finish her pigfoot fajita.

It did not matter whether prayer or a pigfoot was involved—it was about to get worse before it got better.

The cranky-and-stuck-on-menopause church mother, Mother Pray Onn, had just left her house located at 000 No Mercy

Boulevard. She called a cab as soon as she got the phone call from her daughter, Sister Carrie Onn.

The temperature rose another ten degrees outside. Inside, the church vestibule was about to explode, with several egos getting scorched from the fire.

Suddenly, Brother Tis Mythang's big mouth went into overdrive. "Sister Carrie Onn, don't you think they just look too cute? Both Sister Hellraiser and Sister Betty are wearing the same hats. I think they ought to sing a duet. Maybe they both can get up and give the announcements or something. You know, taking turns."

Sister Carrie Onn continued to ignore him, which was a good thing. Before anyone could shut him up for his own good, Sister Hellraiser had forgotten about how heavy her hat was, but not about his "corduroy suit" reference to her stretch marks. She leaped at him as quick as the sticky tongue of a frog to a fly.

Because she had forgotten how heavy the hat was did not mean it still was not heavy.

Sister Hellraiser's hat took on a life of its own. She tried to jump to the left to grab Brother Tis Mythang's leg, and instead the heavy hat pulled her to the right. Each time she leaped, she bounced up and down like a stand-up punching bag. Sister Hellraiser continued rolling around like an electrified broken Slinky.

Finally, in her blind anger, Sister Hellraiser found enough strength to grab one of Brother Tis Mythang's pant legs, but she couldn't hold on and lost her grip. Now both she and her hat were possessed by the demon of revenge. She continued her electrified-Slinky impersonation as streaks of bright-orange shellacked straw from her hat glistened, as she rolled and re-coiled after each botched thrust.

Brother Tis Mythang looked down in horror as she again kept coming dangerously close to laying hands on him. If her aim was true, he'd have to adopt kids, if he ever decided to re-lease his pent-up male hormones. Glistening beads of perspiration poured from his face as he suddenly developed lockjaw.

Sister Hellraiser went into maniac overdrive as she tried again to tear him asunder.

Sister Betty regained enough composure to silently pray harder, because things were about to get real ugly.

Everyone in the vestibule heard a swooshing sound like a toy helicopter blade as an object flew in the direction of Sister Hellraiser. It was the remains of Ma Cile's large-sized, Louisiana Hot Sauce-covered pigfoot fajita.

Ma Cile did not mean to throw the pigfoot so soon. She meant to throw it only after she had sucked all the meat off the bone. Just like David taking on Goliath. She meant to use the bone to serve a beat-down to the trouble-making Sister Hellraiser.

Ma Cile became angrier because the pigfoot fajita had been accidentally knocked from her hand by the wind from Mother Pray Onn as she raced up the steps, from the taxi into the vestibule, and passed Ma Cile.

For a brief moment, Ma Cile could not move. She could not believe her eye when she looked down and saw her empty hands. One moment she had a pigfoot fajita. Then she did not. She had salivated and waited since last week to be the first on line to get her pigfoot fajita. Now it sat, half-eaten, upon the head of Sister Hellraiser, in the middle of the many red, blue, and mauve flowers on the right side of the hat.

Ma Cile trudged a few steps. She was trying to focus her good brown eye, again, on exactly where in the flowered hat the pigfoot fajita landed. It was difficult because her blue store-bought false eye kept jumping around.

When the crowd saw Ma Cile stumbling across the vestibule, sweating and huffing with her eyeballs playing tag with each other, they scattered until she passed.

Sister Hellraiser lay sprawled on the floor and babbled words no one mistook for praises, because she was cussing. She became coherent enough to see the towering Ma Cile coming toward her.

When Ma Cile finally reached Sister Hellraiser, she stood over her with a hand on each hip. She looked like a two-handled teakettle, complete with a seething-hot attitude.

In slow motion, Sister Hellraiser felt her life flash before her as the big, callused hands of Ma Cile descended.

Someone in the crowd with a sense of humor yelled a line from the *Forest Gump* movie: "Run, Sister Hellraiser. Run, girlfriend. Run!"

Sister Hellraiser's beautiful honeyed complexion took on an ashen hue as she screamed, "Don't hit me! Here, take the hat! Sister Betty can have both hats; I don't want it!"

Sister Hellraiser continued quivering with fear. Her reputation as being a bad mamma jamma had disappeared faster than O. J.'s alibi. The need to live radically replaced the need to be numero uno at the Friends and Family Day celebration.

Ma Cile would not be denied. "Give me that—" she hissed.

Before Ma Cile finished the sentence, Sister Hellraiser took her free hand, the one that wasn't holding her heart inside, and flung the hat to the floor. With that, the less-than-spiritually minded crowd in the vestibule started to point, laugh, and stare at Sister Hellraiser. Almost all of them had a reason to want to see her humiliated. At some time or another, she had verbally maimed most of the congregation.

Ma Cile rose back up. It took a moment for her to get a breath. She straightened her gray pageboy-style wig with one hand and placed the other hand on her temple. She tapped one stubby finger against her left temple to line up her one good brown eye so that it leveled with the store-bought blue eye. "The pigfoot!" she yelled. "I only wanted my pigfoot fahidah back! I don't care about yo' hat. But if ya think ya gonna mess with my best friend Sista' Betty and my food, too, think again!"

After Ma Cile grabbed the hat from the floor, she ripped most of the flowers from it. With the tenderness of a new mother, she removed her pigfoot fajita. She glared back down at the still trembling Sister Hellraiser and flung the hat Frisbee-style back at her.

With the pigfoot fajita retrieved, Ma Cile wobbled back to where she last saw Sister Betty standing. Sister Betty was gone. Stunned, Ma Cile scanned the vestibule. Her head moved back and forth like it was attached by a spring. "Where in the world did Sister Betty go?" she wondered aloud. "Y'all move out of my way! I got to go and find po' Sista' Betty," Ma Cile barked.

They moved.

Ma Cile headed for the church's overflow room. She knew that was where she would have gone if she had been as embarrassed as Sister Betty. Since every one of the onlookers had run to the vestibule to see what was going on, Sister Betty was bound to find it empty.

From across the vestibule, behind the safety of about a dozen drama-hungry congregation members, finally came the taunting voice of Sister Carrie Onn. Her entry needed to be memorable, so she pretended to show concern for the cousin she despised.

"My, my, Sister Hellraiser," Sister Carrie Onn yelled. She saw a chance of a lifetime to further humiliate her cousin. Acting like she had just found a pot of gold or a proposal from the man of her dreams, Deacon Laid Handz, she continued her attack with all the enthusiasm of Mike Tyson on Evander Holyfield's ear.

"I see you and Sister Betty ain't wearing the same one-of-a-kind hat no more. I believed y'all claimed it was an original. That's a real shame. The two of you looked so—how should I put it?—twin-ish." For an extra dig she added, "And you look almost the same age."

Sister Carrie Onn looked like a ghetto Eartha Kitt as she slunk to within about five feet of her shaken cousin. "What's wrong, sweetheart? It looks like you could use a blessing right about now."

"Here, let me do the honors." Sister Carrie Onn stopped suddenly, to extend her middle finger toward Sister Hellraiser, before continuing, "Why don't I go inside the pastor's study and ask Reverend Knott Enuff Money and Deacon Laid Handz to come pray for you? I know they'd love to lay a hand or two on you."

When Sister Hellraiser didn't get up immediately and knock

her down, Sister Carrie Onn felt a sense of power and moved in a little closer for the kill. "Would you like that? Prayer can get you through some mighty rough times. Or would you rather have your own pigfoot fajita?"

The crowd suddenly felt as powerful as Sister Carrie Onn. To show their unity, they crept forward and stood behind her. Several impatient hands pushed her gently, urging her to continue.

Sister Carrie Onn acknowledged the crowd's support with a wink and made a fist. She turned to Sister Hellraiser and raged, "I'd help you to your feet, but how many times, when we were kids, did you help me after you knocked me down? Huh? How many times did you tease me about my fashion sense or lack of it? Huh? Well, you don't look so fashionable now, do you? Feels kind of funny looking up at people instead of always looking down at them, don't it?"

Sister Carrie Onn's mouth was in warp speed overdrive. It was running so fast that she never saw Sister Hellraiser jump up with the now disheveled hat in her hand.

Sister Hellraiser stumbled a couple of steps, but she somehow managed to come nose to nose with her cousin, Sister Carrie Onn.

Sister Carrie Onn and her bravado mentally flew to panic city, using atomic energy brainpower. When she last looked, she thought that there were at least five feet of safety between them. She knew it was one thing to badmouth someone when they were sprawled helpless on a floor. It was quite another thing to do it face-to-face.

Sister Hellraiser was certain Sister Carrie Onn had lost her mind. No sane person would ever criticize her fashion sense. It was worse than Ma Cile publicly knocking her silly with a half-eaten hot-sauce-covered pigfoot fajita. She was so mad, she didn't care that she looked like a jar of spilled jellybeans with her hat of many colors discarded on the church floor. She just couldn't believe her very own cousin, Sister Carrie Onn, had insulted her, suggesting that she didn't have fashion sense.

Sister Hellraiser had not been that insulted since Sister

Aggi Tate had publicly told people that she knew it was Sister Hellraiser that had been calling her house, hanging up, and trying to get next to her husband, Deacon Dick Tate. Sister Hellraiser had to set Sister Aggi Tate straight that same night. She told her that as long as she'd been messing around with her husband, Deacon Dick Tate, she'd never called her house. She hated being accused of something she hadn't done. She had more class than to call the house of a married man she fooled around with.

Sister Hellraiser was not as brave as she wanted everyone to believe. She had already looked around and no longer saw Ma Cile or Sister Betty. She knew it was safe to get up. Sister Carrie Onn was no verbal challenge, and she was going to see that she paid for all the humiliation she had received from the others.

"No fashion sense! You must have lost your mind," Sister Hellraiser snarled. "You are the one with no fashion sense! Look at what you're wearing—didn't you wear this same tasteless outfit last October thirty-first? It was wrong then and it's wrong now."

Sister Hellraiser was giving a verbal paint job, using her vinegar-soaked tongue. Her tongue dipped back into the palate of nastiness as she continued her tirade. "I guess you must have dressed in the dark. In fact, did you ever get your lights turned back on? I know the last time, you were so far behind in your payments that the electric company came out and turned off the streetlights in the front of your house."

Sister Hellraiser's mouth just kept on going, and it whittled Sister Carrie Onn down with each syllable.

When Sister Hellraiser finished, Sister Carrie Onn felt small enough to get a job as a teller at a piggy bank.

Sister Hellraiser never missed a beat. She grabbed her radically redesigned hat, which by then was missing all of the mauve-colored flowers, and had been shaped into a square instead of a triangle. She pulled it down on her head, accessorizing it with much attitude. Without any remorse, she continued her verbal beat-down of Sister Carrie Onn. "And, by the way, your bra size finally arrived at the store. Unfortunately, some-one thought it was a boiled-egg holder, so you'll need to pick it up from the dairy department at the supermarket."

A voice from the crowd yelled, "Ouch and touché!"

All of a sudden, the laughter from the crowd stopped. Everyone but Sister Hellraiser and Sister Carrie Onn was looking at the two figures standing in the doorway. They would have kept chewing out each other, except mighty-mouth Brother Tis Mythang set it off—again—and got their attention.

Brother Tis Mythang just couldn't help himself as he looked back and forth from Sister Hellraiser to Sister Betty. Sister Betty was now standing hand in hand in the doorway with Ma Cile. "Have mercy! Sister Betty, did you and Sister Hellraiser bring two different one-of-a-kind original hats to wear today? Things have been so crazy, I didn't even see you two change into your new hats. I still say, you be workin' them hats. . . ." Brother Tis Mythang's mouth kept going like a peppy little snapping turtle.

Peace and quiet never had a chance to show up, because more pandemonium struck. Ma Cile thought her eyes were playing tricks, too. She kept thumping herself in the temple—a futile effort.

Sister Betty wanted to move and couldn't.

No one would believe what happened next, so it was a good thing some of the spiritually challenged congregation members had been taping the entire event. They were going to show it, complete with commercials, at the next testa-lying service. It didn't seem possible, but there they were, Sister Betty and Sister Ima Hellraiser, both wearing the same hat—again.

Ma Cile had been right. Earlier, Sister Betty had retreated to the overflow room, removed all the mauve-colored flowers from her hat, and shaped it into a square, just to make it different from Sister Hellraiser's hat. And, like a scene from the old television series *The Outer Limits* that just kept on repeating itself, here they stood again—wearing the same hat. They looked at each other, too tired to rehash a losing situation, and decided it was a draw. When Sister Betty saw that Sister Hellraiser was not going to restart the imagined competition, she gave a silent "Thank you, Lord."

From a distance, the hats did look the same, but upon close examination, there was a subtle difference. Sister Hellraiser had a smidgen of hot sauce on the right side of her hat left by Ma Cile's pigfoot fajita. It was about the size of a dime, and most people without a magnifying glass would not have noticed.

Mother Pray Onn had been quiet since arriving on the scene. She was biding her time for just the right moment. The "Don't nobody know God like I know God" church mother didn't leave her home, catch a taxi, and then rush up the steps into the church vestibule for nothing. She was going to have her say, and nobody was going to stop her. Of course, she didn't need a magnifying glass to spot possible chaos and was overjoyed when she saw the dime-size smidgen of hot sauce on Sister Hellraiser's hat. Before the choir could start singing "Holy, Holy, Holy" to start the annual Friends and Family Day celebration, Mother Pray Onn started taunting Sister Hellraiser where Sister Carrie Onn had left off.

"Ima, sweetheart, what is that on your hat? Is that blood?" She squinted as if she needed to see it better. "I guess it could be hot sauce—it's hard to tell." Mother Pray Onn used her walking cane to point toward Sister Betty and continued her taunting. "I don't see the same thing on Sister Betty's hat. . . ." She was just getting started.

Sister Betty had had enough drama for one day. She left Mother Pray Onn pointing her cane. She clutched her big family-size Bible to her chest and held her peace. It was better to be thought a fool than to open one's mouth and prove it. She and Ma Cile walked away and continued praising God. They were determined to enjoy the rest of the festivities. Sister Betty held her head high, yet with humility, as she straightened her new and improved hat. She made the hat; the hat did not make her.

As everyone finally left the vestibule, they heard Brother Tis Mythang remark, "Can you believe that entire ruckus in the church vestibule . . . over a hat?" He laughed as he sashayed into the sanctuary. "Folks need to grow up!"

For ye are yet carnal: for whereas there is among you envying, and strife, and divisions, are ye not carnal, and walk as men.
—1 Corinthians 3:2

Charity suffereth long, and is kind; charity envieth not; charity vaunteth not itself, is not puffed up.
—1 Corinthians 13:4

And withal they learn to be idle, wandering about from house to house; and not only idle, but tattlers also and busybodies, speaking things which they ought not.
—1 Timothy 5:13

The Y2K Christmas Pageant

The invitation sent out to the community read,

> *The Ain't Nobody Else Right but Us—All Others Goin'*
> *to Hell Church, located at the corner of Hell and Re-*
> *demption Avenues, in Pelzer, South Carolina, cordially*
> *invites you to attend their Y2K Christmas Pageant.*

It wasn't the usual Christmas pageant. It was more like a television *I Love Lucy* meets *Good Times*.

Inside, the church looked lovely. The decorations were traditional Christmas colors of green, red, silver, and blue. Even the church's ATM bank machine had Christmas stickers supplied by NYCE, PLUS, CIRRUS, and other moneylenders, such as Big Lenny's Pay or Die. The blessing dispenser, next to it, had a "holiday special" sign posted. In addition to the usual "Mo Money," "Destroy Your Enemies," and ribbons for good health there were two new blessings. The "Git a Man" and the "Git Rid of Your Mate" faux-blessing bottles were the favorites for the holidays. Purchase two bottles of either, and you would get a free, supposedly personalized copy of Chante's *Got a Man* CD.

Even with all the glitz and glimmer of holiday decorations and the spirit of Christmas in the air, it only took one person to dampen it. That Christmas, it was the mouth that roared, the choir director, Brother Tis Mythang,

Looking around the sanctuary, Brother Tis Mythang spotted his nemesis, Deacon Laid Handz. For a long time, he'd secretly suspected the deacon of starting most of the malicious rumors that spread about his sexuality. Usually, he never had much to say to the deacon, but since they were alone, it was Christmas, and there wasn't the usual church drama going on, he gave it a shot.

Brother Tis Mythang turned on his thirty-two-watt smile as he spoke to Deacon Laid Handz like they were old friends. "Isn't the church lovely? We are going to have a wonderful Y2K Christmas celebration." The deacon didn't shoo him away, so he felt safe in continuing. "Deacon, you always seem to know what's going on around here. Let me ask you a question."

Deacon Laid Handz pretended to ignore Brother Tis Mythang.

Brother Tis Mythang whined on, oblivious to the obvious snub. "Why does Brother No Note always have to be the one to lead the Christmas songs?" He hit a piano key with each word he spoke. "I've run my fingers up and down all eighty-eight keys on this piano, and I haven't found his nor Mother Pray Onn's key yet."

Deacon Laid Handz kept on ignoring him. His interest waned because the conversation was not about him.

Brother Tis Mythang gave his own long and well-kept fingers the once-over before continuing. "You know Miss Lo Down at the Nail Pagoda charges a lot of yen for a manicure, and I'm not about to mess up my nails hunting for a key."

There was no use in complaining to Deacon Laid Handz. The deacon still couldn't care less. He was too busy profiling in the hand mirror he always carried. He smiled while putting the finishing touches to his new hairstyle, the "fade," which was about six inches high. He couldn't decide whether he wanted it to lie to the right or to the left. He had gotten the haircut at the Shaky Hands Barber Shop and didn't know that a fade wasn't supposed to lie. No one had the heart to tell him that his hairstyle, as well as his multicolored polyester suits, were as outdated as seamed pantyhose. Someone could have told him, but he had wrecked a few nerves with his displays of undeserved ego, so he remained the butt of many jokes. He finally stopped mentally complimenting himself long enough to reply and to shut Brother Tis Mythang's rapid-firing mouth.

"It's because his great-grandfather on his mother's side donated the first washtub used to keep the beat during choir rehearsal," snapped Deacon Laid Handz. "Every true member of the Ain't Nobody Else Right but Us—All Others Goin' to Hell Church knows that." He looked at Brother Tis Mythang in disgust and then continued, "You donate; therefore, you rule."

Brother Tis Mythang's jaw dropped. "So let me get this straight. Because somebody's great-grandpappy donated something a hundred years ago, that means they get special treatment throughout the millennium?"

Brother Tis Mythang let his eyes roll upward as he forgot about his manicure and pounded the keys on the piano. He thought about talking aloud; instead, he whispered as he looked around to see who might be listening. "That ain't right, and I don't care who hears me say it!" He was flashy and a bit eccentric, but certainly not too stupid—most of the time.

"Well, I guess I must agree with you. I'm also tired of Brother No Note always leading the Christmas Pageant song." Deacon Laid Handz stopped and then smiled again in the hand mirror. He blew himself a kiss in it before quickly changing over to his favorite subject—himself. "I don't know if I've mentioned it before, but Luther Vandross once commented on the sultry quality of my voice. He was fascinated by my voice." He stopped and cleared his throat and wrinkled his brow in disgust. "You know, he stole that riff he does from me."

"Say what!"

"You know, the riff he does when he sings that line . . . *'explodes in ecstasy'*? Making sure that Brother Tis Mythang did not misunderstand what he was saying, he added, "You know, that gimmick he uses with his voice in the song 'A House Is Not a Home.'"

Deacon Laid Handz lied like a cheap thrift-store rug. He squinted his eyes as he spoke, so that Brother Tis Mythang wouldn't see the truth in them.

Brother Tis Mythang looked at Deacon Laid Handz with mock sympathy and, without so much as a hint of whether he believed him or not, teased, "Well, why didn't you sue Luther Vandross. He's loaded with millions. He can't be going around stealing people's riffs."

Deacon Laid Handz mistook Brother Tis Mythang's false sympathetic manner for real feelings and softly answered, "Oh, I wanted to sue, but evidently Luther don't have as much money as people seem to think, or he wouldn't have stolen my riff. Anyway, if he needed it that bad, I was willing to let him sing like me for free. After all, there's enough room for both of us to sing in our unique styles. Besides, he promised not to use it singing any gospel music, and I told him I wouldn't expose him by singing any pop music or Kentucky Fried Chicken commercial."

By now, Brother Tis Mythang's usually flapping mouth was closed tight with astonishment. He couldn't believe Deacon Laid Handz was still going around telling that lie. He thought to himself that maybe he had told it so much that he actually believed it. He knew anyone who had ever heard Deacon Laid Handz sing knew he sounded more like Luther Van*gross* than Luther Vandross. When he sang, he sounded like he had taken lessons at the Roseanne Barr School of Voice and Irritation.

As much as Brother Tis Mythang didn't like Deacon Laid Handz, he didn't want the deacon to embarrass himself any further. He quickly changed the subject. "How about we just forget about Brother No Note, and we can decorate the magnificent tree I'm donating to the church. You can help me bring it inside. It's so huge, it almost made my Yugo roll over on its side," he bragged.

"What tree?" Deacon Laid Handz asked. "This year, I'm donating the Christmas tree. I've got mine tied to the trailer that's hooked up to my Mercedes. And I've also bought the star that's going on the treetop. After all it's my tree, so we'll use my star!" he hissed.

"You must be crazy. I said, I'm donating the tree. And I'm donating it on behalf of the adult choir, the youth choir, the joint choirs, the radio choir, and the fund-raising committee. So therefore, you can keep your little used tree that's tied up to your used Mercedes!" Brother Tis Mythang slammed down the piano lid. "You about to make me lose my Christmas spirit!"

"'Used' Mercedes! I just know you didn't just call my Mercedes 'used' again!" Deacon Laid Handz shouted. His mellow-yellow complexion took on a bright-orange hue as his anger boiled. "Have you lost your mind? A 'used' Mercedes. I've told you more than once: anyone with an ounce of class would know that you don't have 'used' Mercedes. They are 'previously owned'—"

Brother Tis Mythang cut him off with a wave of his finger. He replied softly, "Well, excuse me. You know I most certainly do have class." He then put that same finger in Deacon Laid Handz's face, close to the deacon's nose, and yelled, "Well, then, you can take your previously owned Christmas tree that's tied to your previously owned Mercedes, and you know just where you can drive them both—again."

"My goodness! What is all the shouting about?" asked Sister Betty as she entered the sanctuary. As soon as she saw that it was Deacon Laid Handz and Brother Tis Mythang going at each other, she was sorry she had ever left home. "I could hear the yelling all the way down the hall."

Brother Tis Mythang pouted as he rolled each word in sugar. "It's all his fault, Sister Betty. He knew I was donating the Christmas tree this year. Deacon Laid Handz just trying to start up something by bringing in a tired old Christmas tree he probably got on sale somewhere!"

"On sale! What do you mean, on sale? I don't buy nothing on sale. Everything I get is always brand new." He was so mad, he almost picked up the nearest hymnal to throw but instead decided he'd pound his hands on the back of the pew to put more emphasis on the "brand-new."

"Really! What about that used—oh, I'm sorry, previously owned—Mercedes. 'Previously owned' means you didn't get it brand new. Somebody else had it before you!" He was on a roll. "That's right. Somebody's butt occupied the driver's seat before yours!"

"Fool! You just gonna make it a habit of being stupid, ain't you?" Deacon Laid Handz replied.

He ignored that last statement from Brother Tis Mythang because of its truth. He changed the subject. "Sister Betty, tell me which one of us you think should donate this year's Christmas tree. Especially since this year is a millennium celebration. I'm quite sure that the deacon board would love to donate some of our precious time to helping you. Whatever auxiliary you are working with to make this Y2K Christmas Pageant special, you can count on us."

Without subtlety, the deacon looked back at Brother Tis Mythang and gave him a "see if you can top that" sneer.

Sister Betty really did not want to be caught up in the middle of their silly argument. She decided at least to try to reason with them. She put down her big family-size Bible and stroked one of the several hairs on her chin. She pondered her next move. After a few seconds, for an unknown reason, she thought she had the answer.

"Well, now, let's see . . ." Sister Betty stopped to make sure she had their attention before continuing. "Deacon Laid Handz, you know for a long time, Brother Tis Mythang has donated a beautifully decorated Christmas tree and—"

"That's right!" Brother Tis Mythang interrupted. "You heard Sister Betty. She said, 'for a long time.' That means it's a tradition."

Brother Tis Mythang was all set to whittle down Deacon Laid Handz until he looked over and saw that Sister Betty still had her mouth formed to say the next word. He thought perhaps he shouldn't have butted in while she was making a point in his favor. To save face, he gave another one of his best thirty-two-watt smiles and said gently, "I'm sorry, Sister Betty. Continue. Put that out-of-date deacon in his place."

"Thank you, Brother Tis Mythang." Sister Betty quickly turned to Deacon Laid Handz before he could interject and said, "I want to especially thank you, Deacon, for allowing me the opportunity to try and offer a spiritual and fair solution. Now, since Brother Tis Mythang went under the assumption that he would donate the Christmas tree this year, as he has done for so long, why not let him? You can be the bigger person and take your lovely tree over to Sister Need Moe's house. You know she has several children, and her husband was laid off."

To make her suggestion even more appealing, Sister Betty sweetened the pot. "I'm quite sure that when Reverend Knott Enuff Money hears about it, he will put your good deed on page one of the church's *Daily BLAB* newsletter. Don't you think that would be wonderful?"

Sister Betty stopped stroking her chin hairs and looked very sympathetic as she waited for Deacon Laid Handz to reply.

After two seconds of ego stroking, Deacon Laid Handz crowed, "Well, Sister Betty, when you put it that way, I guess I could be the real man and give Sister Need Moe's family my elegant tree."

He put a little something extra on the words "real man" as he winked in Brother Tis Mythang's direction.

Deacon Laid Handz stopped when he saw a change come across Sister Betty's face. Maybe he had gotten to her, he thought. He stepped closer and whispered, "Why, Sister Betty, it looks like you're crying. You don't have to cry. I said I would give my tree away. Brother Tis Mythang agreed to give his to the church. It's gonna be okay. Come on. We should all be getting ready for the church's Y2K Christmas Pageant. I believe it starts in about an hour." He could not resist getting in a parting shot. "That should give us enough time to bring in Brother Tis Mythang's little old tree and take my gorgeous one to Sister Need Moe."

He turned to Brother Tis Mythang and snapped, "Come on; let's go."

Brother Tis Mythang was happy that his Christmas tree would be the one to grace the corner of the church. He didn't

care how or what the deacon said. He looked over at Sister
Betty, who by now had one big solid tear rolling down her left
cheek, and said, "We'll see you when we return." He gently placed
his hand on her shoulder. "You can stop crying now." He stepped
aside, peeked over at Deacon Laid Handz, and moved in a little
closer to Sister Betty. He whispered, "Make sure that a beautiful picture of my tree appears in the column before Deacon
Laid Handz's little old deed." He twirled, grabbed his hat and
coat, and left.

Sister Betty wiped the tear running down her cheek. Both
those brothers could have used a Tic Tac. Together they put
the *hal* in *halitosis*.

It seemed that every time Sister Betty thought she could go
to a church service and have peace, one of the Ain't Nobody
Else Right but Us—All Others Goin' to Hell Church members
had a problem. But she was determined not to let anything get
her down. The pageant tonight should go off without any problems. It was going to be a special event because it marked the
end of a millennium. The members had decided to add Y2K to
their theme. The children had gotten involved. They had rehearsed, and all had memorized their lines and would need no
prompting.

Sister Betty managed a smile and thanked herself for bringing an end to what could have been an early Armageddon. She
could hardly believe that Brother Tis Mythang and Deacon
Laid Handz would lose their religion over a small thing like a
tree.

Instead of dwelling on what happened, Sister Betty looked
at her watch and thought about Ma Cile. She should be arriving
shortly. Ma Cile was bringing her ten-year-old grandchildren,
Lil Bit and June Bug. Normally, she would be nervous whenever those two children were in her presence, but tonight was
Christmas Eve. She was sure that if there was ever a time for
them to be well behaved, tonight was it. She went into the rectory to wait.

As Sister Betty waited, the next hour passed quickly. Various
church members, along with the "special event" members, ar-

rived in a festive mood. The "special event" members were those who only came to church on Christmas, Easter, Mother's Day, and Father's Day and, with a few exceptions, put in an appearance at the annual Friends and Family Day celebration.

Sister Betty heard the sound of a door opening.

It was the Reverend Knott Enuff Money peeping out of the pastor's study. He was dazzling in his new pink-and-red iridescent cape with a green lining. He was also donning a newly coiffed Jheri-curl wig. He was a legend in his own mind.

The Reverend Knott Enuff Money always made sure that various handpicked members stood up and told of his goodness during the devotional service. Those chosen to testify on his behalf were not the smartest. Some of them acted as if they had fallen out of a "stupid tree," hitting each branch on their way down.

After each testimonial, the Reverend Knott Enuff Money would take up several collections for one ridiculous cause or another. He then made his remarks very brief and turned the service over to the hands of Bishop Was Nevercalled.

The bishop, who had no formal schooling, did what he always did. He misread and misquoted verses from the Bible. The one time he did try to bring a message on his own, he told the congregation that David took the thighbone of a monkey and slew one hundred Philadelphians. One time he taught the children in Sunday school that Adam and Eve came from the Garden of Egypt. After eating a whole watermelon, Eve produced seeds, which became God's children. Many children from Sunday school were deprogrammed along with avoiding several lawsuits.

After the devotional, the Christmas Pageant went on as planned. Everything was beautiful. Even Brother No Note, in the spirit of Christmas, decided that he would let someone else lead the Christmas carols. For that gesture, he was given several standing ovations. It also made several folks stay in their seats. Those people were angry. They were going to use his singing as an excuse to use the rest room.

The Y2K Christmas Pageant was a spectacular event from

start to finish. They even had live animals for the manger. Someone had the foresight to keep a pooper-scooper nearby, but even the animals behaved.

Someone dimmed the church's overhead lights for the finale. As customary, four handpicked children came down the center aisle. They dressed in Christmas colors of red and green. They looked like little angels as they held their candles high.

When they reached the front, two of the children stood perfectly still while holding their candles. These two children symbolized the passing of the old year. After saying their parts, they would turn to the other two children standing behind them. They were as one as they reached over and lit their candles. As soon as the candles were lit, the two children in the back would then step to the front. Their newly lit candles symbolized the welcoming of the New Year.

The New Year's Eve ritual had been performed countless times. The same children had participated for the past five years. Of course, Ma Cile's grandchildren, Lil Bit and June Bug, were two of them. They were known as "those two mischievous ten-year-olds." Some of the members, behind Ma Cile's back, called them "Satan's spawn."

Lil Bit and June Bug, true to their reputation, thought they would add a new twist to the formalities. As the first two children turned to light Lil Bit's and June Bug's candles, their precious little smiles slowly turned to terror. They stood paralyzed in their tracks as they saw the impish grins on Lil Bit's and June Bug's faces.

The Reverand Knott Enuff Money, who was at the podium, never understood anything going on around him, so naturally he mistook the look of terror on the first two children's faces for stage fright. He prompted them to go ahead and light Lil Bit's and June Bug's candles, but the children still did not move.

Sister Betty suddenly got a chill in her arthritic left knee. Usually that meant a storm was brewing, and her left knee was never wrong.

It wasn't wrong, because another big storm was about to hit the church.

Rather than let the joyful event turn sour, June Bug turned to Lil Bit and whispered, "Follow me and do what I do." He then leaned forward and took the candle from the other child. The child was still petrified and offered no resistance. Lil Bit did the same to the child who stood in front of her. In unison, they turned to the congregation. They shouted as they lit their candles, "We welcome you to the Y2K Church Pageant!"

Sister Betty could not believe her eyes. When she did believe them, she almost passed out. Even in the dim light, she saw that there was something wrong. The candles Lil Bit and June Bug carried were definitely different. They were bigger than usual. They were Roman candles left over from the Fourth of July.

By the time Sister Betty recovered, it was too late. Somehow she managed to shout, "Oh, no! Look out!"

In a split second, Lil Bit and June Bug had lit the Roman candles and tossed them into the air. In the spirit of how things were already progressing, the candles fell into the waiting branches of Brother Tis Mythang's beautiful Christmas tree.

The *Daily BLAB* and all the other local newspapers had a field day. The headlines the next day read,

> *The Ain't Nobody Else Right but Us—All Others Goin' to Hell Church brought in the New Year with a bang!*
>
> *Last night's Y2K Christmas Pageant was a blast. The church almost went up, and it wasn't for the rapture. The church building itself did not sustain any major damage, although the same cannot be said for the behinds of two children who caused the chaos. The impish culprits were identified as Lil Bit and June Bug. Their grandmother, Ma Cile, has been quoted as saying, "Since them young'uns love fireworks so much, I'm gonna burn they behinds up. I'm burning they dreams and cashing they life insurance policies, too."*

When the fact that she was supposed to be a Christian was put to her, she answered, "I's a God-fearing woman. I'm not a bad person. I plan on getting' some blessed oil—the double-virgin kind. I'm gonna rub some oil in my hand and lay my hand on them chil'ren. When I git finished, they gonna be healed. Places they used ta go, they ain't goin' no mo'. Thangs they used ta say, they ain't gonna say no mo'."

Our sympathies go out to Lil Bit and June Bug. Those willing to donate new behinds to those two kids should call 1-800-NewButt. It was suggested to their grandmother that she take "time out." She replied, "I am. When I get finished whippin' those behinds, I'm gonna take me some of that time out."

Remember me, O my God, concerning this, and wipe not out my good deeds that I have done for the house of my God, and for the offices thereof.

—Nehemiah 13: 14

The Church's Singles Auction, A.K.A. Love for Sale

The telephone rang as if ringing were a crime. The irritating sound interrupted Sister Need Sum's ten o'clock intense and focused meditation. It was a ritual she performed every Saturday while surrounded by several floral scented candles, two Bibles that lay open to the Song of Solomon, and a chocolate cake. "What now? Who's calling me after I just got down on the floor? And it wasn't easy for me to get down here." She strained to rise by pulling up on the back of a small chair and stepped around her ritual accessories as they lay in a circle in her bedroom with the fan humming and the curtains drawn. "It better be important. I feel today is gonna be my day for potential matrimony." She picked up the telephone.

"Hello."

"Sister Need Sum, it's Deacon Lead Belly."

"How can I help you?" He was the last person she wanted to talk to when she needed to be meditating. He was about two hundred pounds of more man than she ever wanted. The irritation in her voice seeped like snake oil through the phone, and she wasn't trying to hide it. "I'm very busy. I'll ask again: how can I help you?"

"Er . . . Are you going to be coming to church this evening?" He had been waiting to get up the nerve to ask her out for months. He'd called the television psychic, Mizz Cleotis, and she'd assured him her cards never lied. He'd practiced for hours what he would say before he called Sister Need Sum, and now he was sure she thought he was an idiot.

"Idiot!" Sister Need Sum, blurted out by mistake.

All doubt was removed from his mind. She had definitely called him an idiot.

"I'm sorry, Brother Lead Belly. I didn't mean to yell out in your ear. I was watching something stupid on television." She knew she was lying, and she was certain he knew it, too. "Yes, I'm going to church this evening—alone." She was way ahead of him.

His original plan, when he'd called her, was to ask if he might accompany her to church. Suddenly, it didn't seem like such a good idea. He decided to ask another stupid question to cover the first one. "I wasn't sure what time everyone was suppose to be there. Do you know what time we should arrive?"

Now who was lying? She knew he was lying, and she was sure he knew she knew.

"I believe we will start around nine-thirty." She had lied again. With a tiny pang of guilt nagging at her, she added, "I'm not sure of the time, but why don't you come around that time anyway?" She hoped everything would be over before that overweight lover arrived. "I was very busy. We'll chat some other time."

Sister Need Sum didn't wait for a reply from Brother Lead Belly. She slammed the phone down so hard, his ears rang and his teeth shook. His next phone call was to Mizz Cleotis. If he had to spend a hundred dollars, he was going to tell her about her lying tarot cards.

Sister Need Sum fumed and called Brother Lead Belly all kinds of names as she inched her way back onto the bedroom floor. She stroked the candles, read the Bible verses, and bit into the chocolate cake. She did all that with the hope that she could mentally connect with the man she knew must be waiting somewhere for her. Today she prayed in earnest because her thirty-first birthday had just passed and desperation was chasing her like it was a bill collector. All she needed to do was pick out an appropriate man-getting dress for tonight's church singles auction.

Once a month, at the Ain't Nobody Else Right but Us—All Others Goin' to Hell Church, the building fund committee held a single men and women's auction. The auction was to raise money to keep the church building looking extremely prosperous and holy.

The auction was held on an evening set aside for some of the desperate and hard-on-the-eye members to come together. Other than that particular event, they never dated. They had plenty of money to bid. Those who were auctioned kept their dignity, since it was for charity. And, those who had to pay for it anyway could also say it was for charity.

This was a favorite event for a certain group of women who claimed that Jesus was their only man and that He was all they needed. They usually spent the most money. The event gave pleasure and competition for the singles in the church.

The Reverend Knott Enuff Money had his own agenda. His real reason for raising money, by any means possible, was so that the church could stay in the big leagues. Two churches such as Bethel AME in Baltimore, Maryland, on the East Coast, and Church of the Harvest, on the West Coast, caused great concern for him.

The Reverend Knott Enuff Money felt the reason he was never invited to speak at those churches was because his church didn't look prosperous enough. He thought he had proved his church's worthiness when he had the ATM bank machine installed in the vestibule. He couldn't see the difference between his church and the other two. One of the big differences between the three churches was that the last two didn't need a building fund function held every first Saturday in the month to maintain their status. Usually, the Holy Ghost and righteous teaching performed the maintenance.

On the third Sunday, immediately following the fourth collection during the morning service, Sister Petri Fied read the list of eligible bachelors and bachelorettes. She was twenty-nine and a longtime member of the church. She was the poster child for low self-esteem. People often said she had a body by Lucile Roberts, and brains by Mattel. Being very petite usually made it difficult for her to get the microphone set up just right. Since the church had cordless microphones, it shouldn't have been a problem. It was. She was so nervous, the microphone would shake, and feedback would ring through the sanctuary. Everyone had to cover their ears as she spoke, and they barely understood most of what she said, which was okay because she didn't either.

It usually took Sister Petri Fied about twenty minutes to read the list of the date-challenged. Every single from eighteen-year-old Brother Buck Tuth to ninety-year-old Mother Hardof Hearing was on the list. It was usually the same people, so it wasn't because there were many names to call.

By the time she finally got up enough nerve to read in front of the congregation, as she had done numerous times before, she had chewed, wrinkled and balled up the list so many times it looked like it had gone through a paper shredder.

A sign of how that zany auction would turn out.

That particular third Sunday was of special interest to the singles set because there were a few new members in the congregation. Several of the new members were baptized the previous Friday night, and they barely had a chance to dry off and put lotion on before they found themselves placed on the auction block.

Sister Petri Fied trembled as usual. She began to announce the names on the list. "Giving honor to all assembled here under the sound of my weak voice . . . I'm going to attempt to read off the names for next Saturday night's sale—er, I meant auction. I'm so nervous . . . Y'all please take all mistakes for love. . . ."

Of course, the head of the "I ain't got no secrets but my own," Brother Tis Mythang, couldn't wait to sound off. His motto was, "Why make things better—why?"

"We ain't got nothing but some love for you, Sister Petri Fied,"

Brother Tis Mythang laughed. To emphasize his outburst, he played a few bars of Natalie Cole's "I've Got Love on My Mind."

Brother Tis Mythang's outburst and goading melody sent Sister Petri Fied over the top. She stuttered and mispronounced the rest of the names on the list, slipped down the steps from the pulpit, and landed at the feet of Sister Need Sum. Instead of getting up, she sat up, leaned over on the pew, and pretended she suddenly needed to pray.

On Your Mark . . . Let's Go Get Some Luv!

At about eight o'clock that evening, most of the love-deprived females and just a few of the still-tied-to-they-mama's-apron-strings male entrants for the church singles auction arrived and rushed into the church auditorium.

The bidding was scheduled for about eight-thirty, CP (Colored People's) time. However, a few of the physically challenged decided they should get there early and grab the best front-row seats. Leading the bunch was Sister Need Sum. She was not only the president of the singles auction committee, but a lifetime member. Her hormonal posse surveyed the room and made sure everything was set up just right. The lighting had to be at a certain angle and not too bright. Having their numerous flaws highlighted was the last thing they wanted.

Sister Need Sum and the other women checked each other for unshaven armpits, smeared lipstick, and acne. "Am I presentable?" she asked Sister Cill Lee.

"I'd date you," Sister Cill Lee laughed.

Everyone knew she wasn't joking, so Sister Need Sum quickly moved away.

One woman had put on only one long, curly eyelash. The eye looked like a deformed spider. Two other women discovered they needed to keep their arms down because they were not "sure." After several women exited the ladies' bathroom with wet toilet paper hanging from the heels of their shoes, they thought close scrutiny was a good thing.

The most important thing for them was to make certain they had the right denomination of money. All the one-hundred- and fifty-dollar bills were to be placed in front of the twenty-and-under bills. That was just in case the ever evasive, scrumptious piece of eye candy, the six-foot, built-for-endurance, and foine District Councilman Hip PoCrit and any other buffed and single men might stray in at the last minute. Those men came at a high price.

They scanned the list of eligible men, held by a rubber band to a clipboard and hung on a nail. There were only about fifty eligible names on it. Unfortunately, there were more than two hundred eligible women.

It was about to get ugly up in there, and ugly was not just limited to the entrants.

As the love-deprived women complained and wailed about the unfairness of the situation and the slim pickings among the male entries, and the men did the same, Sister Need Sum had one of her famous get-a-man ideas. "Don't fret, my sisters," she said with confidence. "I have a plan. Follow me."

Although many of the women that night were disappointed, and other times almost jailed, they followed Sister Need Sum. They looked like little hypnotized soldiers as they tailed along behind her as if marching off to war.

Down into the basement they went and through the church kitchen, like a platoon of ants. Man-hungry ants.

She finally got to her destination, the media room. Sister Need Sum looked around, and there it was—what she was after, one unused computer. In a box not far from the computer lay the monitor and a printer. "Okay, girls, this is it. Grab the computer and the other equipment. We don't have much time. We've got work to do."

They arrived in the basement like a band of man-hungry ants, and they left the same way—with the computer, the monitor, and a printer.

After arriving back in the church auditorium, the ladies set about hooking up the computer and the rest of the equipment.

"Are you going to tell us why we need the computer?" asked

one of the women as she struggled to figure out the printer port from the monitor port.

"We goin' online! Since there are so few real men here tonight, I don't see why we can't just go into a chat room and ask for a few more participants," Sister Need Sum answered, and winked with a sly look on her face.

"But how will we know what they look like? Don't we have enough undesirable and ugly men here already?" asked another woman. She would have asked another question, but her hands were full of cable cords and she didn't know the computer cable from a power cord.

"We'll only accept entries from the ones who can e-mail a picture real quick," Sister Need Sum answered. "That ought to work."

All the rest of the hormones in the room agreed with her, with the exception of one.

"Wait a minute. I gotta know something," said Sister Good N' Plenty, with a raised eyebrow. "Isn't a bird in the hand better than two vultures in the bush? We know what we got here. We don't know what we gonna really get messing with someone in a chat room."

Before Sister Need Sum could respond, one of the men from the slim-pickings pool called out, "Does anyone know how to put one of these floppies in? I think my hard drive froze."

Sister Good N' Plenty took that as a sign and looked at the man with disgust. "Never mind, Sister Need Sum," she hissed. "Hurry up and hook up that other computer!"

It was almost eight-thirty by the time everyone got finished mix-matching cords, dropping floppies, spilling toner powder on the printers, and hooking up the computer. About thirty of the women had to excuse themselves to go to the bathroom to clean up and scheme.

They found out from the mess they'd made that removing toner powder with a dry paper towel was a no-no. They would be out of the bidding for a while. It was 30 down and another 170 women to go. The hunt was on.

Creepin' on the Down-Low

Meanwhile, some of the old folks had their own thing happening.

The blessing dispenser stood outside the church auditorium, down the hall and around the corner. It seemed grand and intimidating standing right next to the ATM bank machine.

Leaning over the blessing dispenser and ATM bank machine was Old Brother Ilie Alot. He was about seventy years old and bent over like an old weeping willow tree. He was chatting with Mother Blister, who was also about the same age and bent over as well. When they stood face-to-face, they looked like a big Valentine's Day heart.

The old couple had been creepin' on the down-low for about ten years, but they always came to the singles auction to keep folks out of their business.

Old Brother Ilie Alot had been creepin' a lot longer, but he saw no need in telling Mother Blister about it. He was a true playa' back in his day. His game was tighter than a flea's fist. He made sure all his women knew one another by name. When holidays rolled around, he'd gather them together so they could decide what to get him as a gift. He often bragged he was the one who put the *P* in *playa'*.

Mother Blister hadn't been a slouch, either. She would have all her men come by on their assigned day, and if any of them got their days mixed up, she just never answered her door.

They were older, and their playa' days, for the most part, were over. They only crept every now and then, to keep the excitement in their relationship. Being up front with each other would have been too boring.

Old Brother Ilie Alot peeped around the blessing dispenser. "Come on. There's nobody around." He took out his wallet and separated his OTB betting slips from the rest of his bidding money. It was another little habit that he felt was only his business.

Mother Blister took out her blue frilly handkerchief. "Good. These folks around here just too nosy for my taste." She turned sideways, out of the view of Old Brother Ilie Alot, and with the skill of a seasoned pickpocket, had the knot undone and her bidding money retrieved. She quickly retied the handkerchief and placed it deep down inside the wrinkled folds of her breasts, which lay captive to a size forty-two-long brassiere.

Placing a dollar bill inside the pullout slot of the blessing dispenser, Mother Blister asked Old Brother Ilie Alot, "Well, what sort of aphrodisiac help do you think we'll need tonight? I sort of fancy buying the lilac-scented rubbing alcohol. It comes in a little spray bottle. That should limber us up. Do you agree?"

Old Brother Ilie Alot, under the misconception that his hearing was as good as it had been in the old days, misunderstood and, with a sly grin, responded, "Hmmm, that sure sounds good to me. Get a can of that Pam oil spray to grease those ashy places on your feet. You can't seem to reach your feet no more. We can also pick up a bottle of Coca-Cola to use as a chaser."

Mother Blister misunderstood, too. She reached back down inside the folds of her wrinkled breasts and retrieved her blue frilly handkerchief. "Well, if it's a chase you want, then I'd better get two bottles of Lilac-scented rubbing alcohol." She withdrew two more dollars and a quarter slug.

After making their purchases, Brother Ilie Alot and Mother Blister wobbled on into the church auditorium. They greeted several other members so that folks would think they'd been there all the while, and took their usual places near the back-row exit. Sometime during the sure-to-be-riotous bidding war, with a prearranged signal, they would slowly sneak out and end up back at the senior citizens' home.

Their routine seldom varied. She would first go into her room, fill up a hot-water bottle, change into her high-necked frilly gown, and then just wait. He would go into his room, put on a pair of his Michael Jordan pastel-colored boxers, and grab a *TV Guide* and a bag of marshmallows. After half an hour past bed check, they'd have a little rendezvous.

They have never told what they did with the hot-water bottle, the *TV Guide* and the bag of marshmallows. Whatever their reason or purpose, it worked. They had been creepin' on the down-low since they were in their sixties, and she never once got pregnant. He never got tired. They even on occasion discussed one day going on late-night television and doing an infomercial. People may want to know their secret. However, if they did that, then it would no longer be a secret. Secrecy to them was their real aphrodisiac.

Old habits were hard to break.

Hitting the Information Highway

Back in the church auditorium, Sister Need Sum took at least twenty minutes to log on to the Internet. After butting in on every chat ranging from "Married Bachelors" to "Men Whose Family Trees Have No Branches," she finally found something she could work with satisfaction: "Men Who Make Six Figures."

The buzz about the wealthy, eligible men in the chat room flew around the church faster than an SST jet plane. Some of the church's single men who came to bid on the women became a little jealous when they found out that men from cyberspace were also eligible to enter.

Sister Need Sum told the men in the chat room that they only had fifteen minutes to send a picture and a few sentences about themselves.

Out of the thirty men in the chat room, only two decided to enter the church auction. It would have been more, but Sister Need Sum had secretly jumped the gun and downloaded her own picture. It was a picture she took when she visited the Museum of Natural History in New York City. She had been standing to the right of a statue of a stooped Neanderthal man and woman holding hands with a small child. Unfortunately for her, when she downloaded the file, only the picture of the Neanderthal woman appeared on the screen. That sight scared off the other twenty-eight men with weak stomachs and no desperation. Of the two who did decide to enter, one was blind and the other loved a challenge.

To make the auction a bit more interesting, Sister Need Sum suggested that they not look at the pictures of the men from the chat room until after all the bids were in. She didn't want to totally infuriate their room of last-chance single men who had taken the time and effort to come out that night.

Deacon Laid Handz, one of the church's most handsome, egotistical, and eligible bachelors, had vowed to forgo marriage or any type of commitment. Therefore, he felt he was the perfect choice to lead the auction. No matter how dry the dating pool had gotten, he was not about to endorse one of Sister Need Sum's scatterbrained ideas of dating a stranger from a chat room. He was glad she did not want the men to do the same thing.

Ever since the buzz went around the auditorium about her hooking up a computer to complete her scheme, Deacon Laid Handz had been laughing to himself. He couldn't wait for that bid to come in. He usually had an ax to grind, and the once-a-month bidding platform was his sharpening tool.

Deacon Laid Handz was at a disadvantage. The only time he had been near a computer that day was earlier in the evening when he accidentally walked in the church's library, where Bishop Was Nevercalled was doing his usual Internet "surfing." The bishop swore that his social life increased 100 percent since he started driving on the Information Highway of Love. The deacon only had to peek at the screen one time to know the information the bishop typed was about as true as Bill Clinton was to Hillary. If he'd been hooked up to a lie detector, he'd have caused a citywide blackout. The fact that there was a picture of a stooped-over Neanderthal woman to the left of the screen only made the deacon even more confused as to what the bishop was really up to.

The deacon raced back to the church auditorium. He couldn't wait to get started. "All right, we're gonna dispense with devotional service tonight. Let's just sum it up by saying that each one of you wants the Lord to send you somebody. Anybody. A warm body. He knows that all of you are needy, and tonight we'll see if somebody's prayers will be answered. Let's start the bidding." Deacon Laid Handz picked a slip of paper with a name on it from, of all things, a collection plate. It seemed appropriate. They were there to collect money and a date.

"The first one up for grabs tonight is—wait a minute." He stopped and smiled. "I got an idea. Brother Tis Mythang, how about a little drum-roll music before I call the name?"

"How do you expect me to play a drum roll on my new Roland six hundred electric piano? There were hundreds of boiled fish and sautéed chittlin' dinners sold to get this! I ain't pounding no keys trying to give you a stupid drum roll!" Brother Tis Mythang snapped. Instead, he delicately sat down on the piano stool, flipped his jacket tail back Liberace-style, and began to play. He did a medley of thirty-two bars of "Camp Town Races" and "Just Don't Ask Me to Be Lonely" just to irk Deacon Laid Handz. He'd never liked Deacon Laid Handz, so any chance he got to work the deacon's microscopic raw nerves was one he never passed up.

Deacon Laid Handz was determined that even the effervescent Brother Tis Mythang would not spoil his fun for the evening. He looked around and made sure that all eyes were on him before continuing. He took his time unfolding the white piece of paper that held the first name to start the bidding. Nothing moved but the ceiling fans, and even they seemed to whirl at rapid speed, yet they emitted little more than a whisper.

Deacon Laid Handz continued looking at the small piece of paper in his hand. He was truly having his moment. He would have continued looking at it and basking in the glow, but Sister Aggi Tate started whining. Her voice, sounding like a crow with a bad nasal drip, was excruciating to the human and animal ear.

"Why don't you take a picture of it and then you can look at it when you by yourself? Now, call out the name! Let's see what kind of money we got up in here tonight!"

Her husband, Deacon Dick Tate, had recently died from a "whine" overdose. She'd supplied the whine. It was rumored that he willed himself to die just to get away from her voice.

It had been only two weeks since his funeral. She was ready

to jump back in the dating game and play with pent-up vengeance.

"You sure you didn't rig the plate? It's your name I've picked," lied Deacon Laid Handz. He would say anything not to hear her voice.

"Yes! I knew it! This is a sign that I'm supposed to be a young widow, but not for long."

Abandoning his usual slow and methodical manner, Deacon Laid Handz started the bidding at fifty dollars. Nobody bid. They couldn't. Everyone had both hands placed over their ears so they couldn't hear Sister Aggi Tate's voice.

He banged the gavel about thirty times before he finally had a bid of five dollars. It was a mercy bid from one of the elderly single men from the back of the church. Someone stepped on his bad baby toe, and when he hopped, his hands went up.

Deacon Laid Handz wasn't taking any chances. He banged the gavel: One, two, three, sold! He didn't even bother to add the word "going" each time the gavel dropped.

It was poetic justice. Old Brother Yucan Trustme, whom most people could not, got the date with Sister Aggi Tate. A date made just right for a night in hell. With their reputation, hell probably wouldn't give them a reservation.

The evening wore on, and most of the bidders were a disappointing bunch to the men and women who were auctioned. The worst were the men who still lived at home with their mamas. They didn't have their names listed on any of the leases or mortgages, so they were basically just homeless.

The women were no better. They ranged from perimenopausal to full-blown. There were several who had been diagnosed with chronic PMS, which stood for probable marriage syndrome. They were the most dangerous ones.

The mismatches that resulted that evening were a surprise to no one but the few who had been recently baptized. They found themselves clueless and unceremoniously sacrificed on the singles auction block.

There were several unusual love connections made between a few men and women who, during the previous week, couldn't stand each other; however, this was a once-a-month Saturday night event. A Saturday night date was a date, and any date would do. After their dates, many of them would come back, and at the Wednesday night testa-lying service, they would reveal it all. Ninety-nine and a half percent of it would be fantasy, but it made for interesting listening.

From the time Sister Need Sum came up with the idea of having strange men from chat rooms enter the auction, she had already made up her mind that she would hold off for one of them. Of the two men who had originally entered, one had accidentally been bumped offline by America On Line.

The bidder would one day write AOL a thank-you note.

"Okay, now we are down to the last entrant for the evening. As you know, our own Sister Need Sum had previously put in a sealed bid for one of the chat room entrants. And since she was the only one to bid on a pig in a poke, so to speak, she's won that bid. Of course, the man in the chat room knows what Sister Need Sum looks like, but Sister Need Sum opted not to look at his picture. So we are all going to see, for the first time, just what and who Sister Need Sum won! Step on up here, Sister Need Sum. Show everyone what you have to offer this lucky gentleman." He extended his hand and urged, "Come on. Show 'em what you working with."

Before Sister Need Sum could speak—and, of course, without being asked—Brother Tis Mythang decided to be playful. He started playing and singing at the top of his voice, a soulful version of Ben E. King's "I Who Have Nothing." By the time she finally ascended the steps to the stage, he was at the verse, *"He can take you anyplace you want, fancy foods and restaurants . . . "* He changed a few words to fit the occasion, but upon hearing them, Sister Need Sum was about to faint at the idea of what she could be getting.

Sister Need Sum was so excited that she didn't care to comment on any of the off-color commentary offered by Deacon Laid Handz, or on the fact that Brother Tis Mythang was singing that song at her expense. Tonight was her night. Tonight, she would be going outside the church masculine pool and dipping her love spoon into new waters. Tonight, she was surfing the Internet!

"Okay, Sister Need Sum. You have described yourself as a spiritually uplifted female, attractive, with modest means, and only a couple of years past your twenty-fifth birthday." Deacon Laid Handz stopped speaking and looked over at Sister Need Sum in disbelief. "While you were spinning your web of deceit, did you tell this man to what church you belong?"

"No, I didn't. But he does know that it is a dating event for charity," she protested. "You see, I wasn't being deceitful."

"For charity. Whose charity? Yours or the church?" He gave a deep belly laugh as he looked at the name on the slip of paper and then back at her.

The same name on Sister Need Sum's slip of paper suddenly appeared on the computer screen in an instant message. The chat room bidder was anxious and wanted to know had he won yet. Deacon Laid Handz took a last glance at Sister Need Sum and was about to go into a shout, but then caught himself as she began to put one hand on her hip and the other hand toward him.

"What's so funny?" she fumed. "I know you ain't laughing at the reference to my true age. You were at my birthday party the other week. So you know I just celebrated it."

"Yeah, I know," Deacon Laid Handz answered, "and it took two cakes to hold all the candles!" He was not about to give up one delicious moment of what was about to go down.

The only thing that saved the deacon from a full-blown butt elimination from Sister Need Sum was the interruption by Brother Tis Mythang singing a verse from the country-and-western tune "If You Don't Like My Peaches, Don't Shake My Tree." That seemed to lighten the mood, and it brought Sister Need Sum and Deacon Laid Handz back to the task at hand.

"Okay, I'm sorry," Deacon Laid Handz said. "Your date is described as the following: He too is a spiritual man. Just so happens that he is a local man here in Pelzer, South Carolina. He is about six feet tall, light-skinned, with a sexy bald head. He's a working man who makes six figures."

"That's all I need to hear!" Sister Need Sum interrupted. "Tell him I can't wait to meet him. Ask him, can we meet tonight?"

"But, the picture—don't you want to see it?" Deacon Laid Handz smirked as he swiftly hit the button marked *Delete.* "Oops."

"What did you do?" Sister Need Sum pleaded. "Never mind, move out of my way. You can't type as fast as I can."

With fingers moving so fast that she would have made typing legend Mavis Beacon proud, she asked and received a resounding *yes* to all of her questions. They agreed to meet at ten o'clock at the El Diablo Soul Food Shanty downtown on Tomaine and Poison Streets. He was familiar with it and was on his way out the door. It was nine-forty-five. No time to waste.

She didn't even wait for the benediction. In about fifteen minutes, she would be with a new and eligible man. A man who made six figures. Echoes of "Hallelujah!" rang throughout the church.

Before Sister Need Sum made it to the auditorium exit, she already had the china pattern picked out, but not before she gave herself the once-over again in the hallway mirror. She thought she looked fabulous. She had on just the right man-seeking outfit with just the right amount of glistening chocolate skin showing. With the swiftness of a seasoned cowboy, she pulled out her Never Alone Again cologne. She sprayed on enough to cause an ozone alert.

Sister Need Sum looked at the others as she departed, as though they were something she wanted to wipe off the soles of her shoes.

In the meantime, Deacon Laid Handz raced off to call the high priestess of havoc, Sister Ima Hellraiser. He pretended he just had to see her because he suddenly needed to get a few things off his chest and she was the only one who could help him. They agreed to meet in about ten minutes at the El Diablo Soul Food Shanty.

It's Gonna Git Hot at El Diablo's

Sister Need Sum's cab arrived first. She raced inside El Diablo's and demanded a table with ambience. She was surprised that she'd never noticed the missing ceiling fan blades, the ripped checkered tablecloths, and the fact that you had to walk through the narrow, antiquated kitchen to reach the small bathroom. But then, she'd never dated someone who made six figures.

The waiter didn't know who or what ambience was and sent her over to speak with Chef Porky LaPierre, the owner. Porky, in between belching, chomping on his twice-chewed cigar, and stirring some strange concoction, told her he didn't know anything about ambience and wasn't going to look up the recipe. If it wasn't on the Saturday night menu, then obviously he didn't serve any. The best he could do was to send over one of the off-duty kitchen helpers with a straw broom tip to shoo away any annoying flies.

Sister Need Sum gave up on the ambience and settled for a table by a big elephant ear plant near the window. The plant by itself took up more than half the visual space. It was the best she could do. When her date arrived, at least she could see him first, and then she would make herself known.

Before Sister Need Sum's butt could hit the seat, she heard the sound of a car door slam. To her shock and dismay, out stepped Bishop Was Nevercalled. She thought to herself, of all the times for him to eat at El Diablo's, why tonight? She moved farther behind the elephant ear plant, so he could not see her. With any luck, her Internet chat room date would arrive shortly and she would suggest another place to eat.

The bishop entered the restaurant and was about to slip the waiter a twenty for some of the ever-elusive quality when he spied Deacon Laid Handz and Sister Ima Hellraiser walking toward the entrance. He dashed to the first empty table he saw. It was one on the other side of the big elephant ear plant.

Sister Need Sum didn't see him, and he couldn't see her.

Deacon Laid Handz and Sister Hellraiser entered and were escorted to the last empty table.

They'd barely been seated before Sister Hellraiser started nipping at Deacon Laid Handz like he was unwanted lint on a sweater. "I thought you said that you had a surprise for me. Something other than some petty things you might have on your chest." She threw in a snide remark for free. "You need to replace whatever they are with a few muscles. You don't exactly have a six-pack working for you."

Sister Hellraiser droned on and on while Deacon Laid Handz tuned her out and scanned the restaurant for Sister Need Sum and Bishop Was Nevercalled. Where were they? The only reason he had asked Sister Hellraiser to come with him was because aside from her sharp, acid-laced tongue, she did look good. And no woman who didn't look good would ever be seen in his company on a "pretend" date.

After about twenty minutes of being shooed away by both Sister Need Sum and Bishop Was Nevercalled after delivering eight glasses of water, the waiters decided to leave them alone. The two of them sat there and played peek-a-boo from behind the big elephant ear plant as they waited in vain for their blind date to appear.

Despite his need to control every situation, Deacon Laid Handz finally told Sister Hellraiser the real reason they were there. She could hardly control her laughter. "You mean to tell me that neither of them knows?" she whispered.

"Nope. And he told her that he makes six figures!" The deacon laughed.

"Well, now, he didn't really lie. I mean, he does work down at the Printer's Plot Animation Studio. Isn't he responsible for twisting different figures shaped into the number *six* to be used by the *Sesame Street* television program?" she asked.

"Well, yeah. But talk about twisting something, he sure twisted those facts." Deacon Laid Handz whispered, "If they don't show up in the next five minutes, we're out of here." He did not want to pay for dinner if he didn't get the floor show he had come to see.

Behind the elephant ear plant, Sister Need Sum and Bishop Was Nevercalled continued their charades and peek-a-boo. This continued until closing, because neither could bring themselves to even go to the bathroom to let out the water they'd been drinking all night. They even invented excuses for their no-show dates rather than admit that they were to remain dateless on another first-Saturday night.

During that time, Deacon Laid Handz and Sister Hellraiser left disappointed. Waiters had been shooed away more times than the restaurant's resident flies and Chef Porky LaPierre had had enough of both of them. It was time to clean up and go home. The dining areas had to be mopped. The kitchen helpers raced to clear away all the chairs and stack the tables in a corner, including the chairs and tables where the still sad and lonely Sister Need Sum and Bishop Was Nevercalled sat.

Rather than be thought of as desperate—which, by that time, she felt—Sister Need Sum got up and decided to use the ladies' bathroom before she departed. It was through the kitchen, so she never got a chance to see what or who was on the other side of the elephant ear plant.

Bishop Was Nevercalled sat there feeling dejected. He couldn't even depend on getting a date with someone who looked like a stooped-over Neanderthal woman. He grabbed the wilted bouquet he had brought with him, and rushed out the door into the warm, moonlit night. He started toward the corner to hail a taxi.

When the kitchen helpers' heads were turned, Sister Need Sum walked out the door without ever looking back. She was too embarrassed. As the warmth of the moon enveloped her chilled spirit, she walked, head down, to the corner taxi stand.

When Sister Need Sum looked up, she was surprised to see the bishop. She still wanted to avoid him. However, there was only one taxi available, and both Sister Need Sum and Bishop Was Nevercalled wanted it. After it was determined that neither of them was going to let the other have it, they compromised. The taxi driver would make two trips. Sister Need Sum's house would be first. They rode in silence. Neither was in the mood to make small talk or even find out why they were both in that neighborhood at the same time. Even though Sister Need Sum was not particularly the bishop's type—she never seemed needy enough for him to control—he did like the smell of her perfume. She, in turn, was so angry about being stood up, she started talking aloud to herself.

"I can't believe I couldn't get someone with six figures."

"What was that?" asked the bishop. "Did you ask about six figures? You know, I make six figures."

"You *what?*" asked Sister Need Sum with sudden interest. She didn't hear everything he said, only that part.

"I said, I make six figures," the bishop replied.

Again she interrupted, not believing her good fortune, and said, "You doing anything tonight? You want to come up and perhaps we can chat? Maybe we can watch a movie. Have you ever seen the one *Indecent Proposal?*" She went on and on until the taxi pulled up in front of her house. "Six figures. How come you never said anything before?"

"Well, I thought everyone knew—"

She didn't wait for him to finish his sentence or pay the taxi. She slid a ten through the money slot and opened the door herself. She almost caused the bishop to bump his head as she snatched him from the cab.

Up the flight of steps to Sister Need Sum's apartment they went. The bishop was ecstatic. He'd never found a woman who was as much interested in how he made six figures as Sister Need Sum. Perhaps she wasn't so bad after all.

By the time they got to the top of the steps, Sister Need Sum had made plans on how she was going to spend the bishop's six figures. As the bishop's wife, she had to be presented in a certain way.

Sister Hellraiser hissed. Her voice cut through the night air like a seasoned karate chop. "The next time you invite me out on another one of your little I-spy escapades, you'd better be prepared to go all the way."

The deacon almost broke the little pocket mirror in his side pocket as he reached into it. "All the way! Why didn't you say something before? There's a No-Tell Motel Six, not too far away. I'm sure they still have the light on. . . ."

"Fool! Are you crazy? What are you talking about? I meant dinner and the theater. Maybe throw in a fur coat or something. Not some greasy spoon like El Diablo's." She twisted his arm and spun him around. "I *know* you didn't think I was talking about—"

"Of course not. I was just testing you. I don't want you!" Deacon Laid Handz lied.

"Really. What's that in the palm of your hand?" The little square, flat package seemed familiar, with the word *Irregular* written on it.

"What, *this*? It's nothing. It's just a folded up Wet Wipe," he lied again.

They fought about their expectations all the way to Sister Hellraiser's house. As she got out of his car, she asked, "Are we still on for this Friday night?"

"Of course. I'll pick you up about seven. Wear something sexy."

> *Be ye not unequally yoked together with unbelievers: for what fellowship hath righteousness with unrighteousness? And what communion hath light with darkness.*
>
> —2 Corinthians 6:14

> *Wherefore come out from amongst them, and be ye separate, saith the Lord, and touch not the unclean thing; and I will receive you.*
>
> —2 Corinthians 6:17

Shoutin' for Appearance' Sake

The words on the yellow lined paper read:

"Don't be embarrassed by your shout!
Shouting is an art form.
Enroll in Sister Carrie Onn's Shouting for Appearance'
   Sake classes
Learn how to shout—for appearance' sake"

"You sure that's exactly how you want it to be printed?" asked the clerk behind the counter as he stared at Sister Carrie Onn in disbelief. He had taken his glasses on and off, even cleaned them, to make sure that he was reading the text correctly.

Sister Carrie Onn placed her hands on her hips and slowly removed the reading glasses from her dress pocket. She leaned over the counter and flipped a stray strand of dyed-brown hair from her face. She snatched the now wrinkled paper from the clerk's hand. She read each word aloud, placing emphasis where needed. With the attitude of a Nubian queen, she peered over the rainbow-colored rim of her eyeglasses at the clerk and shot a look of contempt. After placing her glasses back into her dress pocket, and with the stare of a sexy cobra, she leaned over the counter to within an inch of the petrified clerk's face and replied, "Exactly!"

"Okay. If you're sure that's the way you want your flier to read, I'll do it." After seeing the look on Sister Carrie Onn's face, the only thing he wanted was for her to pay and leave. However, as badly as he wanted to see the back of her as she left his store, he had to ask, "Just what kind of folks are you going after? Who would take shouting lessons? What is it—some kind of hollering contest you holding—"

"Ahem!" She cleared her throat. Before the clerk could continue, Sister Carrie Onn's stare caused the questions to stick in his throat. She took advantage of his involuntary silence and answered, "The folks at my church need to take my shouting classes. I was voted the most likely to be asked to dance in heaven, by the usher board, just based on my personalized style of shouting." As if suddenly getting a flash of brilliance, she added, "Put on the fliers that members of the Ain't Nobody Else Right but Us—All Others Goin' to Hell Church will get a ten-percent discount. Hurry up! Add that line to my flier and tell me how much this is gonna cost!"

The clerk nervously scratched his egg-shaped head and counted the cost of printing the flyer. After counting the money from Sister Carrie Onn, he wrote out a receipt. Looking her over carefully, he handed her the piece of paper as if he were feeding a starving mountain lion.

As she looked over the receipt and placed it in her pocketbook, she gave him one last evil warning look and said, "I'll be back around five this evening. You'd better have my fliers ready. I want to hand them out tonight after the gospel concert. The Mighty Clouds of Joy are coming to my church to give a concert tonight, and I know there's gonna be some shouting. If I'm lucky, a lot of folks will have their toes smashed and perhaps a few seats will be knocked over."

She seemed to be lost in ecstasy as she continued to talk to herself, strutting out of the store. "I'm gonna be rich. But first, I got to find the choir director, Brother Tis Mythang."

The clerk still had his mouth wide open as he watched Sister Carrie Onn exit the store. He suddenly remembered what was so familiar about her and why he had become a nervous wreck.

It wasn't just the outrageous flier; it was her! She reminded him of his ex-wife. His ex-wife who was so unpredictable, he used to fall asleep with his hands balled up into fists. It was the only way he could protect himself during the times she had bad dreams. She would beat him almost into unconsciousness and claim she had no idea why she did it. He had his suspicions because she only used him as a punching bag whenever he'd said no to whatever she wanted to do. Sister Carrie Onn, he suspected, was capable of doing the same thing and more. He flew into the back room and cranked up the printing press.

While Sister Carrie Onn waited for five o'clock to come around, she busied herself talking nonstop on her cordless telephone. During the time she waited, she managed to baste and clove a ham, clean and cut up collard greens, pour enough Karo syrup on her yams to make bees envious, and make sure that she called everyone on her speed-dial list to tell them about her special event—all at the same time. The only thing left undone was the baked cheese and macaroni, á la Patti LaBelle, and, of course, her man *du jour*, Deacon Laid Handz's favorite dessert, pineapple upside-down cake. With the type of arsenal she was cooking up, she meant to show the deacon more than how to shout. She was gonna make him holla' her name . . . if he showed up.

Sister Carrie Onn marveled at her organized kitchen. It was double-virgin white with green-and-yellow accessories, including a big wooden spoon and fork hanging by the side door. The foods in her green-and-white pantry were set up in alphabetical order and color-coordinated. It was a tip she'd picked up straight out of Maggie Stewart's *Guide to a Man's Heart and Wallet, and Other Myths*. Deacon Laid Handz was sure to be convinced; getting to know her better should be his mission in life. She didn't miss a beat. After the concert that night, he would be tired from shouting and would want to be pampered. She would be his ticket to marital paradise. Of course, she would do it all in the name of the Lord.

The big three-foot-high, green-and-yellow-speckled kitty cat clock's tail swung and sounded off five bells. Five o'clock.

Time to get the show on the road. Sister Carrie Onn took one more look at her reflection in the hall mirror. She was amazed at how good she looked in her yellow-and-green sundress. She was a walking hormonal arsenal, armed with the fear of remaining single and the determination to make sure she didn't.

Sister Carrie Onn called the printer's shop from her car and barked, "My fliers better be ready!" They were.

After picking up the fliers and making sure that they were printed correctly, she hurried to the church. She would place a few in the church lobby as well as put some on the bulletin board. As she stapled the last flier to the board, she heard the sound of instruments being tuned. The Mighty Clouds of Joy gospel quartet had arrived and was having a sound check. She tiptoed to the church auditorium and sat in the back row. She didn't mean to be seen. She just wanted to sit and listen.

Knowing she was alone, she whispered her plan aloud. "The Mighty Clouds of Joy will bring the people to their feet." In her mind, she could see exactly how the event would play out. "The people will begin to sway, clap, and move toward the aisles. The shouting will begin, and I'll take notes of whose steps is a little off rhythm. They'll be the ones that would literally step on the toes of the others. Of course, I'll wait until the fervor almost dies down and then I'll jump up."

She continued daydreaming. With the acrobatic agility of a *Soul Train* dancer, she would set it off right. She knew she could shout about as well as she could cook. Both feats were outstanding.

As soon as Sister Carrie Onn saw Deacon Lead Belly enter the auditorium, she knew there was no way her plan wouldn't work. The three-hundred-pound, freckle-faced man was her hidden ace. She watched to see where he would sit. Making sure that she caught his eye before she made her move, she waved at him as she slunk toward his seat. She would work him like Cat Woman always worked Batman.

"How are you this evening, Brother Lead Belly?" she purred. "Do you mind if I sit here next to you during the concert?" she added while batting her eyelashes.

"No, I don't mind. I don't mind at all," the overweight and gentle Deacon Lead Belly replied. He did not try to figure out why the lovely Sister Carrie Onn wanted to sit next to him. From that one little question, he was envisioning a full-fledged relationship with her.

By the time she sat back in the cushioned auditorium seat, he was planning to propose. It wasn't even a minute.

While Deacon Lead Belly was enmeshed in his own wild fantasy and quickly becoming a full-fledged *Fatal Attraction* charter member, Sister Carrie Onn was busy formulating her plan to use the poor unsuspecting man. He was definitely going to be the key to the success of her "Shoutin' for Appearance' Sake" class.

Within the hour, the church auditorium was packed and the overflow room overflowed. The Mighty Clouds of Joy took the stage and did what they did best. They sang the songs of Zion until the rafters shook. The lead singer, Joe Liggon, performed vocal acrobatics worthy of all the thunderous applause he received. He was about midway through his fourth song, with the other Clouds of Joy harmonizing flawlessly, when it happened.

From out of his seat jumped Deacon Lead Belly. He started with just a slight sway of his chubby, freckled hands lifted up toward heaven in praise. Soon his feet felt some semblance of rhythm and joined in. With all three hundred pounds of pure devotion, Deacon Lead Belly started to move toward the center aisle. He responded to the Mighty Clouds of Joy with several shouts of "Hallelujah!" and as if on cue about fifty more attendees joined in.

For the next ten minutes of song and praise, Deacon Lead Belly shouted and stomped, without a rhythmic clue, along with many others, to the pounding and spiritual beat of the pulsating gospel music.

In the meantime, Sister Carrie Onn surveyed the worshippers and took notes. She broke them down according to their shouting capabilities. There were those who were seriously caught up in their praises of God's love. They were immediately ignored. She recognized most of them as congregation members from the little storefront church We Be Keepin' It Real, pastored by the Reverend Honest Tee. It was a church that once fellowshipped with her Ain't Nobody Else Right but Us—All Others Goin' to Hell Church family. For whatever the reason, they could not keep up with the expensive privilege of being under the leadership of Bishop Was Nevercalled. They pulled out and yet seemed to continuously grow spiritually.

Sister Carrie Onn's eyes and mind continued to separate the passionate worshippers into mini-groups of possibilities until she finally found the group she needed. They were about to kill one another as they shouted and stomped all over the auditorium. There were several who had toes hanging over their sandals. These would be perfect. After a few smashed toes, several had started to fight but were quickly separated by one or two quick-thinking ushers. She could not ask for more. They would be the ones to benefit from her Shoutin' for Appearance' Sake classes.

With everything in place, Sister Carrie Onn prepared to make her move. Just as she removed the rubber band from around her bundle of fliers, it happened. The songs of praise faded and the shouts of those dancing before the Lord turned into a stampede. As if someone were speaking through a megaphone, the words "Look out!" were heard. Sister Carrie Onn barely had time to see what the confusion was about before the package of fliers was knocked from her hands. About twenty people trampled them trying to run for safety. Before she could collect her thoughts, she jumped up onto the nearest seat. And that's when it went from bad to worse.

Brother Lead Belly had worked himself into a frenzy. He accidentally fell up against the special row of seats designated for the deacons. The row of seats popped up and did a wheelie. The deacons were thrown into the nearby baptismal pool. The water jumped out and splashed all over the hat of Mother Pray Onn. She had just gotten the hat, shaped like a gray thundercloud, out of layaway especially to wear while she shouted at the Mighty Clouds of Joy concert. All the deacons who were thrown into the pool as dry devils now climbed out as wet devils. They tried to grab poor Brother Lead Belly, but Mother Pray Onn had first dibs.

Together the deacons and Mother Pray Onn ripped Brother Lead Belly asunder. He went from yelling "Hallelujah!" to "Help me!" in just two beats. He struggled to free his three hundred pounds from the angry grips of his attackers. They looked like one long freight train as he pulled them along to his freedom. In the meantime, the Mighty Clouds of Joy thought that they had taken the crowd higher into the spirit and just went for broke. They sang about twelve verses of the same song, flailing and wailing as they wiped the sweat from their brows.

Deacon Laid Handz was the caboose of Brother Lead Belly's angry freedom train. He hung on as the chlorified water quickly shrunk his favorite blue seersucker suit. He was especially angry because he'd bought the suit back in the sixties and planned on keeping it forever to remind himself of how fine he was then and now.

The thought and sight of her man *du jour*, Deacon Laid Handz's muscles rippling through a wet seersucker suit made Sister Carrie Onn change the order of her purpose. She could prioritize on a dime. She flung the last of her fliers into a corner and climbed down from her seat of safety. The thought of helping poor Deacon Lead Belly or her mother never crossed her mind. She had a feast waiting back at her place for Deacon Laid Handz, and this was the perfect opportunity to get him there.

Sister Carrie Onn raced through the crowd, stepping on more toes and, of course, making more people angrier as she made her way to Deacon Laid Handz. Finally, she was there. She latched her arms around his waist. "I'm here to help you, sweetheart." She struggled to pull him from the grasp of the other deacons. However, the hold each deacon had on the other, and especially the hold Mother Pray Onn had on poor Brother Lead Belly, was too tight. She couldn't separate Deacon Laid Handz from the others. So, as Brother Lead Belly pulled the others, he also pulled her.

One of the shocked onlookers happened to look down and

discovered one of Sister Carrie Onn's "Shoutin' For Appearance' Sake" fliers. Thinking that perhaps this was one of the special shouts she advertised, he latched on to her. One by one, as some of the others found the fliers, they did likewise. All around the church auditorium, they shouted, stepped on toes, tugged at weaves, and gave praise. They looked like they were doing the old bunny hop from the fifties. The only ones that didn't look happy were poor Brother Lead Belly, Mother Pray Onn, Deacon Laid Handz, and, of course, Sister Carrie Onn. She was too busy trying to free herself from the grip of the brother who had found her flier and was now latched on to her. "Let me go!" she protested to no avail.

Even Joe Liggon and the other Clouds of Joy joined the shout train; they sang on and on. This went on until finally the Mighty Clouds of Joy looked at the clock on the church auditorium wall and realized that they were only being paid to perform for two hours. They suddenly stopped. Since they were the last ones to join the shoutin' train, it was easy for them to detach themselves. As they did, one of the members of the Clouds reached down and picked up one of Sister Carrie Onn's fliers.

"Now, this is interesting. Why didn't we think of this?" said one of the group members.

"Who said we didn't?" replied Joe Liggon with a wink as he read the flier. "It looks like these folks gonna be busy for a while. We can be on the bus and into the next town before we're missed. We'll grab some White Out correction fluid and make a few changes on the bus. No one will ever know."

"How do you know that whoever this Sister Carrie Onn is doesn't already have a shoutin' class going on?" asked another one of the members.

"Look around you. Does it look like any of these folks ever took any shouting lessons? I'm telling you, I think we can make this work," Joe Liggon said with a smile.

While the Mighty Clouds of Joy grabbed as many fliers as they could and rushed to put all their equipment and themselves into their bus, poor Brother Lead Belly continued to get

his beat-down at the hands of Mother Pray Onn and the deacons. Sister Carrie Onn's sundress got torn, and she accidentally mooned the man who held on to her. The man was shocked,
but he wasn't mad.

On the way out, one of the Clouds looked over at Brother
Lead Belly and sized up his dilemma. Without telling the other
group members, he dodged and weaved past the fists of Mother
Pray Onn and quickly stuffed a flier into the pants of Deacon
Lead Belly, which by then were almost down to his freckled
hips. He thought to himself that perhaps if the poor overweight man had the benefits of shoutin' lessons, he might not
be getting that beat-down.

On the ride out of town, the Mighty Clouds of Joy decided to
write a theme song for their new venture:

> *Wouldn't you like to ride on the mighty, mighty high . . .*
> *Wouldn't you like to shout like the mighty Mighty Clouds . .*
> *. Wouldn't you like to know how we do it . . . Keep on your*
> *toes before you lose them . . . Come on, now, shout! For*
> *appearance' sake, shout!*

Later that night, while he waited to be released from the
hospital emergency room, Brother Lead Belly read the flier he
found in his pants.

> *Don't be embarrassed by your shout! Shouting is an*
> *art form. Enroll in Sister Carrie Onn's Shoutin' For*
> *Appearance' Sake classes. Learn how to shout—For Ap-*
> *pearance' Sake.*

He imagined that his newfound love, Sister Carrie Onn had
probably been the one who put the flier in his pocket. That had
to be the reason why she'd sat next to him before the concert
began. She did care about him. She probably loved him. His
imagination knew no bounds.

Before the doctor could write out a prescription for pain
medicine poor Brother Lead Belly had already mentally writ-

ten out his will to include Sister Carrie Onn, because that's what any good man would do for his future bride.

> *Be not deceived; God is not mocked, for whatsoever a man soweth, that shall he also reap.*
>
> —Galatians 6:7

> *But shun profane and vain babblings: for they will increase unto more ungodliness.*
>
> —2 Timothy 2:16

A Hellraiser at the Fund-Raiser

Sister Ima Hellraiser Tames the Grey Dog Bus

"**F**or the last time, I'm telling you that I am hungry. So I strongly suggest that, rule or no rule, you pull this bus over into the next McDonald's drive-through."

Sister Ima Hellraiser's rough and sexy yet masculine-like voice assaulted Donald the bus driver's ears. Her pitches, her tone, her very presence made him wince with each spoken word.

The round-shaped Donald dribbled nervous saliva down his double chins. He kept one hand on the wheel and used the other to pull at fistfuls of his thick brunette hair. His dark-blue uniform showed evidence that he had sucked on at least two full bottles of pink ninety-proof Mylanta antacid syrup. It also showed that he had followed it with eight cups of lemon-flavored Alka-Seltzer. His suit looked like a pink-and-yellow fizzie. He did it all while driving the 800 miles from Fayetteville, North Carolina, to Pelzer, South Carolina.

At first, Donald did not mind the beautiful and exotic mocha-colored woman who sat behind him. She sat in a seat designated for disabled and elderly passengers. He ignored that fact. Before she boarded, an old man with a cane had occupied that seat and minded his own business. Donald had made the crippled old man give up the seat to the beautiful woman. He impatiently directed the old man to another seat. The black, vinyl-covered seat barely covered a floor hump in the back of the bus. Now the bus driver was getting his payback. Instead of enjoying a few lustful glances of beauty through his rearview mirror, he was sucking on bottles of Mylanta. He and the bus droned on.

From Sister Hellraiser's comfortable seat, she continued her assault. The flowered straw hat bounced around on her head like a broken, spinning top as she nitpicked.

"I see you drinking something. Why the rest of us got to go thirsty?" Sister Hellraiser stopped taunting just long enough to briefly lift her sunglasses. "There's another McDonald's coming up on the left. If you pass this one, consider dying. Do you understand me? I'm hungry, and patience is not one of my finer qualities," yelled Sister Ima Hellraiser.

The emergency call last night from her cousin, Mother Pray Onn, had been right on time. Sister Hellraiser had recently received a reduced sentence of "time served" for a little misunderstanding between her and a few Mormons in Peace Town, Utah. She did not see how it was her fault if they did not believe in Mardi Gras celebrations.

Her sorority sisters from nearby Alpha Witches of Tantrum University had arrived with bright-colored floats and other types of entertainment. The Mormon police arrested the women and charged them with disturbing the peace, soliciting, because they wore strapless outfits, and several other charges. The devious plan that Mother Pray Onn laid out would give her a chance to act out the rage she felt from the arrest. The very idea of some nerdy and unarmed Mormon police officer arresting her and the sorority sisters had made her a laughingstock. Payback was the drug to avenge her character assassination, and she needed a fix.

Mother Pray Onn did not have to summon Sister Hellraiser twice. She was on her way before the receiver clicked in the telephone's cradle. She also hoped that Pelzer, South Carolina had a short memory and didn't hold grudges from her last visit.

Sister Ima Hellraiser kept one eye on the frightened bus driver and the other on the road. Just ahead, a big yellow road sign read, *Food, Lodging and Rest Stop—2 miles.*

"Did you see that sign? " she snapped.

"What sign?" whispered Donald. He did not want the other passengers to know how afraid he was.

"Oh, now you are trying me!" She leaned over and whispered, "Back in my home town they called me Lorena—the original Lorena Bobbitt."

That was all the bus driver needed to hear. He never doubted that she was probably the real Lorena Bobbitt. Although Donald was single and lived with his mother, he did hope one day to have children.

As Donald drove a little farther, he kept looking back over his shoulder, trying to keep his tormentor in sight. With his survival percentages rapidly dropping, he forgot that the height of the bus was over nine feet and the limit for the drive-through was eight and a half.

Donald's head was spinning as he twisted the chain of his Saint Christopher medallion into a knot. Maybe it was the fact that Sister Hellraiser had rallied the entire bus into a hungry mob by singing the McDonald's theme song that had him dripping like a leaky faucet. Whatever the reason, he valued his threatened manhood more than that Grey Dog bus. It was while he was pondering the survival of his manhood that he tried to drive through the Golden Arches. The bus became wedged somewhere between the *ten-billion served* "Welcome" sign and the menu board.

As the passengers screamed obscenities at each other and the bus driver, someone had the presence of mind to call a tow truck. While waiting for its arrival, a crane from a nearby construction site worked feverishly to extract the hood of the bus from the broken Golden Arches of the McDonald's drive-through.

The undaunted Sister Hellraiser and some of the others, who thought it safer to stay friendly with her, went inside to eat. Of course, when she walked past the hysterical bus driver she made it her business to stick out her tongue.

Upon that last insult, Donald completely lost it. "I'm gonna kill you!" He reached out to slap her, knocking over the police officer instead. The police officer, who was in the process of giving the summons, leaped up and stopped him with a mega-sized stun gun. In addition to the summons, as well as a definite lawsuit for property damage from McDonald's, the now electrified bus driver was placed under arrest for aggravated assault on a police officer and a civilian.

Donald came to and started crying. "Please, just let me kick her in the head or something. Let me kill her, please. She needs killing!" He begged and kicked at the air like a cockroach on its back and continued his tirade until the ambulance from the local mental hospital arrived. He was only two months away from retirement, and because of her, he would lose his job. Sister Hellraiser had reduced the poor man from wearing a Grey Dog bus driver's uniform to wearing a hospital straitjacket.

The passengers, about twenty of them, led by Sister Hellraiser, continued to file into McDonald's to eat and wait for the arrival of another bus and driver.

For as long as the McDonald's restaurant had been in existence, with the exception of a weekly special, their menu rarely changed. There were three menu boards listing the same information. Sister Hellraiser took her time reading each one, line by line, blocking and refusing to let anyone order ahead of her.

There were four cashiers; because of Sister Hellraiser's stubbornness, three of them had lines reaching back to the front door. The fourth cashier was a young black girl. Her name tag had her name, Caroline, scribbled in pencil. That should have been her clue. She stood her ground. Caroline, while placing one hand over the missing top button of her striped blouse, fiddled with a nappy strand of pink-colored hair. She rolled it up and down from her bangs that peeked out from her black-and-pink weave. With all the attitude she could muster, she rolled her eyes skyward. Sucking her teeth while smacking her lips, she stared down the annoying Sister Hellraiser.

"Welcome to McDonald's. May I take your order, please?" said the cashier for the fifth time. She clipped her words to let the others know that she was not the cause of their inconvenience. "Sometime today would be appreciated."

"Well, tell me something. If you really believe I'm welcomed," yelled Sister Hellraiser, "then why you acting so snippy? Answer me that one!"

The girl would not back down. "You've been reading this menu board for the past twenty minutes. They all say the same thing. You won't step aside and let anyone order while you make up your mind. This ain't Burger King, so you're ain't gonna have it your way."

Misreading the surprised look on Sister Hellraiser's face and thinking she had got the best of her, she continued. Only this time she spoke with more authority, "As a matter of fact, you took so long that now the breakfast service is over!"

She stopped, looked Sister Hellraiser straight in the eye, then leaned over the counter, past her, and announced to the hungry crowd that lunch was about to be served. As the people surged forward, Sister Hellraiser held her ground. She smiled at the cashier before saying, "That's good, because lunch is what I've been waiting for. Who would want to eat those old two-inch-thick dry biscuits and powdered eggs?"

It was almost a blur as Caroline reached behind the back of the counter and smeared a handful of butter on Sister Hellraiser's face. She quickly removed her giant looped earrings from each ear. She had completely lost it and was about to leap across the counter to slap the wide grin off Sister Hellraiser's face. That's when the assistant manager, Brian, came out of hiding. He caught Caroline's slippery hand in midair. "Let me go!" Caroline screamed at the top of her lungs. "I ain't the one." She wrestled her oily hand from the assistant manager's grip and lunged again. "I'll jack you up. Somebody give me a knife, a rug cutter, or something!"

A few sneaked a peek in their pocketbooks and pockets and then realized that for security reasons they'd left their weapons at home. They gave her a collective "I'm sorry—can't help you" look.

The assistant manager grabbed Caroline again and held her against him with her greasy arms and hands twisted behind her back.

Sister Hellraiser didn't budge. She took advantage of the situation and started yelling, "I'm gonna sue! This is definitely going to be *my* McDonald's! Is this how you treat your customers?" She could barely speak with a straight face.

The red-faced assistant manager, Brian, decided to avoid any more embarrassments or verbal attacks from the obviously deranged yet gorgeous woman standing before him, so he did a complete about-face. With pretended outrage, he yelled at Caroline, "Caroline, go to my office. You pick up your check. You're fired!" He let Caroline go and pushed her aside so it would seem that he was serious.

He knew that Caroline was not at fault. He had been standing in the parking lot when Sister Hellraiser caused the emotional breakdown of the Grey Dog bus driver. After seeing her and the others go inside, he had gone into his office to hide. It was only when he saw that the cashier was about to go one on one with Sister Hellraiser that he came out. He thought that by firing the cashier he might have saved her life. No matter how much "home girl" training Caroline had, she was no match for the crazy woman. He felt sorry for Caroline as he watched her crying with shoulders hunched and head down, as she walked away to his office.

The assistant manager turned to Sister Hellraiser and, with his best professional and patronizing yellowed smile, he said, "Please let me apologize for that cashier's poor and tasteless behavior. She's new and I'm certain that you know McDonald's reputation with our customers. So let's not have any more conversation about lawsuits."

He paused, hoping that his sweet manner had disarmed her, before he went further. Her face was like a blank piece of paper. She stood like a zombie before him. Thinking that perhaps she was pondering what he had said, he continued speaking and squirming. Each word was slow and deliberate.

"As a matter of fact, as a McDonald's special guest, you can order whatever you want. Anything at all—free of charge."

Brian thought a few sweetened words and a free meal were going to disarm Sister Hellraiser. He also thought the red polka-dot tie he wore and the name tag that read, *Assistant Manager* meant something. He was completely wrong. "You see, I have authority."

"Really. The only thing I see is that you shouldn't be dressing yourself."

He started to say something but decided against it.

Of course, Sister Hellraiser was not about to leave well enough alone. Her motto was to kill the spirit, kill the body, and destroy the mind. So she decided one more little dig was necessary.

"Well, I guess I could let this one insult slide." She turned on her best and brightest cobra smile.

She waited with silent anticipation as a nervous smile replaced the concerned look of the assistant manager. It was all in the timing. She chewed on her bottom lip with anticipation. She felt like a tomcat playing with a mouse before it killed the unsuspecting victim.

"Okay, if you insist. I was waiting for lunchtime because I wanted to use this "free Happy Meal" coupon. It says I can use it at any McDonald's as long as it's for a lunchtime meal."

She flashed a frayed piece of paper from her pocket. It looked like a mass of termites had fed on it. She slowly and methodically put the coupon back in her pocket, placing it beside a rubber-banded roll of other coupons.

Sister Hellraiser never took her eyes off the man. Her use of that particular coupon was legendary. Its appearance always came after she had started mass confusion at most of the Southeastern McDonald's restaurants. The result would usually be, at best, an eviction. She'd promise never to return and then go on to the next McDonald's and do the same thing. Sister Hellraiser had no reason to believe that the result of this little escapade would be any different, but she would be on the alert.

The assistant manager had no knowledge of Sister Hellraiser's past pranks. He was beyond caring, and his body language said just that.

Many of the other customers had already privately thought

about choking and stomping the beautiful yet obnoxious woman. They fantasized cutting her into small pieces, hiding each piece under tiny pebbles in Kathmandu. None would have snitched on the other. Thinking about doing it was one thing, committing the act was another. Hesitation saved them because they were not prepared for what happened next.

Sister Hellraiser, on the other hand, had caused worse reactions from many nonviolent people. She saw the first bead of sweat on the assistant manager's brow, the first twist from the corner of his mouth, and instinctively moved aside, just in time.

The assistant manager had had enough. Brian had disciplined a good worker, and for what? He had gone out of his way only for a frayed and used-up "free happy Meal" coupon from a woman who was a psychopath. She had made a fool of him. He completely lost it and miscalculated as he did a flying leap over the counter to choke her. He looked like a dirty rag doll lying on the garbage-strewn floor. He toppled over the trash bin and knocked the half-eaten hamburgers from the clutches of unwary customers. With the aid of several customers, the assistant manager got to his feet smelling like day-old Chicken McNuggets and rotten Value Meals.

Sister Hellraiser saw that this man was about to activate her death certificate. She needed to do something quick, so she clutched her heart and started yelling for help. She yelled right on time. The man jumped up, eyes blazing red, and he was coming straight for her. Before he could reach her, the general manager, Jerome, heard the commotion. He ran from his office and accidentally fell against Brian, knocking him down again. Both men tried to get up, but they were slipping and sliding in a puddle of strawberry shake. They landed facedown in an open tarter-sauce-fish-fillet sandwich.

There was pandemonium. Both the assistant manager and the general manager were screaming like trapped guinea pigs. The manager screamed the loudest because he had broken his arm, and when Sister Hellraiser saw the bone protruding, she pretended to faint. There was so much noise that no one heard the first announcement of the bus arrivals. No one heard it, that is, except Sister Hellraiser. She always kept one eye and ear alert for escape. She heard a male voice say, "The bus for Pelzer, South Carolina, is about to leave in five minutes." She managed to step over the fallen men and got the attention of the other passengers. On her way to the exit door, she grabbed a few bags of McDonald's Choco Chip cookies from the unattended counter. She slowed to take one more look around, gave everyone a look of disgust, and then swished her hips out the door. In her mind, she had suffered; after all, she never got her Happy Meal, so she deserved a little something for her inconvenience.

Several of the other customers followed her lead, and a few, knowing a good thing when they saw it, used the five-finger discount system as they passed the unattended counter. They stole the hamburgers, pickles, lettuce, and the special sauce before running for the bus.

Caroline, the cashier who had been fired earlier, saw them in the parking lot. In a blind rage, she ran from the office into the parking lot and tried to board their bus. She did not care about the stolen food; she just wanted to get a piece of Sister Hellraiser's butt. Caroline wanted to beat her all the way to Pelzer. She did not have a ticket, so the newly arrived bus driver would not let her aboard. She'd have sold tracks from her pink-and-black weave until she was baldheaded for a ticket. Instead, she stood on the hot pavement and sobbed at the unfairness of the situation and banged on the side of the bus as it pulled away.

If the poor replacement bus driver knew who he had on board, then no doubt Caroline would have been welcome to ride and beat Sister Hellraiser until Armageddon ended. He would have pulled into the bushes and let the cashier—and anybody who wanted to—fight Sister Hellraiser and beat the demons out of her. He didn't know, so he thought the one hundred miles left to Pelzer would be peaceful. The reason for him having to relieve the other driver was not important. He needed the overtime, and that was reason enough for him. He drove and hummed while trying to catch a glimpse of the beautiful woman who sat near him.

Sister Hellraiser just winked at him and sat back in her seat. To her, he looked as stupid as the first bus driver. A quick nap would refresh her before she decided on how to toy with him.

The bus was quiet as the driver hummed softly in his fool's-paradise state of mind while an armed female bomb slept peacefully in a nearby seat.

Meanwhile, Inside the El Diablo Soul Food Shanty

It was dark and dusty in the vermin-infested back room of the El Diablo Soul Food Shanty, located at the corner of Tomaine and Poison Streets, next door to Shaqueeda's Curl, Wrap, and Daycare Center, in downtown Pelzer. Five silhouetted figures stood in the doorway on that hot Friday summer night. They looked ridiculous roasting from the clinging humidity as they tried to hide their identity behind matching dark-colored trench coats and hats. They were not the brightest bulbs in the pack, which only complicated matters as they pulled their hats down over their eyes. Of course, this caused them to bump into each other as they entered.

The cigar-chomping, runny-nosed chef, Porky LaPierre Matthews, owned El Diablo. He was tired of picking up his used, chipped china, knocked to the floor by the overdressed clowns every time they closed the door behind them. "Watch where you stepping!" So, like any good seeing-eye dog, he steered them to their seats.

After removing their coats and hats, they sat down. Chef Porky served their usual order. A deep-dish faded blue porcelain platter held a magnificent feast of parboiled rooster wings and blackened baloney, smothered with Jamaican yellow Louisianan-root hot sauce. Of course, no meal would be complete without their favorite Kool-Aid flavor: red. In the dimly lit room, they looked like five hungry weasels. All you could see were heads bobbing and cackling. After every other forkful, they would flick what looked like an unsuspecting crawling raisin off the table.

Every six months, it was the same routine. One of the five would rent the back room for the secret meeting that was a secret to no one. They would give Chef Porky their dinner requests in advance, because he only cooked what was handy and they were very particular. The advance notice was necessary since Chef Porky had once told them that he didn't cook particular and wouldn't look up the recipe for it, either.

Watching them slurp and burp proved to be too much even for the steel-stomached Chef Porky. He needed to get the ball rolling, so he scratched his hairnet-covered, dandruff-filled head and went outside to check out the seldom-filled parking lot. The lot seemed safe, so he went back inside and stuck his nose briefly into the smelly bathroom. The coast was clear. He gave the go-ahead signal by banging a crusty soup ladle against the blackened and grease-covered stove. He waited to get their attention, and when they had stopped eating and licking their fingers, he placed the ladle back in a pot of unidentifiable boiling liquid.

From out of the shadows, a hoarse voice announced, "The biannual Ain't Nobody Else Right but Us—All Others Goin' to Hell Church building fund-raising meeting is now called to order. I like to call it 'biannual' so if anyone finds out what we're doing, they won't know we do it twice a year. First business of the day is to take attendance. Will each one of you state your name, your office, and your purpose for being here?"

At first glance, the blurred figure that stood and began to speak looked like a faded old zoo peacock and wore glasses that made his eyes look twice the size of his face.

Most people thought he looked like a sixty-year-old cocky peacock with astigmatism and a huge ego.

"Assistant Pastor, Reverend and Most Righteous All About-Me. I am here, and I am accounted for, and of course, before we go any further, there are some things that I must have." He was never satisfied, and it was always about him.

Next to stand up was a short, stubby man of about fifty-five—
forty-five, to hear him tell it. To make sure that he looked im-
pressive, he turned his head to the side, exposing a curly hairpiece
dripping with Jheri-curl juice. He was dressed in a drab-gray
polyester-based silk sweatsuit embroidered with a large, twenty-
two-carat gold dollar sign. He thought he was the cat's last
meow.

"Reverend Knott Enuff Money—y'all know I'm the pastor.
I'm here and I'm rich!" He snickered and whirled around, ignoring the crash from the plate he knocked down. "And I'm also
here to talk about making mo' money!" Feeling he had grand-
standed enough to get his point across, he sat down with a thud
that sounded like he'd passed gas.

The next one to rise was a tall, lean figure dressed in a yellowed T-shirt and matching chino pants; he towered over the
others. He acted as if he needed permission to speak the English
language, so he spoke it sparingly as he stuttered, "Ah, well,
everybody here knows who I am, but I'll say it anyway. I'm
Bishop Was Nevercalled, the overseer from the mother church,
Mount No Hope Here Assembly, over there on Pilate's Blood
Avenue."

Thinking that he might have said too much, Bishop Was
Nevercalled grabbed his chair and sat down.

Raising a little handheld pearl-rimmed mirror that he always carried, Deacon Laid Handz spoke boldly as he mocked
the Bishop.

"If—if you—you finished stuttering, Bishop, I'll make my in-
troduction brief and be through, 'cause I got stuff to do. I am
Deacon Laid Handz." He praised himself for his perfect mimicry. "I'm here and always accounted for!"

He liked what he had said, and gave a wide, silly grin of confirmation as he snapped his fingers to the rhythm of music
echoing inside his head. He put the handheld mirror back inside
his purple-and-yellow sleeveless polo shirt and was just about
to speak again, when a strong, no-nonsense voice voice interrupted. "Sit down and shut up, you dim-witted fashion disaster!"

Without hesitation, Deacon Laid Handz did just that. He did it so fast, he almost missed his seat.

"Yada, yada, yada, y'all know who I am. Let's get on with this. It's too hot for this nonsense. And another thing"—she turned toward Chef Porky and glared—"can't we get some air-conditioning in here? If you ain't gonna open a window, at least turn on that air conditioner!"

"It *is* on!" Chef Porky barked, and then mumbled, "You probably can't feel it because we don't have it set on 'menopause.'"

He would have said it aloud, but he remembered that he had recently sold her another toxic refill for her infamous mace spray canister. He also knew she was not shy about using it. So he, too, sank back into the shadows, shut up, and let the meeting continue.

"Mother Pray Onn, can you, for once, adhere to protocol and state your name and office?" the Reverend Knott Enuff Money scolded, but in a nice manner.

"Well, I guess I don't have to now! You said my name, and church mother is my position!" the strong voice replied from its shadowy cover.

Mother Pray Onn was in her usual foul mood. She was dressed in an orange-and-blue duster with deep pockets that held her infamous cocked-and-ready mace spray. She knew she was old, and she definitely ruled. She pushed her short frame closer to the table and laid her custom-made Bible with its sharp serrated edge toward the pastor. Without saying a word, she gave all the men a warning stare, which, when translated, read, *Haven't you been introduced to my Bible before? If not, I can lay the Word on you right now.*

The Reverend Knott Enuff Money read Mother Pray Onn's silent stare loud and clear and humbly replied, "Didn't mean to rush you, Mother Pray Onn, but whenever you are ready we will proceed."

Mother Pray Onn knew she could produce a tai chi chop that could crumble any one of them, and that made her happy. Tonight was different. She did not want to be happy. She did not want to be there, and of course, somebody was going to suffer for it. She suddenly remembered that the chef was still in the room, and yelled, "Chef Porky, you can leave now! We need to get this meeting started, and this is confidential money business we are discussing, which means, it ain't none of your business!"

Hoping to get on Mother Pray Onn's good side, the Reverend All About-Me whined, "Please see when you leave that the extra food is covered. I don't know about the others, but Mother Pray Onn and I are pretty particular about our cuisine. In other words, we didn't bring no bugs and we ain't taking none back."

Deacon Laid Handz added sarcastically, "Yeah, and be quick about it. Besides, ain't you got a tomcat or something that needs skinning so you can serve it to your breakfast crowd? Maybe you might wanna fry up that rottweiler you got tied up in back. Give the folks a little sumpthin' with some bite!"

The deacon had a reason to be angry with Chef Porky. He would never forgive him for selling that last batch of toxic spray to Mother Pray Onn for her spray gun. She had used it on him a few days ago when he pretended to try and help Sister Connie Fuse avoid her. Sister Connie Fuse had made a mistake and taken Mother Pray Onn's grave layaway payment to the We'll Haul Your Ashes Crematorium instead of the They All Dyin' to Git Here Cemetery. Mother Pray Onn had assaulted him on a darkened street, and he still had not recovered from the humiliation or odor.

As if Mother Pray Onn had read Deacon Laid Handz's mind, she kicked his leg to warn him. "You look like your mind is taking a little stroll down memory lane." She laughed, and forgetting that she had just screamed at Chef Porky, she turned and sweetly reminded him to turn up the air conditioner on his way out.

Rather than argue with her again, Chef Porky said okay, and then, to get even with her, he pretended to turn the dial. Letting out a wicked laugh, he told them where to leave his tip, to which the deacon told him where he would put his tip if Chef Porky did not hurry. As Chef Porky closed the door behind him, he overheard Mother Pray Onn remark that she could feel the difference already.

Since the Reverend Knott Enuff Money never trusted anyone, he got up and checked the door to make sure no one was listening. He officially called the meeting to order again and inquired if there was any old business that needed to be finished before starting anything new. When no one responded, he looked at Bishop Was Nevercalled and winked.

The wink was a prearranged signal that the bishop should make a preconceived recommendation, and of course, the reverend would act surprised.

"Ah, excuse me. May I have the floor, Reverend Knott Enuff Money?" The bishop shuffled from side to side as he struggled to keep a straight face.

"Well, certainly, Bishop Was Nevercalled. What fine and necessary order of business do you have for us this evening?" the reverend innocently asked.

The bishop cleared his throat and replied while trying to control his stutter, "I've been thinking about something. Er—er, of course, you wouldn't know anything about this," he said, returning the reverend's wink.

Mother Pray Onn, the Reverend All About-Me, and Deacon Laid Handz could not believe what they'd heard. They gave each other sly looks that read, *Those two must think we are three new fools.* Suddenly feeling that perhaps they should stick together, they smiled and turned back to face the bishop. Mother Pray Onn offered the deacon an olive branch by massaging his bruised leg.

"We—Er, I mean, I—noticed that at this past Wednesday night's prayer and testimony service that the church was packed with people that had not been to church for months. Some of them had been absent for years. Now, perhaps these people lead very busy lives, and because they do, we must accommodate them." The bishop proudly stuttered, "Er—er, that's my own opinion, and I'm just saved like that."

"And how do we do that?" urged on the Reverend Knott Enuff Money. "I'm sure you must have give it some thought."

He wanted the bishop to get the point, because Mother Pray Onn had made it very clear when she beat the two of them up that past Wednesday that they had better be really careful when crossing her. That and the fact that she, Deacon Laid Handz, and the Reverend All About-Me had moved closer together also gave him cause for concern. They looked like Mount Rushmore figures all huddled together.

The bishop recognized the urgency in the reverend's voice and became nervous. His stuttering worsened.

"Ah—ah, well, I was thinking that perhaps we could build a drive-through on the side of the church." He paused to let the idea sink in a moment before continuing, "We could have a bulletin board on the side with a microphone and everything. The people could choose what kind of prayer service or preaching they need, and the price would be printed next to it."

The room, already hot with waves of heat dancing across the sooty tiled floor, seemed to heat up another degree as the Reverend All About-Me's, Mother Pray Onn's, and Deacon Laid Handz's mouths dropped open from shock. They thought they were hearing things until the shifty and greedy smile that stretched from ear to ear on the Reverend Knot Enuff Money's face told them differently.

The bishop mistook their incredulous looks for encouragement and began to stutter less as he continued. He was, for the moment, in his element.

"As I was saying . . . for example, if someone needed a financial blessing, they could select from the "No Money to Mo' Money" prayer column. We could offer weekly specials. For instance, we could offer a two-for-one plan for those who are divorced. They may need money for alimony and child support to stay out of jail or something like that. We could also sell them bottles of double-virgin blessed oil in the small, medium, and large sizes, and for an extra five dollars, we could super size it."

Before the bishop got too excited and spoiled everything, the Reverend Knott Enuff Money jumped up, laughed, and said, "That sounds like a wonderful idea, Bishop. Why didn't I think of that?"

Mother Pray Onn and Deacon Laid Handz looked at each other and jumped up so fast they almost kissed.

"Have you two fools lost your minds? A drive-through added on to the church? That's unbelievable!" Mother Pray Onn yelled and pounded the table, causing the hot sauce to spill onto drops of Kool-Aid. An angry Mother Pray Onn and drops of Kool-Aid plus hot sauce: a nuclear explosion waiting to happen.

"Yeah, what you gonna do next? Offer the congregation fries and a kiddie's toy? What has this world come to? Is there no limit?" the deacon added.

"And what about me?" was all that the Reverend All About-Me could say.

The bishop and the reverend, feeling that perhaps they had gone a little overboard, slowly sat down, leaned back in their chairs, and tried to submerge themselves in the darkness of the back room. Before their butts could fit comfortably in their seats, they heard the others discussing the idea among themselves.

"Do you know how much something like that would cost?" Mother Pray Onn whispered to the deacon.

"No idea what the cost. What I'd like to know is, do we need to put up an arch so people will know how many have gone through?" Deacon Laid Handz bubbled.

Neither had all the answers, so they decided to ask the Reverend All About-Me what he thought.

Since the Reverend All About-Me had not figured how he personally would prosper, he answered carefully, "Now, I don't know for sure. I'll have to check it out and get back to you with some estimates. I know a few *low* people in *high* places." He stopped and raised one bushy eyebrow as he pondered further. "We may have to spend a little extra for the large letters I need to spell my name and have it hoisted on top of the drive-through. I'll call my good buddy, the Reverend Over Priced. Perhaps we can buy it wholesale; after all, we do tell folks that we are a no-profit organization."

"That's nonprofit, fool!" Mother Pray Onn scoffed.

The plotting continued as the three of them kept throwing ideas at one another. Each idea was more outrageous than the last. Finally, to take the arguing to another level, Deacon Laid

Handz suggested that he be adorned in sequins and anything that glittered. He would also do the praying and, of course, the laying on of hands in the "express line."

Mother Pray Onn said, "I want to be in charge of the 'one-on-one personalized service.' Y'all know I have people skills, so I would be best qualified for that position."

With faith renewed in their cohorts, both the bishop and the Reverend Knott Enuff Money jumped up, eager to join in.

"We knew we could count on you folks. Of course, it is gonna cost a lot of money, and that's why we gonna have a special kind of fund-raiser. Deacon, would you mind pouring us another round of red Kool-Aid? Tonight we are gonna celebrate."

On into the night, they slurped, burped, and plotted. They assigned duties to one another. It would take some serious conniving to convince the members, but they had successfully pulled off other ridiculous building fund fund-raisers. Although over the years the building fund hadn't purchased so much as a doorknob, the event became a tradition. Any improvements that were done were donated from the estates of deceased members.

This time, they did not have help from Sister Betty. With her recently acquired true Christian attitude, she was no longer a part of their clique. Also, this year, Sister Carrie Onn wanted to be the fund-raiser chairwoman. That could never be permitted. She was too unstable. With that sobering thought in mind, the treacherous five knew that they would have to be extra careful. They needed to have a distraction, something to keep Sister Betty, Ma Cile, and a few other selected, goody-goody congregation members busy. What or who could do that? They quieted down to think.

The sun was almost up when Mother Pray Onn thought she had the perfect plan. They would need help, and she knew where to get it. After she went over the details, she went to the pay telephone, dropped in a slug, and placed a long-distance call. The others sat there and grinned like devious hyenas in a zoo as they heard Mother Pray Onn say, "Hello. May I please speak with Sister A Real Hellraiser? This is her cousin, Mother Pray Onn."

After several seconds passed, Mother Pray Onn spoke again. "A Real, cousin dear, how are you? . . . You're doing fine? That's wonderful. I heard what happened when you Hellraisers visited that *Jerry Springer* television talk show in Chicago, Illinois." She stopped to laugh before continuing. "I know you must be thanking God that your car had enough gas in the tank to get out of town."

Mother Pray Onn leaned on her cane as she wiped the perspiration from her wrinkled brow while responding, "Yes, God is good. . . . Sister Carrie Onn is doing okay, and thank you for asking. Yes, everybody at the church is doing fine, and no one's doing time, for the time being." She stopped and rapped her cane on the floor. "Listen, be quiet and stop asking so many questions; I'm the one who called you! Did Ima Hellraiser leave for Pelzer yet? . . . No apology necessary—just answer my question. . . . Yes, I spoke to her already, but I need her to do me another favor—the plan has been changed, and if I don't reach her, she's gonna mess everything up! . . . I don't care about your problems—just tell me where she's gonna be staying when she gets here."

When the telephone conversation ended, so did the meeting. After deciding that if the drive-through idea did not work they would try something different, the treacherous five donned their dark trench coats with matching hats, put a few IOUs in the tip jar, and crept out into the daylight. It was early Saturday morning, not quite seven o'clock.

The street stirred with town folks running errands, crisscrossing the streets like ants on a hunt. Others set up their wares on portable card tables. The treacherous five believed no one noticed them. The entire town knew that they were not the brightest bulbs in the pack when they knocked over garbage cans as the bright sunlight assaulted their eyes, alerting all to their presence.

They slithered to their cars, dripping with perspiration in

the ninety-degree weather. People were pointing, and some
even called out to them by name, but the treacherous five did
not care. They were dizzy with happiness that Sister Ima Hellraiser was on her way to Pelzer, South Carolina.

They were headed for a disaster, and too spiritually flawed
to know. Inviting Sister Hellraiser to a fund-raiser was like
inviting a weasel to bring the chickens in.

The Grey Dog bus finally made it into the terminal. Sister
Hellraiser was madder than a rooster at a gay chickens' con-
vention because she'd slept all the way into Pelzer and hadn't
wrecked the new bus driver's day. She ignored many whistles
from the men loafing around the terminal, who had neither the
proverbial pot nor window. She rushed from the bus to the
curb and dashed inside a waiting previously owned purple
Mercedes.

"Well, don't we look delicious?" Deacon Laid Handz said as
he eyed Sister Hellraiser from head to toe. "Do you want to
stop by my place before we meet the others—you know, just so
you can freshen up a bit?"

The deacon had almost forgotten how beautiful the honey-
colored she-volcano was. There was only a minor scar over his
left cheek inflicted by her from their last encounter. It had happened at last year's church picnic, several weeks after one of
the church's singles auctions. They were doing his favorite
dance, the electric slide, and she was in the line in front of him.
She dipped. He slid. The next thing he knew, when he woke up
in the hospital, was that he shouldn't have.

The deacon was told that when she dipped backward and he
slid forward, he took a little too long to move away; she wasn't
having it. She raked him across his cheek with her newly man-
icured French silk-wrapped nail. She also broke the nail and
was about to demolish the other nine when her cousins Mother
Pray Onn and Sister Carrie Onn jumped in. Because those
Hellraisers stuck together, among the three of them they
threw him around the grass like WCW wrestlers Hulk Hogan,

Macho Man, and Sting. Each one took a turn performing her favorite wrestling hold. Eventually, all his wounds healed except for that dime-size scar. It remained as a reminder that the next time he decided to do the electric slide, to do it defensively.

Deacon Laid Handz's face suddenly reddened with anger as he ran his finger along the round scar on his cheek. He decided that perhaps he would just take Sister Hellraiser straight to Mother Pray Onn's house before he did something stupid—again. He had a reputation to retain. After all, he was the chairman of the deacon board, but then he remembered he had been the chairman of the deacon board at that church picnic when those women beat him as if he were an unwanted stretch mark.

The deacon looked over and leered at Sister Hellraiser. She silently confirmed that she knew what he was thinking, by taking out an emery board and sharpening her nails. Removing all doubt so that he understood her intention, she leered back as she raked one of her sharpened nails across the fabric on the car seat.

They rode the rest of the way in silence, which was fine with Sister Hellraiser. She needed to think about the plan to keep Sister Betty and the other do-gooders busy while the Reverend Knott Enuff Money and the others put their bogus fund-raising scheme into action.

As they drove down Highway 29 and rocky side roads, they rode past several Pelzer policemen. Her nose for trouble told her that they were probably looking for her. Every time they saw a policeman, she slumped down in her seat. She looked like a human jack-in-the-box as she popped up and down all the way to number 000 No Mercy Boulevard, the home of Mother Pray Onn. If there was no trouble from the police or Deacon Laid Handz, she would be at Mother Pray Onn's house in about twenty minutes.

Mother Pray Onn's house was actually only five minutes away, but they were not taking any chances, so they drove through the shantytown back roads and littered alleyways.

When they finally arrived, there was Mother Pray Onn,

standing in the doorway with a scowl on her face that would make old Satan himself ask the Lord for shelter. She looked like an old woman spawned from pure dynamite and atomic waste.

Deacon Laid Handz, usually Mister debonair, saw the old she-devil standing in the doorway and refused to help Sister Hellraiser out of the car.

Sister Hellraiser, acting like she didn't need help, got out on the passenger side, and before her feet barely touched the ground, she felt the breeze of her luggage whiz past her and land at her feet. She only heard it and didn't see it. She tripped. She fell face first, spreadeagled in reverence before the queen of mean, Mother Pray Onn.

Deacon Laid Handz took off at breakneck speed. He saw Sister Hellraiser fall flat on her face and knew she would blame him. Laughing to himself, he thought, "She's gonna be killer-mad with me, but I'll worry about that later."

Deacon Laid Handz did deep belly laughs all the way back to the highway. The hot and hazy sun beaming directly down on his head caused him to think that the two women were not going to plan something special to get even. He turned on his radio just in time to hear a few choruses of James Brown's "The Big Payback."

He didn't see the irony in the music as he bobbed and weaved his head, trying to do the "cabbage patch," from the waist up, to the music. He grinned as he raced away toward the island of denial, where he loved to spend so much time.

Mother Pray Onn didn't believe in pity, and certainly not for any of her relatives. She threw her hands up in the air in disgust as she hissed, "Ima, you gonna lie there looking like trash on my grass or you gonna come on inside?"

"Mother Pray Onn, you gonna help me up or are you just gonna stand there in the doorway looking like one of the munch-kins from the Wizard of Oz?" Sister Hellraiser shot back.

"You know I'm old and got a bad back! You were always the selfish one in the family. Get up off your face and come on inside. We got work to do. Do you want some of these nosy neighbors to see you and call the cops?" She stopped and stroked the gray bun that was so tight it gave her a permanent scowl. "Now, get in here quick! I've got some hot coffee perking, if you want it."

Mother Pray Onn turned around and went back inside her house as she completely ignored Sister Hellraiser, who fell twice as she struggled to her feet.

Sister Hellraiser decided to hold her peace knowing it took a special kind of ornery to drink hot coffee during ninety-degree weather. She let a sly grin appear. The Hellraisers were a special breed.

Sister Hellraiser wiped the grass and dirt from her hair as she struggled with her luggage. She became angry again and muttered under her breath.

Mother Pray Onn was standing in her kitchen over a hot stove, pouring a steamy cup of lava-hot hazelnut coffee when she heard Sister Hellraiser finally come in the house.

Sister Hellraiser threw her luggage to the floor and kicked a nearby porcelain figurine, which did not break. She ran straight to the kitchen and found Mother Pray Onn. They yelled and screamed at each other, played the dozens (talking about each other's mamas), and then hugged and kissed. Always at odds, but they were truly glad to see one another.

Mother Pray Onn wanted to act like a gracious host, especially when she remembered why Sister Hellraiser was there, but she didn't know how. She winged it. She smiled, straightened the black laced doilies on her couch, and almost sang the words, "Did you want to put your things in the large guest room?"

The effort was wasted on Sister Hellraiser. "I don't know why you keep calling that closet a large guest room. Sleeping in there is like sleeping in a coffin."

It took a lot of control not to be as nasty as she could be, but Mother Pray Onn sweetly replied, "Well, if you'd rather use the deluxe lockup accommodations offered down at the Pelzer

Police Plaza, I'd gladly give them a call. They do make pickups, you know! If you're hungry, they should be serving the special of every day: bread and water."

Sister Hellraiser's scowl slid from her face. "Oh, cousin, you so sensitive. You know I didn't mean no harm in what I said. I just calls a closet a closet if it looks and feels like a closet."

"Oh, Ima, sweetie, I know you didn't mean anything by that. It's so hot, I guess I'm just a little uncomfortable today. Between me and you, although I'm not old enough, I'm going through a 'change.' "

"A change of what?" Sister Hellraiser teased.

"Menopause!" Mother Pray Onn hollered and then smiled innocently. "I'm flashing faster than a neon sign on Broadway." That last part was the truth.

Mother Pray Onn wanted to rush and get the job done. She knew the sooner the trouble-making heifer was out of her house and Pelzer, South Carolina, the better off everybody would be. She smiled again at her cousin, like an old, scheming Cheshire cat, and led her into the living room. It was almost time for them to put their new plan into action. She added a teaspoon of salt to the hot coffee. Mother Pray Onn was so ornery, she never used sugar in anything. Her entire family was mean and evil. They were the fuel that would keep the hell fires burning for at least two years past eternity and months after the devil burned to ashes.

Through the Streets to Sister Betty's We Go

"Ma Cile, Lil Bit's sticking her nasty tongue out at me!" June Bug whined.

"You's a liar and the truth ain't in you!" Lil Bit shouted back with her favorite accusation.

The kids were so busy teasing each other that they had not noticed that Ma Cile, not one to wait until she returned home to handle her business, had stopped in the middle of the sidewalk. She had one hand dangling by each hip, and before the kids knew what happened, those hands magically slapped each one of them upside their heads. She hit them so hard, they stumbled a few feet in front of her as if she had just shot marbles. By the time she had fussed, huffed, and puffed her way to where they landed and was ready to deliver round two, she heard Sister Betty call her name.

"Hello, Ma Cile."

Fearing Sister Betty had seen her actions, Ma Cile quickly cocked her head to the side and looked at the trembling children. Shaking her head ever so slightly so she could line her eyes up, she gave them her "I'll drop-kick your little behinds right out here in the street, and when I sweep up the pieces, I'll give a quarter to anyone who wants to call the Bureau of Child Welfare and then beat them down, too" stare.

The children understood what Ma Cile's eyes said. They tried to wish invisible angelic halos would appear over their heads.

"Praise the Lord, Sister Betty. We were just on our way to ya house," Ma Cile sweetly said as she moved her huge frame nervously from side to side.

Ma Cile was trying to block Sister Betty's view until she was sure the kids had stopped sniffling. All the "toughness; don't care if you call the Bureau of Child Welfare; here's a quarter" attitude vanished with Sister Betty's sudden appearance.

"I tried to call you, but I got a busy signal. It seems like you still trying to get used to having a telephone. You need to make sure you got it hung up properly. I thought I would just come on over and save you the trouble of coming to me." Sister Betty grinned wide, which caused her teeth to slip. She pushed them back in and, without missing a beat, said, "Besides that, we got some trouble brewing, and me and you gonna have to put a stop to it."

The thought of getting in cahoots with Sister Betty gave Ma Cile a rush, and she quickly put aside any thoughts of the children's welfare.

Sister Betty looked over at the children. As usual, she could tell when they had pushed the envelope and worked their grandmother's last good nerve. "What's wrong with my sweethearts today? Why your eyes looking so red? Do you have allergies?" she asked with a wink.

For the first time that day, they felt as if their tongues were glued and could not respond.

Rather than let one more person on the street know that they had just been physically corrected, the children just pretended to sniff, cough, and nod their heads in unison. They walked about ten paces behind Sister Betty and Ma Cile, in case their grandmother decided to give them a refresher course in South Cackalacky, Behavioral Science 101.

"You hungry, Ma Cile?" Sister Betty asked. She figured out what had really happened with the children by the fresh red slap marks on their prepubescent cheeks. She needed to put their joy back.

Happy for the distraction and feeling just a tiny bit guilty for the public discipline action, Ma Cile quipped, "Yeah, I could use a little somethin' to eat. I guess these here li'l heathens could probably use somethin', too."

"Well, I was thinking perhaps we walk over to that McDonald's in the mall; that way the children could eat and play while we eat and talk. Is that all right by you?"

The idea had all the ingredients for an adventurous afternoon: a mall, two smart-mouth kids, and two snippy, no-nonsense old ladies in a McDonald's restaurant on a Saturday afternoon. Déjà vu! After Ma Cile had just finished backhanding them in public, perhaps the kids couldn't do any more harm at a McDonald's than Sister Hellraiser wherever she went.

Ma Cile and Sister Betty ordered for themselves and the kids. While they waited, Sister Betty told Ma Cile about the vision she had had while praying. Ma Cile could feel her blood pressure rise as she listened closely.

Sister Betty leaned over and whispered, "Are you all right, Ma Cile?" Sister Betty asked with concern. "Is your blood pressure up? Is your sugar up?"

Ma Cile happened to look down at her sagging breast laying on the table and quipped, "Not ever'thang."

The concerned look on Ma Cile's face told Sister Betty different.

Ma Cile looked at Sister Betty and frowned. She didn't want to believe that the Reverend Knott Enuff Money and his greedy cronies were about to pull another scam using the annual fundraiser, their favorite event. Ma Cile placed her hand on her forehead. She felt her blood pressure soar.

Ma Cile pushed her chair back from the table, and without saying a word, she waddled into the bathroom. She was about to enter one of the stalls, when the intrusion of a needling female voice caught her attention.

"Lady, that will be a quarter. Please." The woman had a hump on her back that looked like an umbrella protruding from her spine. She appeared frumpy and old.

"What did you say?" Ma Cile turned and snapped.

Ma Cile was not in the mood for beggars and did not come into the bathroom because her face needed to be powdered. There was a specific purpose, and if this woman did not move, the purpose would be running down her legs any moment.

"A quarter. You need to pay a quarter if you're gonna use the bathroom." The woman used her hunch as a barrier. She spoke the words with all the conviction of a starved kitten threatening to beat the tar out of the neighborhood pit bull.

"Ya got half a second to move outta my way or ya gonna be smelling worse than this here entire bathroom. Now move outta my way!" Ma Cile's hips barely touched the woman as she attempted to pass. The little touch was enough to knock the woman past the second basin and land her under the paper towel rack, facedown in a puddle of unknown but smelly liquid.

Ma Cile's bladder directed her to the closest stall. She entered and slammed the door behind her. She grabbed at the door as it swung back and forth without a clasp to keep it shut. She tried to get herself hovered over the toilet while she held the door in place with one hand to secure her privacy. It wasn't easy, but she managed.

After finishing her honorable duty, she discovered there was no toilet paper. No toilet paper at all, anywhere inside the stall.

There wasn't even a toilet paper dispenser. With long cotton bloomers hanging around her fat knees, Ma Cile panicked and she shot out of the stall as if a Scud missile had been launched before she got off the toilet.

Happy that the small, two-stall, dingy bathroom was empty except for the hunchbacked, elderly beggar woman, who somehow had managed to get up and lean against the graffiti-filled wall, Ma Cile ambled into the next stall only to find that it, too, was toilet-paper-free.

The beggar woman saw Ma Cile's dilemma and spoke with more confidence. "A quarter, please. You have to give me a quarter or you gonna go around with your butt stinking and dripping." She smiled and commanded as she straightened her torn skirt.

With her dignity still stuck in the toilet stall, Ma Cile snapped, "What! I ain't paying ya for the honor."

She was going to stand firm, with bloomers around her knees like a senile superwoman, until she saw what was in the beggar woman's hands. It was a soiled brown paper bag, filled to the brim with sheets of toilet paper held below a wide, snaggled-toothed, know-it-all grin on the hunchback woman's face. Ma Cile was about to say something else, but the sight of an automatic hot-air blower attached to the wall caught her attention.

The woman was way ahead of Ma Cile. "So, what you gonna do with that blower? You gonna stand on your head and let the hot air blow down on you to dry you off? I'll pay *you* a quarter if you can do it!"

Ma Cile thought about it. All she could do was think about it.

The woman grinned with more confidence as she saw the look of defeat spread across Ma Cile's chubby face. She took another peep at Ma Cile's big hips with the bloomers hanging and laughed so hard she almost dropped the bag. "I betcha you'll pay that quarter now, won't you?"

The beggar woman knew she was about to be paid. A quarter for one sheet would not do. Ma Cile needed at least three or four dollars' worth.

After giving in to the bathroom robbery by the toilet-paper-holding, hunchbacked old bandit, Ma Cile lumbered from the bathroom fit to be tied. She wanted to tell, but the details would have been too embarrassing. She sat down in her chair with a thud. Sister Betty took one look at her and knew something was wrong.

"Ma Cile, what's the matter? You look like you just got finished doing hard time. You probably just need a little bit more fiber in your diet."

"It wasn't as easy as I thought it would be, but I'm okay," Ma Cile said unconvincingly.

"That's good. I thought it might have been too hot in here for you. Anyway, do you want to get a little something for dessert? I could use one of those thick shakes or a hot apple pie."

"Well, uh, as a matter of fact, Sister Betty, I'm gonna jist wait until me and the kids get back home to eat dessert. I had ta do my Christian duty and give all my money to a beggar woman in the ladies' room."

"All your money, Ma Cile? You felt a need to give her all your money?"

Ma Cile suddenly rocked back and forth in her seat like a snake trying to shed its old skin. "Uh-huh. The truth be told, I didn't have enough money. I really needed to give her at least a dollar more."

"A dollar more? Why a dollar more?"

Ma Cile was used to controlling situations, and the humiliation she felt could not compare with her anger. Rather than turn McDonald's out, she simply replied, "I don't wanna talk about it. You supposed to do your givin' in a closet, so it's just between you and heaven." Ma Cile knew that on Judgment Day, if God didn't read it aloud from the Book of Life, she certainly would never tell it. She looked at Sister Betty to see if she believed her story. She seemed to.

"Well, seeing as how you gave your last dime to the homeless, this will be my treat for you and the children."

"Thank ya, Sister Betty. Where is them heathens, anyway?"

"They ate and then went outside to play in the children's

area. I figured you and I could talk without being disturbed if they weren't here. You don't mind, do you?"

"That's real nice of ya, Sister Betty. Why don't ya finish telling me what needs to be done and how we can fix them greedy folks?" She wanted somebody to pay for what had just happened to her in that bathroom. The reverend and the rest of his cronies would do.

They finished their discussion and decided to drop the children off at the Young People's Willing Workers program at Blessings to Go Church. It was a little storefront building where Brother Tis Mythang taught music appreciation every Saturday.

Ma Cile was happy the children were out of the way. She felt things could get ugly and she did not want the children in her way. She did not want to feel angry, because anger was not the right feeling to have when trying to fight a battle for the Lord, but it was what she felt.

The Upper Room, A.K.A. the Nosebleed Section

Later on that early evening, the high-ceiling section of the third-floor overflow balcony was empty.

On Sundays and special occasions, all those who did not get to the church on time were unceremoniously directed to walk up the winding staircase, past the second floor, where those who did not want to get involved in the church action sat. To further add to their harsh treatment, the elevators were roped off to teach them a lesson.

The ushers refused to accompany the latecomers, complaining that those who came late did not deserve to be escorted. However, when it came time to collect for the many offerings, the ushers simply took the ropes down and rode the elevators back and forth. The same stoic faced ushers would not bring a fan, a glass of water, a tissue, or even a Sunday program—but a collection plate, they would.

It was around eight-thirty that evening when four of the

original treacherous five—the Reverend Knott Enuff Money, Deacon Laid Handz, Bishop Was Nevercalled, and the Reverend and Most Righteous All About-Me—arrived. Instead of going into the church, they stood in a circle, chatting. Several yellow lilac bushes kept them from public view. They waited until the last janitor left before they crept into the church.

It was still hot and humid, and they were still wearing the same ridiculous outfits of matching hats and trench coats that they had worn the day before at the El Diablo Soul Food Shanty. They rode in silence as the elevator creaked its way up to the overflow balcony. As they exited, their bodies hugged the hallway's darkened stucco-covered walls. Each bumped into the other, bloodying knuckles as they tried to find a light switch to illuminate the balcony. It was not easy, since none of them had personally visited that section of the church before. After several minutes of searching, they still could not find the switch and continued to stumble around in the dark.

Bishop Was Nevercalled, without thinking, decided to light a match. Unfortunately, he stood behind the Reverend Knott Enuff Money, whose hair glistened and dripped oil from freshly sprayed Jheri-curl juice. The bishop tripped over a hymnal, bumping into the reverend. The match set the reverend's Jheri-curl-juiced hair on fire.

The reverend felt the heat and smelled the acrid stench of his burning hair. He also felt the searing pain. He started running around the balcony. He looked like a candle waved at a Michael Jackson concert.

Deacon Laid Handz rushed around trying to tear some of the pillows from the pews to smother the flames. He needed something to throw on the burning reverend. Sacrificing his favorite purple Nehru-collared shirt was not an option. He felt helpless. He felt useless. He *was* useless.

Bishop Was Nevercalled became scared and started stuttering as he yelled repeatedly to the reverend, "Dro-dr-op and ro-ro-roll."

In the meantime, the Reverend and Most Righteous All About-Me took advantage of the situation. He followed behind the still-burning and galloping Reverend Knott Enuff Money. He used the light from the flaming Jheri-curl to locate the light switch. He followed the flaming scalp like the wise men followed the star to Bethlehem.

Deacon Laid Handz finally found an old greasy towel left by one of the janitors and wrestled the reverend to the floor. He threw caution to the wind and hoped his shirt would not be singed as he straddled the reverend's back. He swatted at the flames until finally putting them out as well as knocking the reverend's head around in the process.

The Reverend Knott Enuff Money was in shock, but not to the point where he could not get up. He knocked away the deacon's hands and grabbed the head of the bishop in a kung fu headlock. Everybody was kung fu fighting.

The reverend's eyes were growing wide as he started screaming, "Somebody give me a match!" He wanted desperately to return the favor to the bishop. He suddenly realized a match would be useless.

The bishop was bald, with just a tiny bit of blond hair fuzz that was a remnant of what was, so what was the use?

Just as the reverend was about to do a TKO on the bishop, he looked up in time to see Mother Pray Onn in a karate stance.

In all the confusion, no one had heard her arrive. She stood there looking stunned yet ready to attack. From the outside, there came a sudden clap of thunder and sounds of hard-pounding rain.

It seemed as though Mother Nature took it upon herself to announcing the entrée of the radiant yet always lethal Sister Ima Hellraiser.

Sister Hellraiser trekked in with hands on both hips, and an attitude. "Y'all doing each other's hair? It smells like you singeing pork hide up in here, or a press-and-curl gone terribly wrong! You need to turn on an air conditioner or something. Boy, it stinks!"

A mocking look covered Sister Ima Hellraiser's face like makeup as she slunk her way over to face the reverend. His still-smoking Jheri-curl told her everything she needed to know—that and the hysterical look on the bishop's face. "It looks like you boys had a little accident up here. Don't worry, Reverend, if the good deacon will run out to the car and bring my large cosmetic bag, I think I can fix you right on up."

"Why you still standing there like mud on a rock?" the reverend barked to Deacon Laid Handz as he got up with most of his wig hair still smoldering on the floor. "Get out to her car and be quick!"

Deacon Laid Handz started toward the door.

After a few moments, the Reverend Knott Enuff Money started to calm down. Just looking at the stunning beauty of Sister Hellraiser helped to take his mind off the pain. He was but a mere man.

Sister Hellraiser turned sideways to the reverend, to give him a better look. She used her profile as temporary balm for his burns. Just as quickly as she turned sideways, she turned around and taunted the deacon. "Oh, by the way, Deakie, sweetheart, the elevator's acting funny. You'll have to take the steps down and back up."

Sister Hellraiser took her time turning away from the deacon. She was going to be on the Deacon's case like funk on a skunk. His payback for dumping her at Mother Pray Onn's was going to be special, unique—a work of art.

Slithering over to the reverend, Sister Hellraiser continued to purr like a ghetto Eartha Kitt as she touched his shoulder. "Let this little Hellraiser make it better for you. I've got a red Jheri-curl wig in my cosmetic bag. I keep it for special occasions, like Halloween. This seems like it's going to be special. Very special."

"Ima, I'm glad you've got some kind of wig or something to cover your real hair," Mother Pray Onn laughed. She was never one to be ignored for too long.

Sister Hellraiser spun around and growled, "And what's wrong with my real hair?" She flung her long, red synthetic mane around for emphasis.

"Oh, nothing much. I know you think you real cute. Of course, it must take some effort to try to keep that little bit of hair of yours underneath in cornrows. But I gotta tell you, the last time I saw your hair, it was very short. Those cornrows look more like stitches."

Sister Hellraiser took only two steps before she reached Mother Pray Onn. She stood over her and hissed, "For your information, you crusty old biddy, my real hair is short because I choose to keep it that way. You know I usually keep my hair long, very long. We cousins, so you know I'm mixed."

"Yeah, you mixed all right. Your mama was black and your daddy was blacker. I don't see where you get the nerve talking about how mixed you are. If anything, you mixed up."

"Old lady, now I know you crazy. As black as your daddy was, he was the lightest one in his family, and they used to call him high yella! You must have forgotten who you messing with."

"Excuse me. I'm still smoking over here." The Reverend Knott Enuff Money whined and patted his scalp. "So do you think you two could just shut up and put aside your stupid petty differences and insults?"

"Oh, no. He did not just jump up in family business," Mother Pray Onn and Sister Hellraiser chimed. "Yes, he did. Let's forget about him and forgive one another, again."

Although the Reverend and Most Righteous All About-Me enjoyed the verbal insults thrown between the women, he felt left out. He also wanted attention. He chimed in, trying to make light of the situation, "You know, Reverend, if you can't achieve it, you should weave it. I think I might have, in my pocket, some Royal Crown hair grease to put on what's left of that dry-looking wig. I carry Royal Crown around with me because I like to keep my do tight." He opened the red-and-silver round cardboard canister. It smelled like cheap alcohol and old corn chips.

The room got very quiet as everyone turned and looked at the Reverend and Most Righteous All About-Me. Everyone, including the Reverend Knott Enuff Money, suddenly burst out laughing. The very thought of him trying to touch up his James Brown-styled pageboy with the heavy gook of Royal

Crown hair grease was too much to imagine. The mystery of why his sculptured hair never moved lay in a small round red container with a silver top.

Deacon Laid Handz returned, just in time, with Sister Hellraiser's bag.

The Reverend Knott Enuff Money had stopped laughing and was just about to pimp-slap the Reverend All About-Me all over the overflow balcony when he saw the henna-red Jheri-curl wig in the deacon's hand.

Sister Hellraiser jumped at the deacon. "Did I tell you to go in my bag? You ain't got no business going into a lady's bag!"

"I didn't go into a lady's bag; I went into yours," the deacon smirked.

The reverend ignored the arguing and sneaked a sucker punch, which dropped the bishop into a heap on the floor. "Give me that!" snapped the reverend as he turned away from the bishop. He snatched the wig out of the deacon's hand and put it on lopsided.

None of them liked him enough to tell him. No matter how he put the wig on, it looked better than the half-plucked-chicken look he had without it.

Despite the fact that the balcony smelled like an old hair-processing salon, and although the Royal Crown hair grease did not make it smell any better, the meeting of, now, the treacherous six proceeded. It was important that they plan everything down to the second.

As long as Sister Hellraiser played her revised part, the se-cret and illegal fund-raising for the building of the drive-through attached to the church would be successful. They chatted away and waited for the meeting to begin.

The Pelzer, South Carolina, Library

Earlier, Sister Betty and Ma Cile had arrived at the down-town, glass-enclosed Pelzer library about twenty minutes be-fore it closed. It only took them a moment to figure out which door from among the many glass panels would be the one they needed.

Sister Betty, with her lithe body, was the first to go through the rotating glass door, and she did it with no problem.

Ma Cile was another matter. First, she tried to go through with her big shopping-bag-size pocketbook tucked to her stomach. She couldn't. She then tried to lay it on her side and push forward. She got stuck. With her patience whittled down to about the size of a dime, she gave the glass partition a hard shove. The rotating door turned. It turned and turned again. It kept on turning with Ma Cile trapped inside. The doors kept spinning her until she looked like a chocolate shake in a blender.

It finally took four security guards to bring the door to a stop, but not without their getting all kinds of nicks and scratches. Of course, Ma Cile was fit to be tied. However, once she found out that the cheese fries she had secreted inside her pocketbook had not been smashed during the mishap, she quickly forgave the library door for trapping her. She didn't have time to stay angry. Sister Hellraiser and the others had to be stopped.

They made their way to the archives located on the second floor. As soon as they got off the elevator, Sister Betty heard someone call her name.

"We're over here, Sister Betty. Hurry! We got the information you needed."

Sister Betty and the others rushed over to where Minister Breedin' Love and Sister Loose Gal sat.

"Have you two been waiting long?" Sister Betty asked as soon as she saw them. "We were detained by a minor mishap."

"What ya mean, 'minor' mishap?" Ma Cile snapped. "Them doors tried to kill me. I tell ya, I was fearing for my life. First they tossed and then they turned me. I was scared to death!"

"No, you weren't," Sister Betty laughed. "You thought you were gonna lose them cheesy fries."

How she know about them? Ma Cile thought.

"Well, we're glad everyone arrived safely. Sister Betty, Ma

Cile, come and see what we found." Minister Breedin' Love pointed to a wooden desk in a corner.

"Before we get started, how are you feeling, Sister Loose Gal? I was so happy to see Minister Breedin' Love the other night at testimony service when Sister Connie Fuse had her breakthrough, but I didn't see you."

"I was attending revival meeting at another church last Wednesday night, Sister Betty," Sister Loose Gal spoke softly. At the age of thirty, she had decided to give up a life of hard drinking, harsh conversation, and prostitution. Yet, through it all, she had managed to keep her good looks and take on the mannerism of a high-society woman. Everyone loved her soft speech and polite conversation. "Thank you for asking, though, Sister Betty."

Sister Betty and Ma Cile found a seat and looked at the documents spread out on the table before them.

"Sister Betty, you were right. I think we found a way to stop the reverend and his cronies," Sister Loose Gal whispered. "This is so exciting. Most of the information we found, I never knew existed."

"We don't have much time. Can you print out everything that we need?" Sister Betty asked anxiously.

"I cain't wait till we git them," Ma Cile said as she pounded the table. In her mind, the image of the reverend replaced the one of the homeless, hunchbacked woman back at McDonald's withholding that much-needed toilet paper. Suddenly, she needed to use the bathroom again. "I'll be back." She checked her pocketbook, made sure she had a wad of napkins in it, and then proceeded to the nearest one.

While the others waited for Ma Cile's return, Minister Breedin' Love made a preplanned telephone call to the local television station, Channel Six (YLIE).

He spoke into the receiver. "Everything is going like clockwork." After hanging up the telephone, he had a wide grin on his face.

"Are you sure this is gonna work, Sister Betty?" Sister Loose Gal asked.

"It will definitely work. I have it on good authority," Sister Betty answered. "I prayed."

"When are you going to tell us who told you about what the Reverend Knott Enuff Money and the others were up to?" Minister Breedin' Love asked as he carefully refolded the documents and placed them back on the library shelf.

"Right now, I can only tell you that I prayed," Sister Betty replied. "You'll just have to continue to trust me."

"Okay, I'm back. Is everythang taken care of now?" Ma Cile asked as she tried to catch her breath. Today, using any bathroom was going to take its toll on her.

"They are about to close up here. There's nothing left to do here. We might as well head on over to the fund-raising meeting at church."

Sister Betty turned toward Minister Breedin' Love and Sister Loose Gal. "I'm really depending on you two to do your part. Although, if I know Sister Carrie Onn, she won't be sorry or mad if you didn't show." She laughed. "She thinks it will be less competition for her campaign for chairwoman."

After finding another exit out of the building, one with just a plain, simple door and not one with possessed turning doors, Sister Betty and the others poured out onto the sidewalk. Confident that their plan would work, they accepted a ride from Minister Breedin' Love. They took advantage of the long ride home and finalized their plans.

The plan given to Sister Betty in her dream gave her unwavering confidence to win the upcoming battle. And, of course, her faith in God never wavered.

Let the Fund-Raising Begin

Outside, that night, the weather was about one hundred degrees. However, inside the huge, high-ceilinged church auditorium, the temperature was a comfortable sixty-five degrees. In just a little more than an hour, at eight o'clock, the annual fund-raising meeting would begin.

The planning of the annual fund-raiser was every bit as entertaining as most events held at the church. The procedure was simple. After selecting a chairperson, suggestions for ways to raise moneys would be entertained. Hopefully, they would not be as ridiculous as the previous year's suggestions. The congregation wanted to do everything from selling jars of crunchy peanut butter to the toothless old folks at the local nursing homes to selling bifocal glasses to the blind. To their credit, a few managed to rent out free handicapped parking spaces to several handicapped people. They gave those people a discount, especially those with bunions; after all, they were handicapped.

Soon a few grumpy and overheated volunteers from the fund-raising committee arrived early. They began to push the pews back and unfold the much sturdier metal folding chairs. They then made sure the latches on the baptismal pool were secured. At one of the previous meetings, three hundred-pound Brother Lead Belly had started shouting and stomping when he couldn't get his way. He accidentally pushed up against the deacons' bench, causing it to flip, spin, and pop a wheelie. All of the deacons were thrown from the bench and landed in the baptismal pool. They reminisced and giggled at the disastrous results.

One good thing came out of the incident. Brother Lead Belly joined Sister Carrie Onn's "Shouting for Appearance' Sake" class. After a few classes, he learned how to shout correctly and became the head shouter whenever "Stretch Out" was sung.

Several hat pins, Bibles, hymnbooks, fans, and any object that looked like a weapon were locked in the supply closet. After the injuries sustained from last year's fund-raising meeting, no one took chances.

After a short welcome address by one of the deaconesses, and a fast-paced congregational hymn, the meeting began. It seemed simple enough. Sister Hellraiser was not around then, and simple she was not.

After setting up the auditorium and making sure that the atmosphere for the meeting would be safe, a few of the glum-faced ushers opened the doors.

About two hundred congregation members, as well as others who had no business being there, rushed inside. Most of them were drenched with perspiration and had left their patience behind in their comfortable air-conditioned homes. They wanted to start the meeting on time and get it over. However, they did not know Sister Hellraiser was coming. If word had gotten out that the trouble-making Hellraiser was going to be there, more than just those two hundred people would have attended.

There were a few of the members who had attended other fund-raiser meetings, they came through the door suspicious of the quietness that blanketed the church.

One of the members, Sister Aggi Tate, a woman who always lied about being over fifty, and chairwoman over the Bible study group, broke the silence. She spoke with the same drone and annoyance as a stinging wasp. People said it was her voice. It was rumored that once, before he died, it sent her husband, Deacon Dick Tate, over the edge. He did a short vacation stay at the Delusional Arms home.

"You know, earlier, I was in my garden. I was tending my tulips and annuals. They are quite lovely this time of year. You know, I do have a green thumb. The sun was perfectly positioned over my tulips . . ." she droned.

"Hey, is there a point to your story? You're taking too long," Sister Need Sum snapped. She was a thirty-one-year-old former cheerleader. She felt that life was passing by too quickly. She never wanted to miss any opportunities. She was also the head of the Circle of Friends committee and, at that moment, did not feel friendly. She took an open hymnal and slammed it shut. "I've got a date. A date with a man that I finally got back into my life."

A strange voice from the crowd cried out, "Does that man make six figures, too?" Everyone laughed, and even though the place was lit, some tried to make finger puppet shadows on the wall to add to the teasing.

Sister Aggi Tate adjusted the charm that was shaped like a cross on her bracelet. She twirled the bracelet around her skinny wrist as she spoke. "You mean the man who Sister Hellraiser left chewing on his empty wallet and didn't know why his teeth hurt?" She stopped and eyed the crowd to see who had interrupted. When no one looked guilty enough, she continued, "Well, if you'd stop interrupting and let me finish . . ."

"Please finish!" the church members chorused.

Sister Aggi Tate tried to pretend she was hurt by the verbal assault, but nothing was going to steal the moment from her.

"Okay. Like I said, I was tending my garden . . ."

"We mean, right now!" the members chorused again.

"I saw Sister Hellraiser standing—well, actually, lying—facedown in Mother Pray Onn's front yard. If she'd been laying a few feet to the left, she'd been facedown in the bed of orange jack-o'-lanterns. You know, Mother Pray Onn's garden isn't half as lovely as mine . . ."

Sister Aggi Tate droned on while most of the other members almost passed out.

Like an oncoming ocean wave, all through the room the news spread. Sister Hellraiser had offended, at one time or another, practically everyone in Pelzer, South Carolina. She aggravated the young and the old, the blacks and the whites, as well as the rich and the poor. She was the one person they loved to hate. Everyone had a reason to reach out and touch her. If it were not a crime to do what they really wanted to do to her, she would have been dead long ago.

While the meeting was getting ready to begin, the now treacherous six sneaked in through the side basement door. The Reverend Knott Enuff Money and the others secured Sister Hellraiser in one of the rooms and proceeded to the steps leading to the church auditorium. They told her that after a pre-arranged signal, she should emerge and then join them.

On their way up the stairs, the Reverend Knott Enuff Money asked The Reverend and Most Righteous All About-Me for his compact mirror. The Reverend Money wanted to check out the red wig he had borrowed from Sister Hellraiser.

As was his habit, he had sprayed the wig with too much Jheri-curl activator and moisturizer. It kept sliding to the back of his head. He refused to let Mother Pray Onn pin it with a bobby pin to his remaining hair. That would not be masculine.

The Reverend and Most Righteous All About-Me did not want to share his compact mirror. Everything he had was just for himself. Sharing was not in his vocabulary.

The Reverend Knott Enuff Money knew that the Reverend All About-Me never traveled without a mirror, and he was determined to get it. He was not going to go into the meeting with a bright-red Jheri-curl wig sitting lopsided on his head.

Quickly the Reverend Knott Enuff Money hurled himself at the Reverend All About-Me. He reached out several times, attempting to search the man's pockets for the mirror. With each thrust of his Jheri-curl-juice-smeared hands, they slipped. He was only successful at telegraphing his moves.

The Reverend and Most Righteous All About-Me slid to the side. When he slid to the side, he stepped on Deacon Laid Handz's new purple wing-tip shoes, and it was downhill from there.

The deacon jerked back to bend down to wipe off his shoes. By accident, he managed to place his butt right in the face of Mother Pray Onn.

Mother Pray Onn took her cane by the tip and used the curved handle to reach between his legs. It served to remind Deacon Laid Handz of the difference between men and women.

The deacon jumped up and grabbed himself below the belt. He screamed out in his new soprano voice. He reached out to keep from falling down the steps and palmed the bald head of Bishop Was Nevercalled. The deacon's hand slid off and he went sprawling down the steps, but not before he managed to grab the pants pocket of the Reverend All About-Me, which made the compact mirror fall out. It landed right beside the Reverend Knott Enuff Money.

"You idiot! All you had to do was give me the mirror when I asked for it!"

"It's *my* mirror," the Reverend and Most Righteous All About-Me griped. "Now look at my pants pocket. I'm gonna look tacky tonight. What about me? What am I gonna do?"

What about you! What do you mean, what about you? I'm

laying here somewhere between pain, hell, and misery, and you want to know about you! Deacon Laid Handz thought. All he could do was think, because his voice as well as his manhood were still traveling somewhere in outer space.

"You fools get on my last good nerve. You're down here causing all this noise when we got business to attend. Have you forgotten what's really important tonight? Bishop, you pick yourself up and pull that spider web off your bottom chin."

"My chin."

"Yes. You have spider webs on your third chin down."

She had to be specific because they would have been there all night waiting for the bishop to figure out which one of his many chins contained the spider web. He had more chins than a Chinese phone book.

"Reverend Money, all the compact mirrors in the world ain't gonna stop you from looking like a red ghetto poodle with that wig on. Reverend and Most Righteous All About-Me, it ain't always about *you!* Deacon Laid Handz, as soon as you can, please stand, and let's move on with the plan. Anybody wanna disagree with that?" said Mother Pray Onn, pointing her cane at the men.

Those who could just nodded in agreement.

"I didn't think so," Mother Pray Onn hissed. "I guess the one good thing about all the racket going on upstairs in the auditorium is, no one has heard the commotion you made in the basement. So I guess all is not lost."

By the time Mother Pray Onn and the others finally made their way upstairs to the auditorium, pandemonium from the meeting had begun to spread. The ushers had ganged up against the floral club. The Pastor's Aide Society had turned on the deacon board. The youth choir members had started "playing the dozens" against the gospel chorus. The mothers' board, the missionary board, and the Evangelist Willing Workers Auxiliaries were throwing hymnbooks and ripping prayer hats off one another.

Standing in the middle of all the chaos was none other than Sister Carrie Onn. She looked like the musical director Igor

Stravinsky leading all four sections of the orchestra at the Metropolitan Opera House, as she raised her hand like a baton, and her voice, to spur them on.

Sister Carrie Onn felt she was in her element—carrying on. She yelled to the missionary board that the mothers' board had insinuated that they were a bunch of greedy hormones in long dresses. She told the youth choir that the gospel chorus said they sounded like handicapped pigeons limping on C notes.

Nothing Sister Carrie Onn said made the gospel chorus half as mad as when she also said that everyone knew that their robes were made of foreign and cheap polyester and that they had spent a lot of money to look so cheap.

She continued the mayhem. She screamed out to the deacon board that they were only "pastor wanna-bes," and "ghetto versions" to boot.

Sister Carrie Onn was tossing accusations and lies around as if she were playing one-woman handball.

When the Reverend Knott Enuff Money and the others saw what was happening, they smiled. It seemed as if most of the treachery that Sister Hellraiser was going to perform had already started. He fingered the dollar-sign emblem on his chain and said softly to Mother Pray Onn, "Ah, I can always depend on your daughter, Sister Carrie Onn, carrying on."

Mother Pray Onn ignored him and surveyed the melee. She was about to move toward the vacant podium when one of the hymnals, randomly tossed by an irate member, fell at her feet. She stopped short when she realized it had fallen open to display the hymn "Just a Closer Walk With Thee." She felt no one could possibly walk as close to God as she did, and was angered by the implication. Her displeasure was short-lived due to her appreciation of Sister Carrie Onn's chaos skills.

Mother Pray Onn straightened her little white crocheted cap on her head and continued walking slowly toward the podium. A wide grin suddenly appeared on her brown, leathery, and wrinkled face. *Lord, just give me strength. You know I'm doing this to better the church.* She stopped short when she thought about the many members who did not appreciate her heavenly visionary gift. *Lord, help me show them the way.* She could not wait to give the signal for Sister Hellraiser to appear. With both Sister Hellraiser and Sister Carrie Onn provoking the congregation, it would be a double whammy. The ungrateful congregation would never know what hit them! The fact that neither her daughter nor her cousin knew the other's part in the plan was simply delicious. She was about to laugh herself into a headache.

In the meantime, Bishop Was Nevercalled and the others continued to hug the auditorium walls as they crept along trying to duck flying books, fans, and an occasional communion glass. By the time they finally made it to the podium steps, Sister Hellraiser was barreling through the side door with the subtlety of a Mack truck.

The air in the church crackled, and the hairs on the back of Sister Carrie Onn's neck started to rise. She knew there was only one person on earth who had that effect. She turned slowly, trying to get a sense from whence the eerie feeling came. It didn't take long for the source to reveal itself. It stood with elegance, arms spread in welcome like the Statue of Liberty, and draped in Gucci from head to toe—her archnemesis and second cousin—Sister Ima Hellraiser.

"What in the world . . . ?" She was so outdone she could not continue.

Sister Carrie Onn could not understand what had gone wrong. She had made the anonymous call to the police station as soon as she had overheard her mother make the bus reservations for Sister Hellraiser. "Those dim-witted policemen couldn't catch a cold." She had given them the exact route she knew her cousin would take: Highway 29.

After years of near-death experiences at the hands of her cousin, Sister Carrie Onn knew it was too late. She sucked her teeth. "Shucks." The pseudo-Christian barroom brawler could not have arrived at a worse time. Sister Carrie Onn had just about eliminated most of the contenders from the various auxiliaries for the fund-raising chairperson position, with the exception of Sister Loose Gal. She searched the crowd again and still could not find her. She turned her attention back to her cousin. Getting rid of Ima Hellraiser would not be so easy. Anything short of murder would be a wasted effort.

Flashbacks of treachery flooded Sister Carrie Onn's mind. One devious plot after another, all perpetrated by Sister Hellraiser, crept into every crevice of her being. She was determined that for every time Ima Hellraiser stole a boyfriend, told a lie, or set up a trap that caused her pain, she would pay her back.

Sister Connie Fuse was totally consumed by her anger and ready to scream. However, she was not to the point where she was ready to give up being the fund-raiser chairperson. Giving an event that would make her the Queen of Pelzer, South Carolina, would engrave her name in fund-raising history. It would also make Ima Hellraiser angrier than Hillary Clinton at the mention of pizza and cigars. She would become known as more sinister than those treacherous and infamous rottweiler twins, Lucianne Goldenburger and Linda Trippwire.

The temperature rose again, this time into a squall.

The sight of Sister Hellraiser and Sister Carrie Onn in the same room at the same time caused everyone to have the same thoughts: panic. Without one word spoken, random notions of self-preservation flashed through the congregation's minds as they cleared a path through the red-carpeted aisle.

Much like the running of the bulls in Spain, both Sister Hellraiser and Sister Carrie Onn sprinted toward the podium and the cordless microphone. *Olé.*

Mother Pray Onn barely made it out of the way of the stampede. The currents from the wind made by the two spinsters in their rapid dash to the podium knocked Mother Pray Onn's little crocheted cap to the side. They also managed to step on the ripened bunion on Mother's right baby toe. The bunion popped so loud that those near her thought a gun had been fired. She screamed so loud, they thought she was the shooting victim. All eyes were on her except the champion, Sister Hellraiser, and the contender, Sister Carrie Onn.

"You're just like dog mess. Everywhere I step, there you are!" Sister Carrie Onn screamed.

Out of desperation and humiliation, Sister Ima Hellraiser screamed back, "Well, you done stepped in it again!" She gave a backhanded slap to the arm of Sister Carrie Onn.

Sister Carrie Onn, unaccustomed to an unsolicited slap, without hesitation introduced her left fist to the right side of Sister Hellraiser's stomach.

The next sight to greet the astonished congregation came in the form of the unveiling of little stubby stacks of overprocessed brown hair that had once lain covered by Sister Carrie Onn's summer blond wig and now resided in the fist of Sister Hellraiser.

Survival reflexes served Sister Hellraiser well. They unconsciously stopped a well-aimed second jab because she was as shocked as the others. Since their late twenties, she'd always thought the luxurious blond hair was her cousin's crowning glory. She knew, of course, the hair was dyed, but that was all. She had always thought it was naturally long; she could not stop looking at the mass of blond synthetic hair sticking to her sweaty hands.

After Sister Carrie Onn got over the shock and embarrassment, she reached over and snatched back her hair. Placing it back on her head with the bangs facing the back, she glared at her cousin through the matted blond tresses, with more heat and hatred than the devil could ever muster.

Then the temperature inside changed into a maelstrom.

Sister Hellraiser never knew what hit her. One moment she was wearing a gorgeous green 100 percent cotton Gucci two-piece suit, and the next it was a tattered green one-piece. She looked like a ghetto Keebler elf that had just lost all her cookies, or a crushed can of Sprite soda.

Pandemonium was the theme for the evening.

The reverend and the rest of his cronies decided it might be too soon to go up to the podium. They, the cowards, slunk back into the safety of the shadows.

Time passed, and the three-ring circus of chaos, orchestrated by the spiritual misfits Sister Carrie Onn and Sister Ima Hellraiser, intensified. Every time they raised their fists at each other, someone in the congregation would mistake it as a cue to do something or say something stupid.

And the premeeting rumble continued.

As soon as Sister Hellraiser started to point her sweaty finger in Sister Carrie Onn's face, one of the deacons grabbed the last edition of the church bulletin and swatted one of the trustees. He laid page one right across the only spot on the trustee's head that had a single hair, and screamed, "Hair today and gone tomorrow!"

Sister Carrie Onn responded to Sister Hellraiser's finger with a well-placed gnaw on its second knuckle.

"You bit me!" Sister Hellraiser yelped, shaking her hand as fast as a hummingbird's wing.

Brother Yucan Trustme sneaked up behind Sister Aggi Tate, tapped her on the shoulder, and yelled, "You're it!" She turned and flipped him like a burger at Burger King and served him up, her way.

The chaos continued.

Sister Betty and the others finally arrived. They'd heard the noise from the outside, yet they thought they could enter the fray without notice. Going unnoticed might have been possible if a tall, good-looking man of about forty had not accompanied Sister Betty. He was buffed, with dark, glistening skin. However, before Sister Betty and her escort could get five feet in the door, both Sister Carrie Onn's and Sister Ima Hellraiser's man-on-the-scene hormone radar beeped.

For a moment, the storm abruptly stopped.

Sister Betty led the handsome stranger and the rest of her party through the fray and up to the podium. The entire congregation, including the treacherous six, stopped verbally and physically assaulting one another.

Once the "available male" radar beeped inside Sister Hellraiser's and Sister Carrie Onn's heads, it didn't take but a moment to register. A new, seemingly unattached piece of eye candy was on the church premises.

Without a word spoken between them, the two man-hungry, hormone-driven women momentarily put aside their petty differences. "Can we finish later?" Sister Hellraiser asked.

"There'll be other times to finish this," Sister Carrie Onn answered, and glared. "Trash will always be around." She'd pushed back enough of the wig to recognize the stranger. She also, for the moment, pushed back her hunger for Deacon Laid Handz.

They rushed to gather up their shredded clothes and plucked wigs. To save time, they decided to dress and primp as they continued their rush to the podium.

Sister Hellraiser now had another mission in mind. She pushed to the back of her mind the plan to get the Reverend Knott Enuff Money's fraudulent fund-raising scheme past the vigilant eyes of Sister Betty and the others. The further back she pushed the plan, the closer she wanted to get to the handsome man with Sister Betty.

With God on her side, Sister Betty reached the podium first. She placed her family-size Bible down on the podium ledge, and without saying a word, she extended her little wrinkled brown hand toward the stranger.

The stranger climbed the steps to the podium with all the magnificence of an Arabian championship derby winner. While loosening his spotless white shirt collar, he smiled and extended a strong hand back toward Sister Betty. He was well over six feet, and with Sister Betty being all of perhaps five feet, he looked as if he were doing deep waist-bends as he planted a kiss on both cheeks. She blushed.

"First, I give honor to God, who is the head of my life. And to my pastor, Reverend Knott Enuff Money, to the overseer, Bishop Was Nevercalled, Deacon Laid Handz, Reverend and Most Righteous All About-Me, and Mother Pray Onn. Before I go any further, I would like to invite them to come up to the podium. It just don't seem right for them to be over there hidden in the shadows with so much happening here tonight. Let's give them a hearty amen and applause as they come forward out of the dark," Sister Betty said while clapping her hands.

From out of the shadows, they slunk forward. All had a surprised look on their faces as if they had just won an award they didn't know they were nominated for, and knew they didn't deserve. But instead of amen's and applause, they were met with thunderous laughs.

The Reverend Knott Enuff Money's dried and now frizzled red borrowed wig had curled up on his head. He looked like he was wearing a fez.

The always-dressed-to-the-nines Reverend and Most Righteous All About-Me's back pants pocket had ripped even more. It revealed one freckled brown buttock slightly covered by boxers decorated with a cartoon character—Pooh Bear. If the air conditioner had been working properly, perhaps he would have felt it sooner.

Whatever Deacon Laid Handz was trying to say, only the dogs outside heard it. The little gender lesson Mother Pray Onn had delivered was still in effect.

If the congregation was not exhausted from laughing, it soon would be. Coming in at record speed to get a closer look at the handsome stranger before the Reverend Knott Enuff Money and the others did were Sister Hellraiser and Sister Carrie Onn.

There were plenty of congregation members who looked worn and frazzled, but none of them compared to the raggedy duo that stood at the bottom steps of the podium. After taking a good look at each other and seeing how neither was in position to snag a man, Sister Hellraiser and Sister Carrie Onn backed down temporarily from the hunt.

A few of the bolder members decided to get a little closer. They quickly changed their minds after a severe look from Ma Cile. "Y'all jist try sumpthin'." She was already mad, and dispensing a little eye whammy would be no problem. They withdrew and managed to step back onto the exact spots where they had been before.

"Let me introduce someone very important to you," Sister Betty said after making sure she had their attention. "To those here that live outside this district, this is Councilman Hip PoCrit. He has some very exciting news to share with us this evening.

I am going to step aside and let him tell you what it is." Looking down at the reverend and his treacherous cronies, she added, "I know it will come as a big surprise to some of you."

Councilman Hip PoCrit stepped forward. He wore a pale-blue suit that fit in all the right places and showed he definitely had the right stuff. Putting one hand in a pants pocket and grabbing the cordless microphone with the other, he dramatically surveyed the room. As if he were addressing Congress, the councilman cleared his throat and began speaking.

"First of all, I must say what an honor and a privilege it is for me to be here with you tonight at your pre-fund-raiser meeting." He looked over at Sister Betty and continued. "When Sister Betty and her friends first approached me about your problem, I did not hesitate to offer my assistance."

He glanced again at Sister Betty, who now had Minister Breedin' Love and Sister Loose Gal standing beside her. Their smiles told him that he would indeed get the necessary votes he needed to be reelected. Confident that Sister Betty would keep her promise of votes, he continued. "I have in my possession a proclamation. I will read it to you:

> *The city of Pelzer, South Carolina, on this day, July 18, 2001 declares the Ain't Nobody Else Right but Us— All Others Goin' to Hell Church and its surrounding land as a cultural landmark."*

Smiling a big broad grin, he then handed the plaque to Sister Betty and continued, "If you had not brought it to our attention the fact that this very church sits upon land that was once part of the Underground Railroad, we might have issued a construction permit in error to the reverend."

He looked over at the Reverend Knott Enuff Money, who was momentarily distracted by the sudden itching from the frizzled red fez-looking hair that adorned his scalp. Trying hard to choke back a laugh, the councilman went on, "Reverend, would you and the bishop, as well as the rest of your party, please step up."

"Oh, that's okay," the Reverend Knott Enuff Money replied with embarrassment. "Let Sister Betty *have* her moment." He was hot! His frizzled, red fez-like hair started sizzling like bacon.

Between Mother Pray Onn and the rest of the treacherous posse, they couldn't put together a syllable. They were dumbstruck.

"What could have gone wrong?" Deacon Laid Handz finally whispered. He was just getting his voice back and didn't trust himself speaking any higher.

"Yeah, what could have possibly gone wrong?" they all whispered while turning to stare angrily at Sister Ima Hellraiser like she had a piece of broccoli sticking out of one nostril. "You wasn't worth the twenty-dollar discount ticket it cost to bring you here!" they screamed.

Before she could respond with her usual fiery decorum, the councilman raised his hand and was about to speak. And that's when things went from bad to worse. They went from "ain't no way" to "have mercy" in just seconds.

Someone had finally fixed and turned on the hurricane fan. The Reverend and Most Righteous All About-Me's hands looked like two octopuses as they frantically swept over the back of his torn pants as the cold air from the fan peppered his rump. "Somebody must have tried to take my wallet! Look, my pants pocket's been ripped!" Reality was kicked up a notch when the air finally filtered through the hole in his pants and swept across his butt and down his upper leg. "I've been violated." Not violated, but he was certainly humiliated.

"Lose some weight. You are busting out of your pants," Sister Aggi Tate laughed.

"Look, he's got cartoon characters on his boxers," one of the choir members added while trying to stifle a laugh.

"I'll be dog. It looks like a picture of Mighty Mouse," the mothers' board chorused.

"Here he comes to save the day," the adult choir sang.

"From where I'm standing, I wish he'd save *my* day." Sister Need Sum had moved in closer to get a better look at the Reverend

All About-Me's embarrassing situation and liked what she saw. "Ooh. Now, ain't that just the cutest thing. It's Pooh Bear." She decided she'd repent later, but at that moment, she was enjoying the view.

Suddenly, several of the women from the Widows' Association rushed toward the Reverend All About-Me with offers of help. They wanted to give him everything from packets of needles and thread to personally washing his clean but toddler-looking boxers.

With renewed chaos rekindled, Sister Betty, Ma Cile, and Councilman Hip PoCrit decided they'd be safer off the podium.

Unfortunately, like with a bad car accident, they knew they should not but had to take a peek. And, just like the rest of the onlookers, they could not keep their jaws from dropping when they saw what was going on. The Reverend and Most Righteous All About-Me dashed toward the hallway men's bathroom with the women still in pursuit. He looked like he was being chased by a swarm of man-hungry and widowed killer bees. He was.

Sister Betty and Councilman Hip PoCrit would have been standing there at the podium for a long time, glued to the floor, if it had not been for Brother Tis Mythang. He'd arrived late, and that's why he had not been heard from. He started screaming like he had a toothache after seeing Sister Carrie Onn standing on top of his organ with her blond wig on backward. She was getting ready to stir up the crowd again.

He raced through the congregation, knocking over whatever furniture remained standing. "What's going on? Have you lost your mind? Get off my organ before I snatch you off!" Brother Tis Mythang barked.

"He ain't used to women on his organ." Sister Aggi Tate laughed. She never missed an opportunity to rub someone the wrong way, and she was just getting started.

He backed up a few steps and clutched his chest when he saw that Sister Carrie Onn's weight had flattened the middle C key. He sat down on the broken organ stool and started to cry. From that moment on, he decided that knocking Sister Carrie

Onn from B-flat to G-sharp would be his lifelong mission. There
were too many witnesses tonight, but he would get her or die
trying. He went on crying because it was all he could do.

Minister Breedin' Love looked away from the whimpering
Brother Tis Mythang and took Sister Loose Gal by the arm and
led her to a corner of the room. "You know, I usually have something profound to say, but not tonight. I'm going to wait until
it's my time to preach. There is enough material brought out
tonight to preach about for the next ten years. Perhaps I can
get the congregation to listen attentively if I present it right."

Sister Loose Gal hung her head. *I'm glad I got here late*, she
thought. Minister Breedin' Love could have read word for word
from the King James Version, The New Kings James Version,
and the Amplified Bible and he still would not have gotten most
of the congregation's attention. He was too good-looking and
dressed in the latest fashions because he used to be a manager
of ladies' nighttime services. He used to be a pimp. Most of the
church members never let him forget it. She knew that the
only one who totally forgot about his sins was God.

Sister Betty didn't bother to respond to Minister Breedin'
Love. She knew deep in her heart that one day he would lead
that very same congregation to a higher place in God. Right
now, he had to go through all the accusations and the torments
like any true man of God. He was still young, not quite thirty-
five; he would be all right.

After surveying the melee and determining which exit would
be the safest, Councilman Hip PoCrit grabbed the cordless microphone again. He smiled and said to those nearest the podium,
"Well, Sister Betty, I have seen enough. This plaque and the
city declaration making this church and its land a cultural land-
mark means that no additions or unusual alterations can be
made to this existing structure. I hope I have been of service to
you, and I know I will see you at the election booth."

Councilman Hip PoCrit climbed down from the podium without shaking any hands. He took one last look at the Reverend
and Most Righteous All About-Me and his posse of elderly
man-eaters and laughed.

In the meantime, accusations were being thrown back and forth among the treacherous six. Each one threatened to tell the other's most personal and embarrassing secrets. They blamed one another for the failure of the plan. Things got a little too heated again. Mother Pray Onn's cane was broken, the Reverend Knott Enuff Money's fake red fez-like wig was snatched, and of course, Deacon Laid Handz's soprano voice was returned by another well-placed jab from Mother Pray Onn's elbow.

Bishop Was Nevercalled was so bewildered, all he could do was stand there surrounded by the Sunday school auxiliary and stutter, "Oh, oh, my Lord, what is we gonna do?"

The poor Reverend and Most Righteous All About-Me was totally destroyed because the evening didn't turn out to be about him, the way he had wanted it to turn out.

Little pockets of arguments once again broke out among the auxiliaries. All in all, it turned out to be the same type of pre-fund-raiser meeting it had always been over the past years.

Safely tucked into a corner, Sister Betty touched Ma Cile's arm and whispered, "I was just thinking: wasn't it something the way that Sister Hellraiser just showed up out of nowhere? I wonder who could have told her about what was going on?"

"I don't know. Evil always finds a way to come to church. That ole Satan knows his way around here, too," Ma Cile answered.

"Well, whoever invited her probably wanted to cause more problems in the church." She stopped, looked over at the trouble-makers huddling in a circle, and smiled. "Never mind; I just answered my own question."

Sister Betty and Ma Cile said their good-byes and thank-you's and exited.

Even though they were exhausted and the evening was getting late with the temperature still rising, Ma Cile had one more thing she needed to know. "Sister Betty, did you have us look up all that information at the library so you could save the church? Was that your plan that you say was given you?" She amazed herself at how clearly she was thinking since she'd forgotten to stash her snuff canister in her pocket. However, just

the immediate thought of the snuff caused Ma Cile's cravings
to surface. She tried to ignore it. She tried to turn her attention
back to Sister Betty.

"Yes, it was. I'm glad you trusted me and didn't ask questions.
I told you my plan would work!" Sister Betty giggled. "Although
I have to admit I didn't know about Sister Hellraiser showing
up. I must have got off my knees before the Lord got finished
showing me her part in their devilish scheme."

"Did ya really find out what they were doing while you was
praying?"

"Yes. When you earnestly seek God, He will never fail you."

"But, another thing I need to know. Why did ya have the rest
of us going through all them books and looking up newspaper
clippings while ya fiddled around with that 'puter? I didn't know
you knew how to use one of those thangs," Ma Cile chuckled.

"Of course I know how to use a computer. I'm on the Internet,"
Sister Betty replied.

"You on what net?" asked Ma Cile. She looked at Sister Betty
as if there were something truly wrong with her best friend.

"I'm sorry. I forgot to tell you," Sister Betty confessed, and
then added, "Do you know Sister Pat G'Orge-Walker from the
Blanche Memorial Baptist Church?"

"Yeah, I think so. I heard that whenever she comes here to
visit, she writes down ever'thang she sees goin' on here," Ma
Cile answered.

"That's her. She's real smart and talented," Sister Betty said.
"She says she takes notes so she can show people how to really
praise God in the spirit and not worry about skin color or denomination. She says if we can't love one another, then we're
not following God's plan for His people. Judgment begins at the
House of God, she always says."

"Really! I always knew when I joined Ain't Nobody Else
Right but Us—All Others Goin' to Hell Church, that we was
the ones praising God the right way. But what does that have
to do with you?" Ma Cile asked.

"She put me on the Information Highway and in her books.
I, Sister Betty, am now on the Internet and in bookstores!"

That started Ma Cile thinking, so she just had to ask another question. "Do you think that Sister Pat G'Orge-Walker gonna put me on the Net and in one of her books one day? I see her watching me and chatting with Lil Bit and June Bug sometimes."

"I don't see why not," Sister Betty answered, and then muttered to herself, "If you gotta problem with it, too bad. It's already too late. She's already done it."

"What did ya say?" Ma Cile asked, suddenly wishing she had her snuff canister.

"Oh, nothing," Sister Betty answered.

"Well, she'd better not," Ma Cile hissed. "I don't need nobody knowing about how I dip snuff or what happened to my eye or my bad-behind grandchil'ren . . ."

Sister Betty looked over at Ma Cile and could predict another storm about to erupt. She hugged her oversized Bible to her chest and silently started praying for Sister Pat G'Orge-Walker's safety if she ever decided to visit the Ain't Nobody Else Right but Us—All Others Goin' to Hell Church again.

Sister Betty decided to change the subject. "Ma Cile, did I tell you the news about Mother Eternal Everlastin', from the Church of No Hope and No Mercy?"

"Naw. What happened to her?"

"She died."

"What! Nobody told me about it. She was such a good person." Ma Cile dabbed at one eye, trying to start a tear going. She almost rubbed it raw. It was her false blue eye. She switched the crumbled tissue over to her good brown eye and started dabbing again. "Is there gonna be a fun'ral soon?"

"Yes," Sister Betty answered. She was sorry about Mother Eternal Everlastin' passing but was glad to change the subject from Sister G'Orge-Walker. "I understand she's going to be sent on home by the funeral director, Mr. Bury Em Deep, because most of her family is dead."

"I'll go to the fun'ral, but I ain't paying no respects at her Church of No Hope and No Mercy!" Ma Cile snapped. "The last time I visited, I took Lil Bit and June Bug for one of they Youth Against Violence conferences."

"What was wrong with that?" Sister Betty asked.

"Nuthin' wrong with what they wanted to do. But when we got there, they waved some type of voodoo stick that hummed all over my body. It was scary. Then they pushed a buzzer and let me in." Ma Cile stopped huffing and looked at Sister Betty. "Since when ya gotta be de-voodooed to be made safe and buzzed into a church for service? That's why I ain't neva leaving our church!"

Sister Betty laughed at her best friend, whom she loved dearly, in innocence. With the sounds of the chaotic fund-raiser meeting fading in the background, she and Ma Cile walked away. They walked cautiously, as old folks will do, toward a nearby taxi stand. Sister Betty had her mind on the Lord and thanked Him for using her again. She looked almost angelic as the rays of moonlight lit upon her tiny body. She wondered what her next heavenly mission would be.

Ma Cile gave silent thanks, too, as she swatted at several annoying mosquitoes. She had her mind on her snuff and wondered where she had put her little tin canister that held her pleasure.

Remember how they praise God at the Ain't Nobody Else Right but Us—All Others Goin' to Hell Church. You do the opposite.

As in Sodom and Gomorrah, you won't find ten righteously doing the work of the Lord. Sister Betty hopes to change that.

> *Let us walk honestly, as in the day; not in rioting and drunkenness, not in chambering and wantonness, not in strife and envying.*
>
>   —Romans 13:13

Death and life are in the power of the tongue, and they that love it shall eat the fruit thereof.

—Proverbs 18:21

If my people, which are called by my name, shall humble themselves, and pray, and seek my face, and turn from their wicked ways; then will I hear from heaven, and will forgive their sin, and will heal their land.

—2 Chronicles 7:14

ABOUT THE AUTHOR

Pat G'Orge-Walker is the daughter of parents who were both preachers and pastors. Besides being a record industry veteran as a part of the radio and retail promotion personnel for Columbia Records, Epic Records and Def Jam Records, and a singer with the R&B group the Chantels, she is also the well-known Christian comedienne Sister Betty. Known for her uncanny ability to improvise, her characters continue to leap off the pages onto the stage through her hilarious routines. Although famous for her Sister Betty character portrayed in her award-winning one-woman show, *Sister Betty! God's Calling You!*, she is just as much in demand for her witty and comical portrayal of other spiritually challenged members from her books such as: Sister Ima Hellraiser, Sister Aggi Tate, and Sister I. B. DeUsher, to name a few. She has performed in venues nationwide including Radio City in New York, Universal Amphitheater in California, Lawton McMann Theater in Oklahoma, Carnival Cruise Lines, Royal Caribbean Cruise Lines, Reno, Nevada, and many colleges, churches and other places. She often claims that any resemblance to her characters, dead or alive, is a doggone shame.

The author is also a motivational speaker. Her testimony, "A Kept Woman," has been used by various religious groups, including the Maryknoll Sisters, as a topic for discussion on how

God will keep you from birth to death. This particular testimony will also appear in *Chicken Soup for the Christian Woman's Soul*. One of her short stories, "Consequences," appears in *Proverbs for the People* (an anthology) along with other noted authors. Another short story, inspired by the death of her oldest brother, Herbert, entitled "Love Went to Heaven" is a resource tool used by many grief counseling services.

Ms. G'Orge-Walker is the recipient of the Black Writers Organization's Gold Pen 2000 Innovative Writer award; an award given to her by her peers for creating a new genre of fiction: Gospel Comedy.

Pat G'Orge-Walker resides in Elmont, New York, along with her husband, Robert, and grandson, Brian. She is a deaconess and attends Blanche Memorial Baptist Church in Jamaica, New York.

For more information visit *www.sisterbetty.com* or e-mail: sisterbetty@sisterbetty.com